DEADLY PREMONITION

Lightning suddenly streaked across the horizon and crackled as it ripped through a tree, tearing off branches and sending them flying. I winced as a loud clap of thunder followed in its wake. The driver cracked the whip again and the carriage pitched forward as the horse raced through the forest at breakneck speed. Great gusts of wind whipped the rain into sheets that blew in front of the carriage, making it virtually impossible to see the jagged path.

"It's only a storm," Forrest said, as I buried my face in his shoulder.

Peering through the rain-washed window, my heart literally stood still, for high on the hillside sat an exact replica of the house that had haunted my dreams since first it had materialized on the ink-splashed pages of my notepaper. I couldn't shake my conviction that fate had ordained my coming here, and that something ominous awaited me at Villa Montelano.

I gasped when I saw it close-up. There was something evil about the villa, and without thinking I turned to Forrest and said, "Please don't make me go in there. I'm afraid."

ANNE KNOLL

THE DARK SECRETS OF VILLA MONTELANO

ZEBRA BOOKS
KENSINGTON PUBLISHING CORP.

ZEBRA BOOKS are published by

Kensington Publishing Corp.
475 Park Avenue South
New York, NY 10016

Zebra and the Z logo are trademarks of Kensington Publishing Corp.

First Printing: September, 1993

Printed in the United States of America

Dedication

*This book is dedicated
to my father,
Robert G. Boarman,
a gifted composer and pianist,
who gave me a wonderful gift
when he taught me to love music,
and
to my mother,
Genevieve,
who used to tell me stories.*

Acknowledgment

*Thanks always to my daughter,
Renee,
whose keen insight and deep sensitivity
never fail to inspire me.*

All seems infected that the infected spy, as all looks yellow to the jaundiced eye.

—Alexander Pope

What loneliness is more lonely than distrust?

—George Eliot

Chapter 1

London, 1899

We had no sooner stepped outside when the heavens opened up and a sudden drenching rain drove us back to the shelter of the awning over the store.

"Shopgirl's shower," my friend Maggie proclaimed. "Why can't it storm *before* six or *after,* I'd like to know."

We leaned closer to the door of Madame's Exclusive French Ladies Shop as the rain came down in sheets and the wind, like some Puckish tease, slammed it up against us.

Maggie rapped frantically on the door. "Madam sees us. I know she does. Oh, why won't the old devil let us back in?"

"Because we're not customers," I said.

"You're right," Maggie quipped, "she'd open the door in a minute to sell a button."

I opened my umbrella and held it out like a shield to protect us, but it was torn from my hand and landed in the gutter, fabric ripped and spokes twisted beyond repair.

"Oh, no," I said, and then, to add insult to injury, the rain suddenly slacked off and the wind stopped.

Maggie squeezed water from the hem of her skirt and

pursed her lips. "Well, I never. Now that the damage is done it clears off. And they say heaven will protect us working girls!"

I looked sadly back to the gutter and my dead umbrella. It was the only one I owned.

"I'm going to make a run for it now, lovey," Maggie was saying. "Me mum's a stickler about supper. Won't take no excuses about being late, she won't." She opened her umbrella and added, "Wish you went my way, Charlotte. I'd share this with you."

I smiled. "I know you would, Maggie, but I'll be all right. It's going to stop soon, and I don't have that far to walk." She hesitated, and I gave her a playful shove. "Go on with you. Don't keep your mum waiting."

"See you in the morning, then," she said, and holding her skirt in one hand and the umbrella in the other, she skittered off down the rain-soaked street.

I stuck my hand out from under the awning. It was still raining, but was also getting late, I thought, and pressing my face up against the shop door's window, I peered back inside. The huge clock that hung above the glove counter showed it to be six-thirty.

It would be dark soon, and unpinning my hat, I held it in the crook of my arm for protection. Bad enough I have to replace an umbrella. I can't afford to replace a hat, too.

At that moment, a carriage pulled up at the curb, and a dark-clad man stepped out. I forgot about the rain and darted out from under the awning. Dusk had fallen, and a sudden premonition of danger overwhelmed me. Without looking back, I hurried around the corner.

"Miss, wait."

My heart leapt into my throat. Dear God, the man was calling me. Had he thought I was waiting for a pickup? Ninny, why didn't you leave with Maggie? There are more things to fear on London's streets than a little rain.

8

He shouted again, but I picked up my skirts and ran, never stopping until I was in front of the dilapidated old brownstone I called home.

Anxious to get out of my soaked clothes and looking forward to a cup of hot tea, I hurried inside, but Mrs. Hill, my loquacious landlady, pounced on me before I could climb the stairs.

"I been waitin' for you." Her beady little eyes took me in from head to toe. "Soaked to the skin, ain't you now, ducky? What ya do—forget your umbrella?" She smiled to herself, amused, I'm sure, at my bedraggled appearance.

Too uncomfortable for words, I nodded, wondering why she had been waiting for me.

"You had a gentleman caller," she said. "I told him where you worked. Did he come to the shop to see you?"

"No," I answered cautiously, recalling the man who had tried to get my attention on the street.

"That's funny. I give him directions. Brewster and Biddle streets, I says. It's a fancy ladies' shop with one of them green awnings outside."

"Not Biddle. Brewster and Barclay Streets."

She shrugged. "I 'spect he'll catch up with you. Said he was a barrister. You ain't in any trouble, I hope."

Annoyed, I shook my head, and she gave me a calculating look. "You look innocent enough, but you can't tell today. Still waters run deep. Ain't mixed up with no married man, I hope."

I gathered my sodden skirts in my hand and started upstairs. "Don't concern yourself, Mrs. Hill. It's probably something about the shop. Madam will handle it, I'm sure."

She looked disappointed. "Oh? Well, don't be takin' offense. I was only tryin' to be motherly, Miss Stone. Young women can't be too careful nowadays."

I acted nonchalant for Mrs. Hill's benefit, but an uneasy feeling crept over me and I felt a premonition

9

that my life was about to take a startling and dangerous turn. What possible reason would a barrister have for wanting to see me?

My rooms were at the head of the stairs, and feeling more uncomfortable by the minute in my soggy clothes, I struggled to fit my key into the rusty old lock. Suddenly my landlady's shrill voice split the air.

"Miss Stone!"

I jumped, the lock jammed, and frustrated to the point of tears, I left the twisted key in the hole and looked down over the banister.

Standing beside Mrs. Hill was a tall elegantly dressed man who couldn't have been more than thirty. Could this be the barrister? I wondered.

I must have made a sound, for they both looked up and Mrs. Hill said, "This is the gentleman who was asking for you, Miss Stone. You may see him in the front parlor," she added primly. Mrs. Hill did not allow ladies to entertain gentlemen in their flats.

"I'll be right down," I said, and before I had reached the last step, the stranger had smoothly dismissed Mrs. Hill. "Thank you, madam," he said firmly. "You've been most helpful."

The silly woman gave him a coquettish smile and curtsied. "Think nothing of it, Your Lordship."

When she was safely inside her own quarters, he handed me a card. "Allow me to introduce myself, Miss Stone. I am Forrest Singleton of the law firm of Pendleton and Forrest in America."

"There must be some mis—mistake," I said, blushing to the roots of my hair. I had stuttered as a child and every now and then the embarrassing affliction returned. "You probably want to see Madam Suzette, the shop's owner." I managed to say without incident.

"I don't think so. You are Miss Charlotte Stone, daughter of the late Henry Stone, are you not?" I nodded and he said, "Then, you are the one I wish to see."

I must have looked frightened, for he smiled in a reassuring way. "There is no cause for alarm, Miss Stone." Giving the cramped hallway a cursory glance, he smiled. "Come, let us discuss this in a more comfortable setting. I believe your landlady offered the use of her parlor."

"Of course. Forgive me," I said, leading him into the front room. I closed the sliding door, though I was positive that Mrs. Hill would soon be bending her ear to it.

The room was plunged into sudden darkness and I hastily lit a lamp whose flickering light cast our shadows on the wall. His, large and distorted, loomed over mine and I shuddered against a sudden irrational fear.

Tearing my eyes away from the shadows, I faced him, a little embarrassed at my childishness, for in reality, he was quite handsome and not menacing at all.

He moved closer and studied me with genuine concern by the light of the lamp. "Miss Stone," he exclaimed. "You're soaked to the skin."

"I got caught in the rain," I said feebly.

"See here, now. We can't have you catching cold. I don't suppose Mrs. Hill would mind my waiting here while you change."

"No, but . . ."

"Please, Miss Stone. I insist. Take your time. I'll sit right here and wait for you."

"Very well," I said, vanity overcoming my curiosity, for I knew I must look a fright.

Hastily I slid the door back and almost toppled over Mrs. Hill.

"I was after gettin' the water off this carpet," she said, straightening herself up.

I hurried past her, and once upstairs I tackled the key that was still stuck in the lock. This time it turned easily and I entered the room and quickly shed my soggy clothing.

I lit a lamp, and standing in my petticoat, I peered anxiously into my closet. A meager assortment of dark skirts and almost-identical white blouses stared back at me, but a flash of color in the back of the closet caught my eye and I pulled out a pink silk shirtwaist. Delicately embroidered with tiny pink roses, it was an expensive blouse I could never have afforded had it not been reduced because of a hole in one of the sleeves.

I had carefully mended the tear, but since the blouse was too dressy for work, it had hung in the closet unworn for almost a year. Now, acting on impulse, I laid it out on the bed with one of my plain black skirts.

Rubbing my hair vigorously with a towel, I brushed it dry and then swept it up on top of my head and knotted it. Little tendrils of curls escaped, but I didn't have time to pin them in place.

I dressed, and giving myself a quick glance in the mirror, I was surprised at the change in my appearance. The rosy-hued blouse added color to my cheeks and made my chestnut brown hair sparkle with red highlights. The wispy curls released by the rain gave me a haphazard air that was disconcerting, but strangely becoming, and though I have never considered myself pretty, I was pleased with what I saw.

Returning to the parlor, I excused myself to Mr. Singleton for keeping him waiting.

"It was worth it, Miss Stone. You look charming and I am sure you feel better." Taking a handsome gold watch out of his pocket, he glanced casually at it. "Nearly seven-thirty," he said, snapping the case shut. "Would you do me the honor of having dinner with me, Miss Stone? I haven't had dinner, and I know I've kept you from yours."

His eyes locked with mine, and I held my breath, feeling myself suddenly transformed like Cinderella into a beautiful and desirable princess.

You have not been properly introduced to this man, my middle-class conscience protested.

No, but he showed me his card. He is a barrister, and besides, this is a business call, not a social one.

"It is rather late," I conceded. "Thank you, Mr. Singleton, I'd be happy to join you.

Once out on the street, he hailed a hack and told the driver to take us to the Savoy.

Leaning back in the plush seat, I tried to smother my apprehension about going to such an elegant establishment. "I don't know if I'm dressed for the Savoy," I said.

"Nonsense. You look lovely, Miss Stone."

I glanced down at his hand and the pearl-handled walking stick it grasped. A diamond ring glittered on his little finger and black onyx cuff links graced the sleeves of his perfectly starched, snow-white shirt. His black suit was of the finest worsted cloth, and my practiced eye recognized the workmanship of a master tailor in its cut. Forrest Singleton was a man of position and importance, I mused, and again I wondered what business he could possibly have with me.

"Is it always so foggy in London?" he asked after glancing out the carriage window.

"Not always," I said and then amended my answer to "Just most of the time."

He laughed. "Spoken like a true Londoner. I suppose you don't even notice it."

"Oh, we notice it, all right, but we're used to it."

"Do you like living in England, Miss Stone?"

"Yes, but then I've never lived anyplace else."

"Ever think about going to America?"

I almost laughed. The idea was so preposterous. "Oh, no," I said.

The carriage stopped, and, with it, our conversation. Mr. Singleton handed me out of the cab, and while he was paying the driver, an elegantly dressed group of men and women emerged from the restaurant.

Chatting and laughing, they sauntered off and disappeared into the fog, on their way after dinner to the theater, or perhaps the opera, I mused. They were people from another world, a world that I only occasionally glimpsed through the eyes of Madam's customers as they gossiped in the fitting rooms.

"Shall we go inside?"

He placed his hand on my elbow and a shiver of excitement raced through me. I felt lightheaded and a little nervous being in the company of such an attractive man.

Once inside, I was pleased when we were given a table that was situated in an alcove. I could see, but not be seen. No doubt my simple shirtwaist attire had prompted the waiter to assign us to this inconspicuous corner, but I was relieved nonetheless.

Service was prompt and I was spared confessing that I could not read the French menu, for my host ordered for us both.

When the waiter had departed, Mr. Singleton said, "I hope my selections meet with your approval, Miss Stone."

"Oh, yes indeed," I replied, and then blushed. "I don't understand French, Mr. Singleton, but I'm sure everything will be delicious."

An unreadable expression crossed his face, and then he smiled and said. "You're like a breath of fresh air, Miss Stone. I'm awfully glad you consented to join me."

"So am I, but my curiosity is getting the best of me," I replied. "Won't you tell me now what this is all about?"

He seemed at a loss as to how to begin. "Did your father ever discuss his background with you, Miss Stone?"

"His background? My father was raised in an orphanage, Mr. Singleton. He didn't talk about the

14

past, but my mother told me that his had been a most unhappy childhood. Orphanages in those days were extremely harsh and repressive," I added.

Perhaps that was why he was such an indulgent father, I mused with the clarity of hindsight, and overcome with nostalgia I felt a tear roll down my cheek.

"Forgive me," I said. "I was very close to my father. Mama died when I was twelve and Papa raised me alone. I only lost him last year."

He put his hand over mine. "I understand, Miss Stone. Believe me, I don't want to distress you. What I have to tell you concerns your father, though."

"I don't understand any of this," I said. "My father was never in America."

"No, but his mother was." The waiter arrived at that moment with our soup, and I found myself overcome with another vague feeling that what Mr. Singleton was about to tell me was going to drastically alter the course of my life.

"His mother?" I repeated as soon as the waiter had left us.

"Yes, she is the client that our law firm represents. Before your grandmother died, she engaged us to locate her son." He tasted his soup, and said, "Delicious. Eat yours before it gets cold, Miss Stone."

Like a child, I obeyed, but excitement had dulled my appetite. "Why would this woman come forward after all these years?" I asked.

"When people grow old, they like to tie up the loose ends, rectify past mistakes," he said. "Your father was mentioned in your grandmother's will, and since you are his only heir . . ."

"Well, Papa doesn't need her now," I said, feeling suddenly resentful for my father's sake. "And I want nothing from her. I can take care of myself."

He put down his soupspoon and gave me an incredulous look. "Miss Stone, I don't think you fully understand . . ."

Nerves on edge for a reason that wasn't clear even to myself, I felt compelled to state my case. "My father worked very hard," I said. "He managed to send me to a very good school. I don't intend working in a shop all my life. I have a teacher's certificate, and as soon as there is an opening, I've been promised a position in a private school for young ladies."

He gave me an indulgent look. "And what do you expect your salary would be then, Miss Stone?"

"Room and board, and two hundred pounds a year," I said proudly.

"Admirable, I'm sure, but listen to me, if you will, and don't interrupt until I have finished."

"Very well," I said.

"I understand your resentment, but I beg you to reconsider your position for your father's sake."

"But that's the very reason why I have refused it!"

He raised his hand. "No interruptions. Remember?"

"I'm sorry. Go on, Mr. Singleton."

He nodded and fixed me with a steely eye. "You had a loving father. Did you not?"

"I certainly did."

"And he wanted you to have a better life, wouldn't you say?"

"Of course."

"Then, don't you think, Miss Stone, that your father would want you to consider accepting his inheritance? How can you reject whatever largesse should come to you through a father who loved you so deeply?"

He was confusing me, and I was almost glad to see the waiter return with our meal so I could have a respite from his relentless barrister's logic.

It's true, I thought. If Papa were here, it would please him enormously to spend the money on me. He was a man who cared nothing for material possessions, but he derived an inordinate amount of pleasure from bestowing them on those he loved.

A little calmer now, I took a portion from each vegetable in the divided serving dish the waiter presented to me.

The meal was delicious, and the wine that Mr. Singleton had ordered to go with it was superb. It was making me a little giddy, though, and I was finding it impossible to come up with a rebuttal.

"What do I have to do? Sign a paper or something?"

"I'm afraid it's a little more involved than that, Miss Stone. You will have to go to America."

I was dumbfounded. "Why, the cost of the passage alone would probably be more than the inheritance," I said.

He smiled slowly. "I think not, Miss Stone. Countess Belinski was a very wealthy woman."

I was more confused than ever. "Countess? But I thought you said she was an American."

"No, Miss Stone. Your grandmother was Italian, but her third husband was a Russian count. He died, but she retained the title."

I was shocked. "She had three husbands!"

He laughed. "And countless lovers. Your grandmother was quite bohemian." He leaned back in his chair, and I listened like a child being told a fairy tale.

"The countess, which was what your grandmother liked to be called, had been a celebrated opera star in her day. Her stage name was Gia Gerardo and she appeared all over the world.

"In 1879 she purchased a vast country estate in Maryland. During the next ten years while she was still performing, she transformed it into an exotic mansion, and when she retired, she took up permanent residence there. It resembles a Moorish castle," he added. "She furnished this architectural monstrosity with art treasures from all over the world, and an odd assortment of protégés and stepchildren periodically shared the residence with her. Since it has more than forty rooms, I doubt if the countess was ever certain who had left and who was staying on."

My head was whirling. I didn't know if it was from the wine or the conversation. The whole thing sounded like something out of a book and I found it hard to believe that either my father or myself could be related to such a woman.

"Are you sure my father is this woman's son?" I asked.

"Without a shadow of a doubt, Miss Stone," he answered. "Our firm is very exacting when we conduct our investigations."

The clock struck two. And I had yet to close my eyes. Pulling the blanket around me, I got up and sat in the rocker by the window.

The premonition of danger and change that I had sensed yesterday afternoon still haunted my thoughts. Was that why I hesitated to give Mr. Singleton my answer?

"No one can force you to do anything, Miss Stone, but you would be a very foolish young woman to refuse. I think you have more common sense that that."

"I have been authorized to use funds from my firm's retainer to cover all expenses incurred in getting you to America for the reading of the will. That means passage, Miss Stone, luggage, a suitable wardrobe. How can you refuse such an offer?"

How, indeed? A Cinderella story come to life. A chance to see America, a new wardrobe, and even a handsome prince to accompany me on the crossing, I thought. Maggie, or any other girl, would have jumped at the chance last night.

"I have to think about it, Mr. Singleton. There's my job to consider and . . ."

"Miss Stone, you may never have to work at all after this will is read."

I very much doubted that, but perhaps I'd have enough to tide me over until a teaching position opened up, I reasoned.

Pushing all my vague and disturbing vibrations aside, I turned up the lamp, and dragging the blanket

18

behind me, I pulled a sheet of notepaper out of my desk, and dipping my pen in the inkwell, I wrote:

Mr. Forrest Singleton
The Grand Hotel
Northumberland Street
London, England

Dear Mr. Singleton,

I have decided to accept your offer—

A clap of thunder suddenly exploded like a cannon in my ears, and lightening shrieked across the sky. I jumped and the pen scratched across the page, splashing ink on the paper.

I blotted the page before throwing it into the wastebasket, but the dried inkblot caught my eye. It resembled a Moorish castle and there was something frightening about it. I drew the blanket across my shoulders and shivered as I reached for a fresh sheet of paper.

Chapter 2

Maggie buttoned me into the blue lace gown and whispered. "Lordy, but he's handsome, Charlotte, and so elegant. And you'll be spending two weeks alone on a ship with him!"

She rolled her eyes suggestively and I felt compelled to set her straight. "This is a business arrangement, Maggie. Mr. Singleton is only acting in the interest of his firm."

She shrugged. "You already told me that, lovey, but who says you can't change his interests around?"

"Oh, Maggie," I said impatiently. "He's an important man. I don't expect him to socialize with me. I'm lucky just to be getting the clothes and the trip."

She shook her head. "Whatever you say, love, but thanks for throwing the commission my way."

I waved her gratitude aside. "What do you think of this one?" I asked, looking at myself in the fitting room's long mirror.

She wrinkled her nose. "Too prissy. My granny could wear it. Try on the rose satin."

I stepped into the gown and she smiled at me through the mirror. "Now that's more like it."

"It's a ball gown," I countered.

"So, and what do you think ladies wear on them fancy boats?" Opening the door wide, she shoved me outside the fitting room. "Mr. Singleton," she called in a loud voice.

"Hush," I said, but he was already walking toward us.

His face registered approval and something else. Was it surprise? "Very nice, Miss Stone."

I felt myself blush. "But, it's a ball gown," I said.

He ignored me and looked at Maggie. "She'll need several. Evenings are formal onboard ship."

Maggie nodded and gave me a smug smile. "That green silk that Mrs. Minton had her eye on would do nicely."

I knew the gown she meant. It had a Paris label, and was even more daring than the rose satin.

Two hours later we were finished and my head reeled at the extent of our purchases. Stockings, gloves, shawls, petticoats, and gowns—I had never owned so many clothes. They were all to be sent to my room at the Grand Hotel.

I had moved out of the flat two days ago, and I still bristled every time I recalled Mrs. Hill's ugly insinuations. "You're moving to the Grand Hotel! My, my, that's a new twist to an old story if I do say so, lovey"

What would she think if she knew Mr. Singleton had signed a check for all this finery? I wondered.

Why should I care what she thinks? I asked myself. Everything is proper and aboveboard. My conscience is clear, and I have no reason to suspect Mr. Singleton of any ulterior motives. He has been a perfect gentleman from the very beginning.

Still and all, that strange premonition of disaster would give me no peace. I had pushed it into a dark corner of my mind, but it kept resurfacing and throwing a cloud over my good fortune.

Maggie walked us to the front door. "Good-bye, Charlotte. I'm going to miss you," she said.

I threw my arms around her. "I wish you were going with me," I whispered.

She rolled her eyes in Mr. Singleton's direction and

21

smiled. "No, you don't, ducks, but thanks for saying so."

The ship was so big, I didn't see how it could stay afloat, but Mr. Singleton assured me we had nothing to worry about.

"You won't even know you're at sea, Miss Stone. Come along, let's board, and I'll take you on a tour."

Taking my arm, he led me up the gangplank and we circled the decks. I gaped at the beautiful interiors with their posh salons and intimate little lounges, but when we came to the dining room I lingered in the doorway to admire it.

More elegant even than the Savoy, the walls were covered in rose-colored silk, and drapes in a beautiful shade of moss green velvet adorned the windows. In the center of each table was a bud vase containing one perfect dusty pink rose.

Mr. Singleton brought out his pocket watch and unsnapped the case. "Ready to go up on deck? We'll be leaving shore soon and that's something you won't want to miss."

Passengers crowded the rails, and taking my arm, Mr. Singleton said. "Let's go to the next deck. You don't mind a little breeze, do you?"

I had to hold on to my gigantic new bonnet with all the violets on the brim. "Better take your hat off," he warned. "It might land in the Atlantic."

The wind whipped through my hair, dislodging hairpins and undoing my knot. "Oh my," I said, trying to pin it back with one hand.

"Don't," he said. "You look beautiful like this, and besides, it won't stay."

My heart did a somersault. Just a figure of speech, I told myself. He didn't really mean it.

Sometimes Mr. Singleton shocked me. He was a worldly man, and I suppose he found my values outmoded, but nevertheless, we liked and respected each other.

The blast of the ship's whistle caught me off-guard, and I almost dropped my hat into the yawning sea. "We're moving," Forrest shouted. "Wave good-bye, Charlotte."

Leaving England seemed to mark a turning point in our relationship, for he had called me Charlotte, and I had likewise thought of him as Forrest. After that, it just seemed natural that we move permanently to a first-name basis, and without thinking about it, we did.

My cabin fascinated me. The furniture was built into the walls, and though the room was comparatively small, it was so compactly arranged that there was plenty of room for everything.

Forrest had told me it wasn't necessary to dress for dinner the first night out, so I needed only to comb my wildly tangled hair and pin it securely in place.

I loved the ship, but dreaded docking in Baltimore and being forced to confront the odd assortment of people that resided in my grandmother's house. I knew nothing about artists, but I imagined them to have volatile temperaments and mercurial moods—characteristics that I was at a loss to deal with. No doubt, they would resent my presence, I thought, which was understandable.

I smoothed the skirt of my navy blue suit, and made a pact with myself. I would not think about Maryland or the Villa Montelano, which Forrest had informed me was the name of my grandmother's estate. I had two wonderful weeks at sea to look forward to, and a charming man to share them with. I was going to enjoy myself and live like a queen for the first time in my life.

Pining the huge hat back on my head, I picked up my purse and left the cabin. I was to meet Forrest in the Red Salon and then we were going to dinner.

I spotted him immediately, but paused in the doorway to feast my eyes on his handsome face: a

23

strong jaw, straight aristocratic nose, and blue eyes that would have been the envy of any woman. They were a decided contrast to his coal black hair, and the combination bespoke an Irish ancestor, though I hadn't thought Singleton to be an Irish name. But Americans, I recalled, were usually mixtures of several nationalities.

He was seated at a table for two, and just as I was about to enter the lounge, a woman joined him. She was tall and very attractive with pale blonde hair and classic features. My mind still focusing on nationalities, I placed her ancestors in Greece. *Helen of Troy, the face that launched a thousand ships,* I mused.

Forrest had risen and they stood together talking, two tall, good-looking people who made a handsome couple. I drew back, and then chided myself for being a fool.

You have no claim on the man. This is a business arrangement. He's been very kind, but he has a perfect right to associate with whomever he pleases. Evidently he knows this lady, and the polite thing for you to do is to plead a headache and order dinner in your cabin.

As I approached the table, Forrest looked up and smiled. "Here's Miss Stone now," he said to the lady by his side.

Close up, she was even more beautiful, and I felt myself shrinking to insignificance beside her. Her name was Kitty Lawrence and Forrest introduced her: "An old friend. We've known each other since we were children. Haven't we, Kitty?" he said.

"I try to forget it," she replied coyly. "You were a terrible tease, Forrest Singleton."

He winked at me. "Don't believe it, Charlotte."

Miss Lawrence turned disinterested eyes in my direction. "Forrest tells me you're from London, Miss Stone. We were there for the whole season. I probably met you at one of the soirees, but one meets so many people, and I do have a frightful memory."

I was spared making a comment, for she turned

24

immediately back to Forrest with a remark about a mutual acquaintance.

"Let's all sit down and have a glass of wine," Forrest suggested, and I took advantage of the opening.

"None for me, thank you. I'm afraid I have one of my headaches. Please excuse me. I only came down to tell you that I must retire for the evening."

Forrest looked concerned, so I hastened to reassure him.

"Please. I'll be fine in the morning."

"Of course she will," Miss Lawrence hastened to add. "My old mammy always used to say that rest is the best medicine for a headache."

Thanking them both for their concern, I made good my escape.

I awakened at six, and this time, I really did have a headache, no doubt from hunger, for I'd had nothing to eat since lunchtime the day before.

Looking through my new wardrobe, I decided on a gray morning dress with white piqué ruching around the high neck. It was the kind of dress I was comfortable in, subdued, but not unfashionable, and when I had added my cameo pin, I thought the effect one of elegant simplicity.

The violet-bedecked hat added a touch of color to the ensemble, and picking up my purse, I left the cabin, hunger forcing me to brave the dining room alone.

I had spent my solitary evening reading the ship's brochure, and having studied the map, I knew the location of the dining room and every other room on this "floating hotel," as the brochure called it.

My thoughts were on food as I strode purposefully down the long corridor—crispy bacon and scrambled eggs, toast swimming with butter and marmalade, or maybe pancakes and plump sausages . . .

Rounding a corner at a brisk pace, I suddenly collided with something hard and big.

"Oops, sorry," the man said, and when I righted my hat, I saw that it was Forrest.

"Charlotte! I was just coming to see you. How are you feeling?"

"Much better, thank you, Mr. Singleton."

He looked surprised. "Why so formal? Yesterday you called me Forrest."

How could I tell him that yesterday I had forgotten my place? And that after meeting Miss Lawrence, I was reminded of it.

"We're solicitor and client," I said simply.

He laughed and shook his head. "Always so prim and proper. Come along, we'll have breakfast, but I'm calling you Charlotte, and I insist that you call me Forrest."

I took the arm he extended, and let him escort me to the dining room, for I was as hungry for his company as I was for food.

The week that followed was one I shall never forget. Forrest spent all of his time with me. He seemed to have no inclination to renew his acquaintance with Miss Lawrence, and he treated me like I was a beautiful, aristocratic lady whose company he really enjoyed.

I didn't understand his interest in me, but I knew well what my old friend Maggie would say: *"Don't look a gift horse in the mouth."*

Because this accomplished man accepted my lack of accomplishments with such patience and good grace, I blossomed like a flower in the sun.

I played shuffleboard and table tennis, and in Forrest Singleton's arms, I danced the way I'd never danced before.

He inspired me to stretch beyond the tight little boundaries I'd set for myself, and though I realized these cherished days would soon be nothing more than memories, I was grateful for them.

A lavish ball was planned for the evening of our seventh day out and Nellie Melba, the famous opera singer who was on board ship, had consented to sing.

I had as yet to wear the green silk gown that Maggie had insisted I take. Forrest had not forgotten it, though, and he even suggested that it would be especially appropriate if I wore it to the ball.

Gathering courage, I wiggled into it. The low neckline was banded with white satin gardenias and the tight skirt fit over my hips like paper on a wall. There was a pleated train attached to the back and a silver ring at the hem which fit over my finger, allowing the train to be held up for dancing.

Looking at myself in the mirror, I was shocked. I pulled the neckline up, but it immediately slipped right back down again, showing more cleavage than I considered decent.

There is no way I can appear in public like this, I told myself. I'll just have to wear the rose satin again, and as I reached behind me to unhook the gown, someone knocked on the door. "Charlotte, it's Forrest. Are you ready?"

Oh, no, I thought. "I have to change," I said, struggling to find the hooks.

"Are you wearing that green gown?"

"No, it's too . . . No, I'm going to wear the rose satin again."

"Charlotte, do you have the green gown on?"

"Yes, but it doesn't look right. I can't wear it."

"Open the door, Charlotte. We'll be late."

I still couldn't find the hooks, and in desperation, I said, "I'm hurrying, but I can't get the gown unhooked. If I turn around, will you do it for me?"

"Yes, now open the door."

I unlatched it and turned my back as he entered the cabin. "There's five hooks. If you'll just get them undone, I'll change and be ready in no time," I said.

His hands were on my shoulders and he turned me around. "Let me see it on you first."

Tears of mortification stung my eyes. "I look like a tart," I mumbled, and then clamped my hand over my mouth, horrified at what I had said.

He shook his head and smiled. "Charlotte, Charlotte. What am I going to do with you? You look like a beautiful woman, and the gown is in the height of fashion."

"But not for someone like me," I protested.

"Most especially for someone like you." He put his hand up to my face and brushed away a tear. "Trust me, Charlotte. If people look at you tonight, it will only be because they admire you."

I did trust him implicitly, so I picked up the green peacock feathered fan that Maggie had suggested I carry, and gave him a weak smile.

He opened the door and executed a sweeping bow. "To the arena," he said, and I laughed in spite of myself.

Melba—for she was known professionally by her last name—had made her American debut only six years ago, Forrest informed me. "But she has been singing in Europe for more than ten years," he added.

"How old is she?" I asked.

He shrugged. "Fortyish."

"Do you suppose she knew my grandmother?"

"Probably not. The countess retired to America about the time that Melba was making her European debut."

"Are opera singers always old?" I asked him, and he laughed.

"It takes years of training to sing opera," he explained. "Your grandmother was unusual in that she made her debut when she was very young, but then she was an unusual woman with a most unusual voice."

I hadn't understood why it took so long until I heard Melba sing. Her voice was magnificent, but, like an uncut jewel, it had to have been meticulously honed and polished, I realized, for how else could she have attained such unbelievable breath control? Then there was the matter of language. Not all operas were written in a singer's native tongue, so they would have to be linguists as well.

I sat spellbound during the entire performance. I have always loved music, as had my father, I recalled, and now I understood that it was in our blood, a legacy from a woman who had turned her back on her own son.

After the performance, we had a late supper in the dining room before attending the ball being given in Madam Melba's honor.

"I had no idea there was so much to learn. My grandmother must have been a very intelligent woman, even though she did desert her child," I added.

"*Shrewd* is a better word for Gia."

The adjective surprised me. "You didn't like her?"

"Yes and no. Your grandmother could be charming when it suited her. She could also be cruel when it didn't suit her to be charming. Let's forget about the countess," he said abruptly. "I'm more interested in you." Reaching across the table, he took my hand in his. "The nicest thing she ever did was to make it possible for me to meet her beautiful granddaughter."

"Please don't flatter me," I said, and blushing, I tried to withdraw my hand.

But he held it fast and looked deeply into my eyes. "I meant every word I said, Charlotte. You are beautiful, but you're also kind and good. Meeting you is the best thing that has ever happened to me."

My heart sang as he raised my captive hand to his lips and gently kissed it, but common sense warned me to beware. We were on board a ship, and shipboard romances were notoriously fickle.

I had never attended a ball, and I would have been satisfied to just sit on the sidelines, listening to the beautiful music and watching the dancers whirling past, but Forrest would have none of that.

"I want to dance with you, Charlotte. How else can I hold you in my arms?"

I'm certain my feet never touched the floor, but we

29

circled the ballroom, one, two, three times, and I was breathless when the music stopped.

"What you need is a glass of champagne," he said, signaling the waiter.

The bubbles tickled my nose, but the taste was delicious, and being thirsty I drank it right down. "That was refreshing. Could I have another glass?"

Forrest laughed. "Of course, but don't drink it so fast this time. You're supposed to sip it, like this . . ."

"I didn't know. I've never had champagne before."

"You haven't?"

I giggled and shook my head. "If Mrs. Hill could see me now . . ."

"Who's Mrs. Hill?"

"My landlady. Don't you remember, she curtsied and called you *Your Lordship.*"

"Ah, yes, Mrs. Hill, charming lady. I think she was taken with me."

I giggled again. "She was, but she warned me about you."

"Did she really, now. What did she say?"

I imitated her broad accent. "A gel like you, Miss Stone, should be careful when a fine gentmon offers 'er the moon."

He looked away. "She's right, you know, but I'm glad you didn't take her advice."

I thought it a rather strange thing to say, but then I didn't always understand American humor.

We drank more champagne and danced again and again, until Forrest whispered, "It's getting stuffy in here. Let's take a stroll up on deck and see that moon I'm supposed to be offering you."

I nodded, and holding hands, we wended our way past the other dancers and stepped outside.

A whoosh of fresh air knocked me backward into Forrest's arms, and he pressed me to him.

"Sweet Charlotte," he said, assaulting my mouth with honeyed kisses that left me weak. All my inhibitions vanished, and reaching up, I wound my arms tightly around his neck and returned his kisses.

Breaking away, we walked over to the rail and looked out over a moon-drenched sea. I don't think I have ever known such happiness, and so I ignored the little voice that tried to remind me that we were of two different worlds, Forrest and I.

"You're shivering," he said, and taking off his coat, he wrapped it around me. "Better?"

"Yes." But I didn't need the coat. His arms were enough to keep me warm.

He brushed my ear with soft, nipping kisses, and I giggled and leaned back in his arms. Then I hiccuped, and a nagging little voice pricked my conscience. "I think I drank too much champagne," I said. "Please take me back to my cabin."

We circled the deck and came inside through another entrance. Feeling lightheaded and silly, I sat down on the floor. "I'm too tired to walk anymore," I said.

Forrest looked down at me with surprised amusement. "Charlotte, you have to get up."

"But my feet hurt."

"All right, then I'll carry you," he said, swooping me up in his arms.

I knew I was being outrageous, but I didn't seem to care. Winding my arms around Forrest's neck, I laid my head on his shoulder, drinking in his fresh, masculine scent. I was in love, and I didn't want the night to end.

When we got to my cabin, I handed him the key and somehow he managed to balance me in his arms and open the door.

Once inside, though, he stumbled in the dark and we both pitched forward and landed on the bed. The next thing I knew, he was kissing me again, and when his hands roamed possessively over my body, I couldn't bring myself to resist.

"Charlotte, Charlotte," he murmured huskily. "Let me love you."

His fingers were fumbling with the hooks on the

back of my gown, and I didn't protest when he slipped it down and kissed my breasts. I felt it slide over my hips, and when he had unhooked my corset and tossed it aside, I let his hands make me forget that this was a terrible sin.

He left me momentarily and in the darkness I could tell that he was undressing. Before I could protest, he was back, smothering my cries with passionate kisses. I felt the soft hair on his chest against my bare breasts and I trembled with an unknown want when he slipped his hand in between my legs.

"I want you so much, Charlotte," he whispered, and although I didn't know exactly what that meant, I heard myself say, "I want you too, Forrest."

Chapter 3

Sunlight was streaming through the small porthole when I opened my eyes. Disoriented, I sat up in bed and the sudden realization that I was naked hit me at the same time that I spotted my corset. There was something obscene about the way that ugly undergarment dangled half-on, half-off the chair, as if it had been slung there . . .

Oh, my God, I thought. Last night . . . I have to remember what happened last night!

Feeling shaky, I lay back down in the bed and pulled the covers up over me. After the concert, we had had dinner, and then we had gone to the ball. I remembered whirling round and round, and feeling so thirsty. Oh, yes, I recalled. I had been *very* thirsty, and the champagne had tasted so good . . .

Disjointed scenes passed swiftly through my mind then—Forrest kissing me up on deck, carrying me down the long corridor, coming into the cabin, and then—

"Oh, my God!"

Shame and remorse overwhelmed me, and I buried my face in the pillow and cried until there were no tears left. My throat burned and my head throbbed, but I forced myself to get out of bed and cover my treacherous body with a dressing gown.

Checking my watch, I saw that it was ten o'clock.

Forrest was probably relieved that I hadn't put in an appearance in the dining room, I thought, and then wondered how I would ever face him again.

I heard a knock on the door, and for a second, I froze. It must be the maid, I thought with sudden relief. She probably wants to do up the room.

Opening the door quickly, I gasped and took a step back. Forrest Singleton stood in the corridor holding the largest bouquet of flowers I had ever seen.

He was in the room before I could close the door, and giving me an astonished look, he said, "You've been crying. What's wrong, Charlotte?"

"Oh, how c-can you ask such a question?" I said, fighting back a fresh onslaught of tears. "Have the decency to leave me alone, Mr. Singleton, I b-beg of you."

He put the flowers on a table and tried to take me in his arms. "I could be mistaken, but last night I thought you cared for me, Charlotte."

My eyes blazed. "Please don't mention last night again. Unfortunately, I'm not used to drinking champagne, but that is hardly an excuse for my conduct."

I turned my back on him because the tears were rolling down my cheeks, but he turned me around again and said, "Please don't cry, Charlotte. I didn't seduce you, you know, if that's what you're worried about."

"Good heavens, what do you call— What do you call—" My voice broke and I could say no more.

He sat down in the chair and pulled me on his lap. "Listen to me, Charlotte. Last night I got carried away, but I want you to know, I would never take advantage of you. I respect you more than any girl I know. That's why I left when I did."

"You—you left? Still how c-can you respect me after—"

He placed his fingers over my lips. "Because I love you, Charlotte, and I want to marry you."

I shook my head. "You can't marry me!"

"Why not?"

"We're from two different worlds."

"Oh, stop that nonsense, Charlotte. What is that, an excuse? If you don't love me, just say so."

I couldn't deny it. "I do love you, Forrest," I said, "And I always will."

A triumphant look suddenly crossed his face, and planting a kiss on the tip of my nose, he stood me on my feet. "Dry your eyes and get dressed, sweetheart. I'm off to tell the captain he has a wedding to perform today!"

I gasped. "Today!"

"Of course, today. We'll have the rest of the week for a honeymoon."

It was impetuous and wild, and the very thought of it made my head spin, but I was in love and the man of my dreams was waiting for an answer.

One week later, we stood at the rail as the ship slipped slowly into Baltimore's harbor.

I wished these halcyon days at sea could have gone on forever, for here time was suspended and we existed in a world that lay outside reality.

But the best of honeymoons—and ours had surely been the best—must someday come to an end and one must resume living in the real world again.

I loved Forrest and I wanted so much to fit into his life and make him proud of me, but as the ship slipped closer to shore, that nagging old premonition cropped up like a sleeping snake and slithered around my mind. I pushed it away. What could possibly go wrong now when all my Cinderella dreams had come true?

Mrs. Singleton, I mused, still finding it hard to believe that the name belonged to me, and glancing down at the third finger of my left hand, I smiled. Forrest's ring was too big for me, but I had wound string around the shank to keep from losing it.

Following my gaze, he said, "We're stopping at the jeweler's today and getting you a proper wedding ring."

"This one did fine," I said. "We're properly married, aren't we?"

"Absolutely. Our marriage is legal in the eyes of the law. I made certain of that, my dear."

He lapsed into silence then, lost in his own thoughts. Wanting to bring him back to me, I squeezed his hand and said, "I'm anxious to see my new home."

"I told you it's just a little townhouse, so don't be disillusioned when you see it. At any rate, we shan't be there long," he added.

"What do you mean?"

"I mean, we'll probably move somewhere else. Find something bigger and nicer," he added.

The thought made me nervous. I should have preferred living simply, cooking and cleaning for the two of us with no servants to intimidate me, but I knew Forrest would never be content to live in such a way.

Although my husband had very little money and was struggling to succeed in his uncle's law firm, Forrest had been used to finer things.

The American Civil War had played a tragic role in my husband's background, for his mother and father's families had been on opposing sides of the conflict. Maryland had been a divided state, Forrest had informed me, and when his Confederate mother eloped with a Union officer, her family had disowned her.

Forrest was named for his mother's family, but that overture along with his birth went unnoticed and unforgiven by the Forrests.

His mother had died when Forrest was two years old, and his grief-stricken father rejoined the army and went out west to fight the Indians. It was then that his paternal grandparents took Forrest into their home and raised him in their sprawling mansion on the outskirts of Baltimore.

"They spoiled me rotten," he'd confessed, "but I loved them dearly. Their home was called Lauraland

36

after my grandmother and it was just about the loveliest house I've ever seen." He had paused a little sadly and then confided that his grandfather had lost all his money and died when Forrest was ten. Lauraland had been sold, and Forrest and his grandmother had moved to the house in Baltimore.

"A penny for your thoughts, Mrs. Singleton."

Forrest's voice broke through my reverie and I said, "I'm sorry. I was thinking about what you said."

"About what?"

"About moving somewhere bigger and nicer. I think what you really want is to go back to Lauraland."

A strange expression crossed his face and his voice turned cold. "Don't try to read my mind, Charlotte, and stop being afraid to reach for the stars."

His reaction took me by surprise and I must have looked a little hurt, for suddenly he pulled me close, and planting a gentle kiss on my forehead, he said, "You deserve to reach the stars, Charlotte, and so do I."

Remembering where we were, I broke away. "People can see us," I said.

He laughed. "My darling little prude. I'm counting on you to keep me on the straight and narrow."

The ship docked at noon, and after a delightful lunch at the Stafford Hotel, Forrest hailed a cab and had the driver take us to an elegant jewelry store. When we came out, I was wearing a beautiful diamond solitaire and, more important to me, a traditional gold wedding band.

The next time the carriage stopped, we were in front of an imposing townhouse on a tree-lined street in Mount Vernon Square. I don't know what I had expected, but this was obviously a fine neighborhood, and my naive dream of cooking and cleaning in a servantless household was permanently dispelled.

"This is an elegant neighborhood," I said.

"Oh, it is," he assured me. "In fact, Mt. Vernon is one of the finest areas in the city. There are some magnificent houses here. I just meant that ours unfortunately is not one of them."

"Are there servants in the house?" I asked.

"Only the housekeeper, Mrs. Chaney, and a maid." Hugging me to him, he brushed my forehead with a quick kiss. "Don't worry, darling. Mrs. Chaney will handle everything. She's a bit of a martinet, but you'll get used to her."

Another Madam, I thought. No, I won't get used to her. I'll just learn to tolerate her.

Mrs. Chaney even looked like Madam; both of them with long pinched noses and thin disapproving lips. She acknowledged our introduction with studied courtesy, but her cold eyes proclaimed that I had *shop* written all over me.

The house was charming and much larger than I had anticipated. Forrest had said that his grandparents had bought the house in 1845. "My grandfather wanted to sell it after he built Lauraland, but Grandmother wouldn't hear of it, so they rented it out until we had to move back in."

I gathered that was after Forrest's grandfather had died.

"So, you and your grandmother came back here to live."

"Yes. The house was in her name, which was luck. Otherwise we would have been forced to take a flat."

His words hit home, and I said, "That would have been unfortunate. The accommodations are usually rather poor."

I think it suddenly dawned on him that he might have offended me, and he said, "I told you they spoiled me, and from now on, I am going to spoil you, my darling."

"You already have, Forrest. I'm happier than I ever dreamed of being."

He took me in his arms then and held me close. "Oh, Charlotte. You're so good for me. This is only the beginning, sweetheart. There are wonderful years ahead for us. We're going to reach the stars, my darling."

"I already have," I said, and he picked me up and carried me upstairs to our bedroom.

"Forrest," I protested. "What will Mrs. Chaney think?"

"The hell with Mrs. Chaney," he said, depositing me on the big poster bed and nuzzling my ear with kisses.

A blissful week followed, and though I still felt uncomfortable around Mrs. Chaney, I must confess that we had little contact with each other. I suppose I should have asserted myself and assumed the position of mistress of the house, but I had no earthly idea what was to be done, and since Forrest was home a good deal of the time, I was satisfied to let Mrs. Chaney take charge.

We drove around town in our very own carriage—the height of luxury, in my estimation—but Forrest said the carriage was a disgrace and we should soon be buying another one.

I found Baltimore to be a charming city with many beautiful monuments, but Mount Vernon Place will always be my favorite. Our townhouse stood a stone's throw from the monument, and the stately column with the figure of General George Washington mounted majestically on the top dominated the whole area. Although I was not an American, I found the sight an awe-inspiring one.

The Peabody Conservatory was just around the corner and I felt at home when I gazed on the statue of this famous man, for he had also lived in London, where there is a similar statue of him on Threadneedle Street.

Those early September days were warm, and sometimes a gentle breeze would carry the strains of beautiful music from the conservatory right into our townhouse. What happy days they were, but short-lived, for Forrest returned to work and that very night he informed me that my grandmother's will was to be read the following Tuesday.

I don't know why the news upset me, but I felt like a dark cloud had suddenly swooped down and enveloped us. Forrest seemed preoccupied too, and I wondered if my gloom was contagious.

We took a hack to the law offices of Pendleton and Forrest on Charles Street. All of the countess's presumed heirs would be present for the reading. And I, her only blood relative, am more the outsider than any of them, I mused.

"What are their names again?" I asked Forrest when we were seated in the carriage.

He seemed impatient with the question. "You'll only forget them again. There are too many to remember, but if it makes you feel any better . . . Victor DeSantis was the countess's manager. He's an ugly old man with white hair," he added. "Then there's Marshall Haines, your grandmother's star protégé. He's a handsome young man with blond hair."

I gathered from the inflection in Forrest's voice that he was not overly fond of either Mr. DeSantis or Mr. Haines.

"Carla Pinetti is another protégé. She's also young, dark eyes, dark hair. She's not important," he said. "But Dorcas is. She's the stepdaughter, Dorcas Belinski Faro. She's liable to contest the will if it doesn't go her way. She has a son, Nicholos Faro. He'll be there, too."

"What about Mr. Faro?" I asked.

"Who?"

"Her husband, the boy's father."

"Oh, they were divorced years ago. He only married her because he thought she had money." He sniffed. "Time might yet prove him right."

We arrived in a matter of minutes and took the

elevator to the second floor of the large office building.

"Damn," Forrest muttered under his breath as we entered the office, for the others were all there ahead of us.

They were seated facing a short gray-haired man who rose and said, "You're late, Forrest. It's after nine."

"Sorry, Uncle. There was traffic in the street." Forrest addressed the assembled group then and said, "May I present my wife, Charlotte."

I felt my face catch fire as all eyes turned to me.

A dark-haired young woman who was seated in the far corner of the room gasped. "Your wife!" She was about to say something else, but a tall, handsome man with blond hair interrupted her.

"Well, congratulations, old man." He shook Forrest's hand and then turned to me. "This is a pleasure, Mrs. Singleton."

"Marshall Haines," Forrest said, and I took the man's extended hand.

Other introductions followed and I was relieved when Henry Forrest said, "It's getting late. Would all of you please sit down?"

It was obvious that our marriage was a complete surprise to the others, but of course Forrest had told his uncle. His was a face that was hard to read, however, which I supposed to be an asset in his law practice.

We took seats, and just before Henry Forrest began, a man and woman entered the office and discreetly took seats in the back of the room. They were handsome Italian people, more attractive by far than Dorcas or Victor DeSantis, but something in their manner told me they had been in the countess's employ. "Gia's housekeeper and her groom," Forrest whispered, confirming my guess.

Henry Forrest cleared his throat and said, "Now that everybody is present, I will commence." His voice sounded ominous as he adjusted his glasses and read. "The last will and testament of Gia Gerardo Belinski."

The first part of the will covered bequests to charities and servants, including a most generous one to the housekeeper, whose name was Sophia Concetta Grazziano.

Since none of this concerned me, my mind began to wander.

The dark-haired girl who had gasped when Forrest announced our marriage must be Carla Pinetti. Why had the news upset her? I wondered. And why did I feel her blazing black eyes boring into my back even now?

Dorcas Belinski Faro and her son were both older than I had expected. He was a grown man, possibly twenty-five or more, and she was at least fifty. She was a big woman with dyed jet-black hair that showed up her harsh features and gave her a sinister look.

Her son, Nicholas, was a decided contrast to his mother. Thin to the point of appearing emaciated, he looked ill and his dark eyes had the haunted look one sees on the faces of consumptives.

I turned my attention to Victor DeSantis. He was indeed a disagreeable-looking man. A member of the countess's own generation, he was probably seventy or more, for she had been sixty-five. I stole a glance at his rigid profile. Wasn't old age supposed to mellow people? I mused.

The only pleasant one in the bunch was Marshall Haines. He, at least, had shown some cordiality toward me. I remembered then that Forrest didn't like him and I smiled to myself. Mr. Haines was very handsome. Perhaps Forrest was jealous.

"An annual scholarship of three hundred dollars will be awarded to the most promising young soprano in the Baltimore area. The competition will be conducted through the auspices of the Peabody Institute every year for the next twenty years, and the annual endowment to the Peabody will amount to three thousand dollars per year for the next twenty years."

Henry Forrest's voice droned on and on, and the heirs began shifting in their seats. Victor DeSantis coughed loudly several times and Dorcas brought out a fan and fanned herself vigorously.

The thought suddenly dawned on me that the others might not know who I was. Forrest had introduced me only as his wife, Charlotte Singleton, and no mention at all had been made of my connection to the countess.

Henry Forrest, of course, knew, but I didn't think he would confide in his client's beneficiaries.

"To my groom, Cal Marcus, I leave my thorough-bred mare, Lady Baltimore, and the sum of five thousand dollars a year for life . . ."

The droning voice paused and a collective gasp broke the silence in the room. Victor DeSantis suddenly stood up. "That racehorse should be mine!"

Dorcas's face turned blood-red and she cried, "Sit down, Victor! That horse was promised to Nicky!" Then she sank back in her chair and said, "The bitch, she was only taunting my poor Nicky."

Using his fist like a gavel, Henry Forrest rapped on his desk. "Ladies and gentlemen, please control yourselves. I'll not tolerate such outbursts again."

The murmurs died down, but the elderly groom was gone. I had noticed him slip out of the room, his eyes brimming with tears while his good fortune was being castigated. I felt sorry for the man and I wondered how my own small bequest would be treated by these greedy people.

"To Carla Pinetti, my ungrateful little protégé, I leave my lovers. I always knew we shared them, Carla. May they be as faithful to you as they were to me, darling. I also bequeath to Carla the emerald broach and sapphire necklace which have been missing from my jewelry collection for over a year. You may keep them with my blessing."

Carla's wrath exploded in Italian. I had no idea what she said, but her message was clear. Storming out of the office in a hysterical rage, she shouted back, "Lies, they are nothing but lies! She was a wicked, jealous old woman."

The door slammed behind her and the others fidgeted in their chairs. It was obvious that they were all uneasy now, awaiting their turn.

"To Vincent DeSantis, my manager, I leave the advice he once gave to me: *He travels fastest who travels alone.* It was bad advice, but take it yourself, Victor. You deserve to be alone."

The old man's face registered no emotion, and dead silence filled the room.

"To Marshall Haines, I leave my music collection and sufficient funds to continue his musical education at an institute of his choice. His voice will take him to whatever heights he cares to climb."

If Marshall Haines was disappointed, he failed to show it, and the droning voice moved on.

"To Nicholas Faro, Count Belinski's grandson, I leave the Belinski castle in Russia and the suggestion that he find some means of livelihood to support it, for it has been a drain on my finances ever since I married his noble father."

Now there remained only Dorcas and myself, and probably only Dorcas, I thought, for if I should have been given a bequest it would have been mentioned earlier in the will. It was just as well. I hadn't wanted anything from this heartless woman in the first place.

"To Dorcas Belinski Faro, my dear stepdaughter, I leave the sum of twenty thousand dollars, which is more than her father brought to our marriage, for his debts, which I paid, amounted to a hundred thousand dollars."

Dorcas's face was again crimson and I thought she was going to choke. The others looked in confusion at one another.

"But who is to receive the bulk of the estate?" Victor DeSantis shouted. "There's no one left!"

The others nodded and spoke among themselves. Henry Forrest's voice rose above the din.

"Ladies and gentlemen! I have not finished reading the will."

44

"There's no one left," someone repeated.

Forrest's uncle sighed. "I'm afraid there is." His steel blue eyes met mine across the room. "Mrs. Singleton, will you come up front, please, so you can hear this more clearly?"

All eyes were focused on me. I saw shock, puzzlement, and the dawn of hate appear.

Forrest reached for my hand. "Go ahead, Charlotte. I'll stay back here."

I wanted to run out of the room as Carla had done, but my wooden legs carried me stiffly to a chair right in front of Henry Forrest's huge desk.

"To my granddaughter, Charlotte Stone, I leave my home, the Villa Montelano, and everything contained within and without the estate; the stables and the horses with the exception of the aforementioned racehorse, Lady Baltimore, the ninety acres of ground that surrounds the villa, and the balance of my assets after taxes and the distribution of bequests mentioned in this will, with the stipulation that she is to take up residence in the villa for at least two years after the date of my death. I also stipulate that all those now residing at the Villa Montelano be allowed to remain there for six months or until they are willing and able to make other arrangements for living quarters. This constitutes the final and complete terms of my last will and testament. Signed, Gia Gerardo, the Countess Belinski."

My heart was fluttering like a fan in my chest and my knees were so weak, I knew I should not be able to stand.

Forrest rushed to my side and whispered in my ear, "Relax, darling. There's nothing they can do."

Like the distant rumble of thunder, the voices of protest grew louder and louder.

Victor DeSantis's gigantic figure loomed menacingly over Henry Forrest. "What kind of hoax is this? How can there be a granddaughter? Gia never had a child!"

"I'm afraid she did. We've done a thorough investigation, Victor. Charlotte Stone's father was Gia's son."

Dorcas pushed her ample figure through the maze of people and chairs. "I intend to contest this will, Henry."

"That's your privilege, Dorcas."

"We don't have to contest it, Mother," her son said softly. "Because this isn't her last will."

The others all stopped talking and turned their attention to Faro. "What do you mean?" DeSantis said.

"I mean there's another will. I overheard Gia talking about it the night she died. She told that stupid maid of hers to call Henry Forrest and have him come out right away because she'd made a whole new will."

"This is the first I've heard of it," Henry said.

Faro smiled an ugly smile. "Maybe someone else in your office got the message instead." He turned to Forrest then. "I seem to remember that you came out to see Gia that night, Singleton."

"That's right, I did, but on another matter entirely."

Victor DeSantis sneered. "I know Gia. She was paranoid about her will. She would never have entrusted it to a *junior partner.*"

Nicholas Faro looked pointedly at Dorcas and said, "Let me take you back to the hotel, Mother. You look exhausted."

The others left with them and Forrest said to his uncle, "I don't believe there's another will, but those leeches are desperate. Charlotte and we had better get out to the villa before they descend on it like a swarm of locusts."

Uncle Henry gave my husband a calculating look. "The Winslow case goes to court on Wednesday. Shall I assign a replacement for you?"

"Certainly not. I'll get Charlotte settled in and drive back to Baltimore in the morning."

I felt the hand of fate reach out and snatch me up.

All the vague premonitions that had haunted me for months suddenly culminated in this moment, and a ghost of a thought brushed eerily across my mind.

Say no. You don't have to go to the Villa Montelano, it whispered, but Forrest was smiling down at me.

"Come, sweetheart. We'll get you packed and be on our way to the villa before those vultures can check out of the Belvedere Hotel."

Love triumphed over caution as I heard myself say, "Whatever you think best, Forrest."

Chapter 4

Forrest stood in the doorway while I packed. "Just take what you'll need for several days," he said. "I'll have Mrs. Chaney ship the rest up to the villa later."

I was still in a state of shock. "What are we going to do with this house?" I asked.

"Nothing."

I felt relieved. "Then this isn't a permanent move. We'll come back here."

"Charlotte," he said impatiently. "Why live here when we can live in a forty-room mansion? This house will be used when I have to stay in town." Then pulling out his watch, he checked the time. "Hurry, sweetheart. We have a long trip ahead of us."

We took a train out of the city, and soon the scenery changed from cobblestoned streets to a panorama of lush, rolling hills and deep wooded valleys. "The countryside is beautiful," I remarked.

"Wait till you see our land, Charlotte." He looked wistful as he said, "There's a woods that borders the estate, and in the autumn when the leaves turn, the colors range from fiery red to molten gold. If you stand on the hillside and look down, it's quite a spectacular sight."

"And the house, is it equally beautiful?" I asked, for I wanted desperately to shake my dark and evil image of the Villa Montelano.

"Oh, the house is a monstrosity."

"A monstrosity!"

He shrugged. "Just my personal opinion, dear. Your grandmother's taste ran to the opulent." He laughed derisively. "Gia couldn't decide what she wanted, so she incorporated everything she saw and liked into the villa. I told you the outside resembled a Moorish castle. Well, the inside is straight out of Versailles." He smiled then and patted my hand. "Don't worry about it, sweetheart. We'll stamp our own images on the villa. Maybe even change its name," he mused.

His words did little to curb my apprehension. Dear God, I thought, will I ever feel at home in such a place?

He jolted me out of my reverie when he said, "While we're on the subject, I want to warn you about the others."

I must have looked terrified, as indeed I was, for he put a protective arm about me and said, "Now, don't look like that. They're not going to murder you in your bed, but they will try to give you a hard time. I want you to stand up to them, Charlotte. Just remember, you're the mistress of the Villa Montelano now."

"When will you be back?" I said.

"As soon as I can wind up this case—but, Charlotte, you have to realize I can't be at the villa all the time. I have clients, sweetheart. Would you want me to desert them?"

I thought, *Yes, I would. Let your uncle take care of them. I need you to be with me!*

But I shook my head and answered, "No, of course not, dear."

The train made stops at several rural junctions, and just when I was beginning to think we would never arrive at our destination, Forrest stood up and retrieved my luggage from the overhead rack. "Next

49

stop is ours," he said jovially.

We pulled into a small station where a handful of people stood on a wooden platform waiting to board the train. Several children hopped up and down with excitement as the engine pulled into the depot, wheels grinding to a halt and whistle shrieking like a banshee.

A small boy raced forward as we stepped down, and his mother grabbed him by the ear. "You got the manners of a goat, Joseph Fisher! Let the lady and gentlemen get off the train first." Then she turned to Forrest. "He begs your pardon, sir. He's just excited he is."

"And why wouldn't he be?" Forrest said, giving the little fellow an understanding smile. "It's not every day a lad gets to ride on a train.

The child smiled back at him with gratitude and I felt a rush of love for my husband. Forrest's warmth and easygoing manner put people at ease, and I wished with all my heart that he could stay and soothe the ruffled feathers of all those vultures who were going to descend on me tomorrow.

A rickety old carriage was parked in a field alongside the station and Forrest said, "We'll have to use the coach. No one at the villa is expecting us."

The driver, as disreputable looking as his vehicle, suddenly stepped down from his perch and approached us. "Can I be taking you to the villa, Mr. Singleton?"

"That you can, Wilson. They won't be sending a carriage since we're not expected."

The coachman reached for our luggage, but Forrest said, "I've got it, Wilson, and by the way, this is Mrs. Singleton."

The old man looked at me with obvious surprise and tipped his old-fashioned stovepipe hat. "Afternoon, Ma'am." He smiled, showing off a gold front tooth that glittered in the sunlight, and I suddenly decided that I didn't like him.

He probably reminds me of someone else, I thought,

for what possible reason could I have for disliking the man?

Wilson opened the door and Forrest helped me into the carriage. "Take the Old Fork Road," he told him. "I want to show Mrs. Singleton the woods."

Wilson looked up at the sky. "We're gonna get a storm," he said.

Forrest ignored him and we were almost jolted out of our seats when Wilson angrily snapped the whip and the old horse lurched across the open field. The carriage careened onto a narrow dirt road, and soon my attention was drawn away from the surly driver and back to the beauty of the rolling Maryland countryside.

The carriage traveled at a brisk pace and then swerved sharply left, and we found ourselves in a grove of tall trees with just enough room to pass in between.

The narrow lane widened out to a clearing with a stream running through it, and on the other side sharp cliffs rose up to meet a dark and threatening sky.

Lightning suddenly streaked across the horizon and crackled as it ripped through a tree, tearing off branches and sending them flying. I winced as a loud clap of thunder followed in its wake. The rural paradise had taken on a menacing tone and I wanted to escape it and run back to the city with its familiar concrete and cobblestones.

The driver cracked the whip again and the carriage pitched forward as the horse took wings and raced through the forest at breakneck speed. Great gusts of wind whipped the rain into sheets that blew in front of the carriage, making it virtually impossible to see the jagged path. I fully expected us to crash into a tree or be struck by the lightning that flashed furiously on and off as it lit up the sky.

"It's only a storm," Forrest said, as I buried my face in his shoulder.

I felt his arms tighten around me like a protective

shield and I wanted to beg him to change his mind about leaving in the morning, but I was afraid he would get angry.

When I raised my head, I was relieved to see that we had come out of the woods and were on the open road again. The storm had not lessened in intensity, but I felt safer now that we were not completely surrounded by so many large trees.

"If you look to your right," Forrest said, "you'll catch a glimpse of the villa as we round the bend."

Peering through the rain-washed window, my heart literally stood still, for high on the hillside sat an exact replica of the house that had haunted my dreams since first it had materialized on the ink-splashed pages of my notepaper.

Like the inkblot, the house resembled a mosque with a series of domes graduating toward a great central dome.

"Didn't I tell you it was a monstrosity?" Forrest remarked with a laugh. "Gia claimed she had the domes transported from an old palace in Persia, but I took that story with a grain of salt."

I nodded solemnly, wishing I could look on the house as an eccentric old woman's joke instead of an evil omen, but I just couldn't shake my conviction that fate had ordained my coming here, and that something ominous awaited me at the Villa Montelano.

The road leading to the house was winding, and tall trees obscured it from my view, but it was there, like a harbinger of doom, and I gasped when I saw it close-up. There was something evil about the villa, and without thinking, I turned to my husband and said, "Please don't make me go in there. I'm afraid."

He looked at me with surprise and then impatience. "Pull yourself together, Charlotte. What will the servants think? You're the mistress of this house. For God's sake, act the part."

"I'm sorry. I'm tired and a little overwhelmed by

52

all of this."

He hugged me to him. "Of course you are, sweetheart, but this is a dream come true. I want you to enjoy it."

Wilson interrupted our conversation by flinging open the carriage door and confronting us with a scowl. "We're here, and small wonder it is—travelin' through the woods in the middle of a storm."

"Go up to the house and tell the servants their new mistress has arrived," Forrest said.

Wilson slammed the door and tramped up the steps to the house.

"He's angry that you made him drive through the woods," I said.

"He's always angry about something."

"Well, he did warn you about the storm."

"So, it came up faster than I anticipated. Don't worry about it. He'll be well-paid for getting a little wet."

Wilson returned then, followed by two male servants from the villa, and while one of them saw to the luggage, the other held an umbrella over our heads and escorted us into the house.

I don't know what I had expected to see, but nothing in my limited background could have prepared me for the Villa Montelano.

The entrance hall alone was larger than my London flat, and the townhouse in Mount Vernon Place suddenly shrank in my mind to the proportions of a dollhouse.

Feeling like a country bumpkin, I gazed upward to a ceiling that must have been fully twenty feet high. It was ornately plastered and gilded, and I had seen a similar one in a grand cathedral in London once.

Gazing quickly around the room, my eyes rested on a large circular window of leaded stained glass. It reminded me of a kaleidoscope with its geometric patterns of gold, red, and blue. Flanked on either side by two matching oblong windows, the three of them sparkled like jewels in the light that filtered through.

"Charlotte," Forrest's voice cut through my day-dreams and I suddenly realized that a woman had entered the hall and was standing before us. "This is Sophia Grazziano," he said. "She was your grand-mother's dresser, and when Gia retired from the stage, Sophia took over managing the villa."

I had seen her in the law office, but we had not been introduced. Close-up, she was even more striking. Her face was unlined, the complexion flawless although she must have been over sixty. Thick black hair, liberally sprinkled with gray and drawn back tightly in a huge knot gave her an austere, forbidding look.

Our eyes met, and the coldness and contempt I saw in hers sent a chill running down my spine.

Speaking with a heavy accent, she said, "I knew your grandmother when she no older than you are, Signora Singleton, but you do not resemble her at all."

"I've been told I favor my mother," I said, feeling a sudden surge of pride in the fact. I wanted no kinship with the Countess Belinski and the knowledge that I had inherited neither her talent nor her temperament suited me fine.

The woman's dark eyes searched mine for a moment and then she said to Forrest, "Congratulations on your marriage, Signore Singleton. I wish you both every happiness." Turning back to me, she assumed a businesslike air and added, "If it is agreeable, Signora, I will call the staff together and you can meet with them tomorrow morning at ten."

Oh, Lord, I thought. Whatever shall I say to them? I have no earthly idea what is expected of servants in an establishment like this.

Postpone it, I thought. Plead fatigue, but Forrest answered for me. "Excellent idea, Sophia. Mrs. Singleton will be happy to meet the staff. And now, we'd like to get settled in. Have the bags brought up to the Blue Room."

She looked at him with surprise, but her expression quickly reverted to one of disinterest. "Certainly, Signore."

The young lad who had brought in our luggage led us up the widest staircase I had ever seen. Thick ruby red carpeting covered the treads and as we mounted the stairs, Forrest ran his hand over the beautiful carved banister. "This is African rosewood," he said. "Magnificent, isn't it?"

I nodded, but made no comment. I thought *everything* was magnificent, but would I ever feel at home here? I wondered.

The young servant showed us to our room, which was a glorious mixture of my favorite color. The handsome Persian carpet combined every shade from indigo to sapphire in a riot of blues against a rich cream-colored background. The heavy crocheted bedspread and matching canopy were also in cream, and velvet drapes of regal royal blue graced the windows.

It was a gracious room with none of the flamboyance I had glimpsed downstairs, and I didn't feel intimidated by it.

Forrest was watching me and he smiled. "You like this room, don't you, Charlotte?"

"Oh, yes, it's the loveliest room I've ever seen."

"That's because Gia had nothing to do with it," he said, and running his hand over the handsome bedspread, he added, "She forgot to do over the guest rooms, otherwise this would surely have been replaced by something gaudy and red."

"Then I'm glad she forgot. That spread is an heirloom, and besides that, I love the blues in this room. Blue is my favorite color."

He stretched out on the bed, and pulled me down beside him. "I didn't know that."

Taking off my hat, he placed it on the bedside table,

and regarding me with an expression that was rather wistful, he said, "There are so many things we don't know about each other, Charlotte."

He kissed me tenderly then and all my fears evaporated. I loved, and wonder of wonders was loved in return. If Forrest wanted me to be a grand lady, then a grand lady I'd be. Or die in the attempt, I thought, and then mentally bit my tongue. I'd soon be sharing the villa with all the displaced heirs, I remembered.

Forrest's mood suddenly brightened and he said, "I'm not surprised that you like blue. The color suits you, Charlotte. It's gentle and serene: ladylike, too," he added with a twinkle in his eye, and reaching behind me he began to unhook the bodice of my dress.

"Forrest." I cried. "It's daylight!"

He gave me a wicked laugh. "The better to see you with, my little prude."

"It's almost four o'clock, teatime. They'll be expecting us downstairs."

He unhooked the last clasp and the back of my gown opened to the waist. "You're in America now, Charlotte," he said, pulling the dress over my head. "We don't have teatime, and who would be expecting us if we did? We're the master and mistress of the villa, darling."

Tossing the discarded dress on a chair, he pushed me gently down on the pillow and slipped my chemise down to my waist. "Oh, Charlotte, you're so beautiful," he said, kissing my naked breasts and making me forget that it must certainly be immoral to make love in broad daylight.

We were dressing for dinner when Forrest said, "Tomorrow, when you introduce yourself to the staff, I want you to select one of the servants to act as your personal maid."

"I don't need one, darling," I said. "I much prefer to

have you hook me up the back."

His face was turned, so I couldn't read his expression, but I thought I detected a slight note of impatience in his voice when he answered. "Charlotte, you are the mistress of the villa. Of course you will have a personal maid."

Oh dear, I thought. You can take the girl out of the shop, but can you ever take the shop out of the girl?

"And another thing," he said, seeming to read my thoughts. "If the others should ask what you did in London, just say you were a teacher."

"But, I never taught," I said.

"You told me you had a teacher's certificate."

"I do, but . . ."

"Regardless, then, you are a teacher," he said.

I don't know where the tears came from, but they suddenly overflowed like a pent-up dam, and I bent my head so Forrest would not see them.

He was instantly beside me, though, and turning me around to face him, he enfolded me in his arms. "Don't, Charlotte, please don't. I wouldn't hurt you for anything in the world."

I buried my face in his broad shoulder, weeping like a child, and as such, I didn't protest when he carried me over to a large fireside chair and sat me down on his lap. Brushing my hair back from my eyes, he cuddled me to him like a gentle father and said, "I don't care what you did in London, Charlotte. I was proud of you then, and I'm proud of you now. But, some of the others can be vicious, especially Carla and Dorcas. They'll come back here ready to fight, and I don't want you to give them any ammunition."

"They can have it all. I don't want it," I said.

"Hush, don't say that, Charlotte. Your grandmother was trying to make amends. Don't deny her your forgiveness." Reaching in his pocket he brought out a handkerchief and handed it to me. "Now dry your tears and let me see you smile."

Feeling like a ninny, I smiled and said, "I don't know what came over me."

"Too many sudden changes in your young life, but you'll adjust, just like you adjusted to your wicked husband." He raised his eyebrow and said, "I do believe you liked making love in broad daylight. Shame on you, Charlotte. What would your Cockney landlady have to say about that?"

I couldn't help laughing. Poor old Mrs. Hill had been convinced I was going to the devil when I left London. Whatever would she think if she knew I was living in decadent splendor in a Moorish castle?

We had dinner in what Forrest referred to as *the small dining room*. I failed to see anything small about it. Both our dining room and drawing room in Mount Vernon Place would have fitted neatly inside it, but Forrest said the banquet hall was three times as big, and was only used when the countess gave one of her large, formal dinners.

We sat at opposite ends of the long mahogany table and I found myself wishing for the coziness and intimacy of our meals together in the little townhouse.

The color scheme in this room was predominantly gold with touches of red. The walls were covered in gold brocade, and heavy red velvet drapes lined in gold satin hung over the long, narrow windows.

The meal consisted of several courses with a side serving of some kind of pasta that was absolutely delicious.

I found it hard to converse naturally with my husband, for we were too far away from each other and my awkwardness was not helped by the two servants who hovered about, constantly replacing dishes and replenishing the wine and water glasses.

I was relieved when the dessert was served, and although I felt as stuffed as a pouter pigeon, I forced

58

myself to eat the rich cake that was placed before me lest it be considered a breach of etiquette to refuse it.

After dinner, Forrest showed me through this wing of the house which consisted of a banquet hall, a theater, a large and small gallery, and a library where he paused and looked over the books that lined the shelves.

There were many rare books, particularly in the field of music, he said, and then he added that the paintings and objects of art that were housed in the two galleries were considered to be quite a valuable collection.

The extent of my inheritance was beginning to dawn on me and I felt even more inadequate to cope with the responsibilities such wealth entailed. Thank God I have Forrest to lean on, I thought, and then remembered that he would be leaving early in the morning and I would be completely on my own until the weekend.

There were several small salons which Forrest said were used in the evening for after-dinner conversation or card playing by guests or those living at the villa on a permanent basis. They were as formal and ostentatious as the large drawing room, which was done in pink and crimson.

The furnishings, Forrest informed me, were a combination of Louis XV and XVL, and the countess had later added several Chinese pieces which she felt lent an exotic touch to the room's decor.

By this time my eyes ached from viewing so much busyness; bric-a-brac and wall hangings in untold quantities, vines and curlicues picked out in gilt; carpets and draperies splashed with every conceivable combination of designs, and all of it orchestrated in strong, brilliant color.

I longed to return to the understated elegance of our blue bedroom, and I prayed that a good night's sleep would miraculously prepare me to cope with Forrest's departure in the morning and the subsequent arrival of the other heirs.

So, I was relieved when Forrest said, "It's been a long day, darling. I want you to go upstairs and get ready for bed. I'll be up in a few minutes and I'll bring you a warm drink to put you to sleep."

I wanted to ask him to come with me, but I knew I was being ridiculous. I was a grown-up, married lady. Surely I could go upstairs by myself. I flashed him a brave smile. "All right, dear, but don't be long."

He brushed my brow with a quick kiss. "Half an hour, and that's a promise."

I left the drawing room and walked down the long corridor that led to the great hall. The villa was as silent as a tomb. Not a servant was to be seen and I had to assume they had all retired to their own quarters in another wing of the house.

The great hall was in semidarkness, lit only by a small lamp which the servants had left burning. In the shadows, I gazed fearfully at the suit of tilting armor that stood guard over the stairway. It was over six feet tall and I was reluctant to pass it, being suddenly seized by a childish notion that someone was hiding inside it.

I stood there for what seemed like a long time and then I picked up my skirts and ran all the way up the stairs, never stopping until I was in the sanctuary of the Blue Room, breathless, but safe.

When Forrest came into the room, I was dozing, my head propped up against the pillows, an unopened book beside me.

He came over to the bed and handed me a tall glass. "Drink this, sweetheart. It will put you to sleep."

I looked at him with drowsy eyes. "I don't need it, Forrest. I'm sleepy already."

"Drink it for me," he insisted.

I sat up and took the glass from his hand. It tasted funny, and I said, "I don't know if I like it. What is it?"

"A milk punch. It'll soothe your nerves. Come on, now. Bottoms up, like a good girl."

I drank it down and made a face. "There, I drank it.

Now you're not going to leave. You're coming to bed, too."

"Of course," he said, disappearing into the dressing room, and a few minutes later, the light went out and I felt the mattress sag under his weight. I snuggled up against him and an instant later, a black curtain descended on my brain and I was plunged into a state of total oblivion.

Chapter 5

I awoke to total darkness and complete disorientation. Where was I? In the ship's cabin? At the townhouse? No, not the townhouse, I thought, sitting up in bed, for there was no street light shining in the window.

The villa! Yes, of course. I was in the Blue Room at the Villa Montelano, and the last thing I remembered was drinking the glass of punch.

Forrest had said it would put me to sleep, and he was right. I must have nodded off immediately, but why had I suddenly awakened?

What difference does it make? I thought drowsily, and turning over on my side, I reached out for the comforting presence of my husband. But the other side of the bed was cold and empty. Forrest was not there!

I stiffened, as a childish, irrational fear spread over me, and then reaching for my robe, I got out of bed and lit the lamp. I was alone in the room and I jumped when the hall clock struck three.

Leaving the light on, I got back in bed, consoling myself with the thought that Forrest would be back soon, but when the clock struck four and I was still alone, I became upset.

I surmised that Forrest had taken my empty glass downstairs and then decided to check the library again.

He had been interested in some of the books on music, I recalled.

Now he's probably asleep in a chair, I thought, and putting on my robe, I stepped out into the corridor and peered over the railing.

A small lamp in the foyer cast an eerie glow over the darkened great hall. "Forrest," I called.

My voice rang hollow in the cavernous depths below and reluctantly I began to descend the staircase.

I was about halfway down when I heard it, a low, ghostly hum. The voice belonged to a woman, but if there was a tune at all, I didn't recognize it. The eerie sound paralyzed me and I stood motionless while every nerve in my body tingled with a raw and primitive fear.

The humming stopped as suddenly as it had begun, and I turned and ran back up the steps as if the Devil himself were behind me.

Once inside the Blue Room, I closed the door and, dragging a boudoir chair across the floor, I lodged it under the doorknob.

Oh, how could Forrest do this to me? He knows I'm afraid of this house. I crawled back in bed, feeling abandoned and hurt, but slumber, like the proverbial sandman, was a stealthy hunter and the next time I heard the clock strike, it was seven o'clock in the morning.

A bright September sun flooded the room with light, and before I could collect my thoughts, I found myself encircled by two strong arms. "Wake up, Sleeping Beauty," Forrest said, planting a kiss on the back of my neck. He smelled deliciously of tooth powder and shaving soap, and I turned my head to taste the freshness of his lips.

He was fully dressed and I said, "How long have you been up?" Before he could answer, my memory returned and I pulled away from him. "Where did you go last night?"

"Go?" He raised an eyebrow and gave me a quizzical smile. "What do you mean?"

63

"I woke up in the middle of the night and you weren't here. Why did you leave me like that, Forrest? You knew I was afraid."

He put his arms around me again. "You were dreaming, darling."

Could I have been? "But, it was so real," I said. "I heard the clock strike. I got up, and started to go downstairs, but . . ."

"But what?" he asked, running his hand through my long hair, his mouth pressed close to my ear.

"I heard a woman's voice. She was humming. Oh, it was so creepy."

"There, there, sweetheart," he whispered, patting me on the back. "A woman humming," he said with a touch of amusement. "That sounds like a nightmare to me."

"You didn't leave the room, then?"

"Where would I go?"

I shrugged. "I thought maybe you were downstairs reading. You seemed so interested in those books in the library."

He laughed. "They're not going anywhere. I can read them anytime. Now get up, darling. A good breakfast will set you to rights. I, for one, am ravenous, and if you don't get up this very minute, I'm going to eat you!"

He gave me a playful bite on the neck, and giggling, I jumped out of bed and ran into the dressing room.

I washed quickly, and, scanning my wardrobe, finally selected an apricot morning dress. The color was becoming and I wanted to look my best, remembering with a touch of sadness that Forrest would be leaving in a few hours. Today is Tuesday, I mused, and I won't see him again until Friday afternoon.

The thought was sobering and I must have looked forlorn, for he swept me into his arms and seared my lips with kisses.

The apricot gown lay over a chair, waiting to be put on, and still holding the kiss, we backed up to the bed and fell into it. Our coming together was swift and sweet and a little poignant because we were still bride and groom and soon we'd be parted for the very first time.

Later, as we descended the staircase arm-in-arm, I again remembered the dream. With unaccustomed clarity, I recalled the spookiness of seeing the great hall bathed in an amber glow that cast dark shadows on the walls. I remembered how my senses had bristled like a cat's whiskers when I'd heard that tuneless hum. "That punch had a strange effect on me," I said. "What was in it?"

"Just an egg, some cream, and a little rum." He gave me a condescending smile. "It wasn't the drink, Charlotte. You just had a plain, old-fashioned nightmare."

We entered the small dining room and I was surprised to see a woman at the buffet table. Her back was to us, but when she turned around, I saw that it was Carla Pinetti, the tempestuous young woman who'd left the law office in such a huff.

Fixing her eyes on Forrest, she smiled warmly. *"Buon giorno."*

"Good morning," he answered, and putting an arm around my shoulder, he said, "You remember Carla, don't you, darling?"

"Of course. Good morning, Miss Pinetti."

She gave me a condescending look and Forrest hastily added, "We're all on a first-name basis here, darling. Carla and Charlotte will do just fine."

"By all means," Carla said. "We're just one big, happy family at the Villa Montelano."

She took her plate to the table and Forrest turned his attention to the buffet. Lifting one silver cover after another, he exclaimed, *"Frittata al formaggio, frittata al prosciutto, salsiccia, crespelle."* Handing me a plate from the warming tray, he said, "You must try a little of everything, Charlotte. Italian food is magnificent. You'll love it even if you can't pronounce it."

I could see where language was going to be another barrier that would separate me from the rest of them. I knew a little French, but I was not even proficient enough in that to read a menu, while the others, Forrest included, probably spoke several languages fluently.

We joined Carla, and as soon as we were seated, she turned to Forrest and began to speak rapidly in Italian.

In a voice as sharp and cold as an icicle, he cut her off. "We will converse in English, Carla. My wife doesn't understand Italian."

Two spots of color appeared on her cheeks and her dark eyes smoldered with resentment as they met mine. "I apologize. We are all multilingual here, but I shall try to remember that you speak only English."

"I don't mind," I replied. "I might learn something."

"I'm sure you will." Pushing her plate aside, she turned back to Forrest and said, "When are you leaving?"

"In about an hour."

"Good. I'll go with you. Some of my luggage is still at the station."

He looked annoyed. "How come?"

"Because that idiot of a coachman refused to take all of it, that's why."

"Did you arrive this morning?" I asked Carla, for like a serpent an ugly thought had slowly slithered across my mind.

Her smile was smug. "No, *cara mia*. I arrived yesterday afternoon."

Forrest closed the suitcase and picked up his hat. "Remember, sweetheart, you're to meet with the servants at ten. And don't forget," he added, giving me an encouraging smile. "I want you to select a personal maid."

Locked in my own thoughts, I nodded absent-mindedly. Jealousy and suspicion, tormented twins of the insecure, hovered like bats in a dark corner of my mind.

Had Forrest lied about last night? Had his absence been a reality and not a dream? Then I suddenly remembered the chair under the doorknob.

Of course it had been a dream! If the chair had really been there, Forrest wouldn't have been able to get back in the room again.

How could I have entertained such disloyal thoughts? And overcome with remorse, I threw my arms around my husband's neck.

"Oh, I do love you, Forrest," I cried. "And I'm going to miss you ever so much!"

My ardor took him by surprise, and he laughed. "Why, Charlotte, I do believe you're trying to seduce me."

I blushed. "If that's what it takes to keep you here."

He crushed me to him and his voice was husky in my ear. "My proper little British bride! How I would love to accept your delightful offer, but duty calls." Then he kissed me and said, "I feel like a beast leaving you here to cope with all these crazy Italians, but don't let them intimidate you, Charlotte. Just remember, you are the mistress of the villa."

I nodded, wanting only to please him, but I didn't think I could ever be the mistress of the villa, for this house reflected the image of a vain and pretentious woman; someone I would not have liked and who, I am sure, would not have liked me.

"For-eest!"

It was Carla, calling from downstairs. Her voice assaulted my ears and made me homesick for the clean, clipped sound of a London accent.

Forrest rolled his eyes. "Gia always said Carla's voice was more timbre than tone." Then he kissed me quickly. "Good-bye, sweetheart. I'll see you Friday afternoon."

I stood at the window and watched them leave. Carla wore a bright green suit and a matching hat trimmed with ostrich plumes.

Forrest handed her into the carriage and then seated himself beside her. The ostrich plumes fluttered prettily against Carla's dark hair and I had a sudden urge to heave the window box down at her head. The violence of my emotions shocked me. It's this house, I thought. The Villa Montelano is saturated with hate, and if Forrest and I stay here, what will happen to our love?

I went downstairs, and since it was only nine o'clock I wandered aimlessly through the empty ornate rooms. Surely, I thought, there must be one spot where I can feel at home, but there was not an informal room in the house.

In the large drawing room, a curio cabinet caught my eye, and to my delight, I saw that it contained a collection of music boxes. Without thinking, I opened the door and withdrew a dainty figurine. The tiny porcelain ballerina was exquisitely crafted, and very carefully, I turned her over and wound the little key.

Holding the music box in the palm of my hand, I watched enthralled as the little figure twirled around and around to a tinkling tune which I didn't recognize, but later learned was from the opera *Lohengrin.*

"Desidera?"

The voice was low, but it startled me nevertheless, for I thought I was alone in the room. I whirled around and the music box slipped out of my hand.

I gasped, and Signora Grazziano said, *"Madre di Dio,"* as the little figurine hit the floor and splintered into a thousand pieces.

Horrified, I stooped down and started picking them up. "I'm so sorry. You startled me and it slipped out of my hand. Perhaps it can be glued," I added, stupidly—for anyone could see the damage was beyond repair.

She looked down on me with contempt. "One does not glue a priceless Pattiere."

I had never heard of the famous French artisan, and I stared back at her like a gauche schoolgirl.

Her black eyes bored into mine. "Monsieur Pattiere

presented that particular piece to the countess after he heard her sing Norma at La Scala."

I stood up and faced her. "I'm ever so sorry," I said, wishing I'd never even seen the music box, much less held it in my clumsy hands.

Reaching for the bell cord, she jerked it impatiently, and in a matter of minutes, a young freckle-faced maid with a shock of bright red hair appeared in the doorway. Her lilting brogue was music to my ears. "Beggin yere pardon, Senior Grazziano, but did you ring?"

The housekeeper glared at her. "Signora, *Signora!* Can't you say it right!" The girl looked confused and Signora Grazziano threw up her hands. "Just get a dustpan and clean up this mess." Then she turned to me with eyes that were cold and dark with suppressed anger. "If you've finished inspecting the music boxes, Mrs. Singleton, we can get on with meeting the servants."

I followed her through a maze of corridors that led to another area of the house, and in a large room off the old-fashioned kitchen the assembled servants stood in line waiting to be introduced to their new mistress.

The Signora introduced the servants, apprising me of each one's duties, and when all had filed past, she said, "Mr. Singleton told me you would be selecting a personal maid. I suggest you choose Anna. I call her back?"

"I thought I would offer the position to the little red-haired maid I saw in the drawing room," I said.

"Fiona?" She followed the name with a disparaging laugh. "Really, Mrs. Singleton. Fiona is just a parlor maid and she's only been with us for a few weeks."

I wasn't going to be overruled, not this time. "Fiona will do," I said simply, and the Signora shrugged.

I managed to find my way back to the main wing of the house, and as I approached the great hall, I heard voices.

Oh, Lord, I thought, the displaced heirs have finally arrived!

I decided to wear peach. It was a brown-haired girl's best color. Madam had said so, and she was an expert, wasn't she?

Put the little hazel-eyed, brown-haired wrens in peach. It's the best we can do for them.

Brilliant green plumes and Carla's jet black hair flashed before my eyes.

A beautiful woman has blond or black hair—maybe red, if it's the right shade—but brown? Never!

Madam's words of wisdom were always followed by a Gallic shrug, and looking at myself in the mirror with Fiona behind me, I automatically hunched my shoulders together.

Fiona's flaming red hair was definitely not the right shade, and the abundance of freckles that dotted her plain little face were another liability, but she was too practical to let it bother her. My own lack of beauty had never bothered me either until now, I mused.

When a plain woman marries a handsome man . . . I let the thought hang. Forrest isn't interested in Carla, I told myself.

How do you know? one of my demons probed. *They could have been lovers before he ever met you.*

But, he married me! I insisted.

The demon's twin laughed. *And why do you think he married you? What do you have to offer a man like Forrest Singleton?*

I covered my ears and Fiona said, "Oh, mum. Do the earbobs pinch?"

"What? Oh, no, Fiona, they're fine," I answered. This is ridiculous. I must stop imagining things, I told myself.

I looked up at the mirror again, and what I saw there paralyzed me with horror. Fiona had changed into a beautiful black-haired witch. I didn't recognize the face, but the creepy seductive smile chilled me to the bone.

Jumping up, I knocked over a bottle of cologne. "Oh, mum, be careful. Don't get it on your gown."

I shrank away from her, but she had changed back again, and was staring at me, her homely little face full of concern.

"There, I caught it. Thank the saints in heaven. I wouldn't be wantin' you to spoil your beautiful gown."

I was still shaking when I left the room. Of course it hadn't really happened. My mind had been playing tricks on me again, but that was small comfort. I have always considered myself a sensible person, so what was happening to me? Was I losing my mind?

It had all started in this very room last night. No, I corrected myself, it had started back in London. Hadn't I experienced premonitions of danger there on the very day Forrest had appeared with an invitation to the Villa Montelano? And what about the inkblot, that haunting vision of evil that had suddenly materialized on the letter of acceptance I was writing?

It all centered around the villa, though. That was plain to see, and I wished with all my heart that my bohemian grandmother had not been so eager to salve her conscience. A token gift would have been sufficient to provide Forrest and me with a little extra comfort and still remain in the charming city of Baltimore.

I slowly descended the wide, magnificent staircase, and when I reached the bottom, a babble of voices drifted out to me. Wrapping my courage around me like a shield, I followed the sounds to the drawing room.

The glittering group of handsomely dressed people looked up as I entered the room and my feet immediately turned to lead and shackled me to the floor. Finding it impossible to move, I merely stood in the doorway while several pairs of hostile eyes stared back at me.

"Ah, Mrs. Singleton, so nice to see you again." The young man came forward, reached for my arm, and by the grace of God my feet were suddenly released from their shackles. I thought I should always be eternally grateful to Marshall Haines for rescuing me that first evening when I had felt myself surrounded by enemies.

His poise and self-confidence soothed my jangled nerves and allowed me to maintain some semblance of composure. "You've already met Carla, Victor, Dorcas, and Nicholas," he said. "And in case you've forgotten, my name is Marshall." He gave me a warm smile. "May we call you Charlotte?"

"By all means."

Leading me over to Victor DeSantis and Carla Pinetti, who were seated beside an elderly man with very long, very white hair, Marshall said, "You've already met Carla and Victor, but now I want you to meet the Maestro."

The two men stood up and I was introduced to the Maestro whose long Italian name was unpronounceable, at least for me. I was relieved to learn that everyone simply called him the Maestro.

Giving me a courtly bow, he kissed my hand and said something about Gia which Marshall translated. "The Maestro says Gia had the voice of an angel."

Victor suddenly cut in. "No Carmen could equal Gia's."

Carla flashed the Maestro a smile. "I would like to sing Carmen someday," she said.

Her thick black hair was piled high on her head in an elaborate arrangement, but I could imagine the sensuality she would project with it hanging down in a disheveled mass of curls against her soft, white shoulders. Oh, yes, I thought, Carla would make a convincing Carmen!

She was wearing a sapphire blue gown with a deep décolletage that exposed those beautiful shoulders and more of her breasts than was decent in my estimation. The blue was perfect on her, as the green had been this

72

morning. Madam was right, I thought, the raven-haired can make any color their own, while we little brown-haired wrens must make do with peach.

Victor DeSantis and the Faros, mother and son, all made it a point to ask when I had arrived at the villa. I gathered they had not expected me to arrive so soon and certainly not ahead of all of them.

"When will Forrest return?" Victor asked, and before I could reply, Carla answered him.

"It all depends on the court. If the trial runs late, he may miss the Friday-night train and have to come up early Saturday morning."

Forrest had made no mention of this to me. His last words had been that he would see me on Friday. "I'm expecting him on Friday," I said.

Carla gave me an indulgent smile. "Forrest told me this morning on the way to the station that there was a strong possibility the trial would run late."

Nicky Faro raised a thin eyebrow. "You went to the station with Forrest?"

"Yes. To pick up my luggage," she said.

"How convenient. By the way," he added, "Aren't you giving a recital at the Peabody soon?"

"Yes, it's Friday evening."

A servant arrived with a tray of drinks, and Marshall said, "We're all ahead of you, Charlotte. Have a glass of champagne."

I pleaded a headache and refused. There was no way in the world that I was going to muddle my thoughts with champagne. My head was already reeling from Carla and Nicky's sly innuendo and I sensed an undercurrent of malice in all the polite conversations.

Dorcas finally spoke in a cold and impersonal voice. "Have you discussed any changes in the household with Sophia, Charlotte?"

"I don't intend making any changes," I said. "I'm sure the Signora has everything under control."

Dorcas's black eyes darted across the room and rested on the curio cabinet. "Not quite. A Pattiere is

73

missing from the music box collection."

I felt a blush creep up my neck and burst into flame on my face. "Unfortunately, I broke the little ballerina this afternoon," I said.

"Why, that was worth . . ." She stopped and looked down at me with blazing eyes. "Very unfortunate indeed!" she said.

I involuntarily took a step back. She is as powerful as any man, I thought, letting my eyes stray to the heavy arms that showed through her sheer chiffon gown. Stealing a glance at Nicky, I found it hard to believe that such an emaciated young man could be Dorcas's son.

Dinner was announced then, and I was escorted into the dining room on the arms of Marshall and the Maestro. There was an awkward moment when they led me to what had obviously been Gia's place at the table, and I could feel Dorcas's eyes smoldering with resentment as I was seated. Marshall and the Maestro took places on either side of me, and although I found it difficult to understand everything the Maestro said, he was pleasant and seemed oblivious to the tension that surrounded us. Much to my relief, the British custom of segregating the sexes after dinner was not observed, so I was spared having to face Dorcas and Carla alone in the drawing room.

I might have been better off, though, for Victor, Dorcas, and Carla decided to play bridge. "We need a fourth," Carla said.

Nicky gave her a sullen look. "Count me out. I'm too tired to think."

Victor said, "How about you, Charlotte? Do you play?"

I admitted I didn't and Carla pounced on Marshall. "That leaves you, darling. Come on, you can be my partner."

Before he could answer, she was across the room grabbing his hand. "Think how much fun we're going to have beating Victor and Dorcas," she said.

That left me with Nicky and the Maestro, and much to my regret, the Maestro bowed and said in his halting English, "Thank you for a most charming evening, Signora Singleton."

"Please, don't go," I said, clinging to this pleasant man like a lifeline.

Clicking his heels, he smiled. "It's been a pleasure, Signora, but an old man needs his rest."

"Please call me Charlotte," I said. "And thank you for coming. I hope we meet soon again."

I thought he looked a little puzzled by my last remark, but he kissed my hand and took his leave.

"The Maestro lives here too," Nicky said, giving me a sardonic smile.

I blushed. Would I never stop making a fool of myself? "I didn't know. I just assumed the Maestro was a guest," I said in a weak voice.

"As we all are, present company excepted," he added. No longer smiling, he stared at me intently. "It can't be pleasant having another woman's guests foisted upon you, but I might as well warn you, Charlotte, none of us plan to leave before our time is up."

His eyes were dark and sunken into his face like the black holes in a skull, and my skin crawled with revulsion. "Please excuse me," I said. "My headache has gotten worse and I think I'd best retire."

He stood up. "Then I'll say good-night, Charlotte, and pleasant dreams."

I made my apologies to the others, and hurried upstairs to the sanctity of the Blue Room. By this time my head was really pounding and I lost no time getting out my clothes and into bed.

Forrest would have been perturbed to know that I didn't utilize the services of my new maid, but I was uncomfortable playing lady. I could undress myself and much preferred to do so, and besides, I needed to think.

It had been a disturbing evening and I wanted to run

over it again in my mind. Had the conversations really been laced with innuendos and double meanings, or had I again been possessed by those relentless twin demons?

All looks yellow to the jaundiced eye.

I had read that somewhere, and the words jerked me back to sanity. I would not let my imagination run away with me again. Carla was wrong. Forrest would be home Friday. He had told me so and I believed him.

Chapter 6

I heard music, not humming this time, but the tiny, tinkling sound of a music box. Straining my ears, I sat up in bed and listened. Yes, the tune was the same. But, I had destroyed the music box, so this must be a dream.

The dead music box kept on playing its ghostly tune and my blood ran cold as the creaking sound of a door being slowly opened rose above it. Straining my eyes now, I peered into the inky blackness of the room.

I felt a presence hovering over me, and recoiling in terror, I mentally willed myself to awaken. Then as my eyes became accustomed to the darkness, a skull-like face took shape and materialized before me.

Paralyzed with fear, I hung suspended in that void which lies between dream and reality, and then very slowly the image receded and disappeared into the shadows. I could have sworn I heard the door creak once more before sleep mercifully rescued me from the void and plunged me into oblivion.

I awoke feeling disturbed, because like the other dream, this one had such vivid sounds as well as images. I don't think I will ever forget the eerie hum that dominated the first dream, and the melody that the little music box had played was now running round and round in my head like a familiar old refrain.

Nicky Faro's face suddenly flashed before me—gaunt, wasted. Hadn't I been reminded of a skull when

I looked at him?

My nerves are getting the best of me, I thought. Surely the man would not dare to enter my bedroom, and what about the music box? Hadn't I destroyed it myself?

I jumped as a creaking sound drew my attention to the door, which was slowly opening. Holding my breath, I expelled it with relief when Fiona poked her head inside and said in her lilting brogue, "Good morning, Mrs. Singleton. I'm after bringin' you a nice cup of tea."

She brought me more than tea, for her presence miraculously banished my dark thoughts and restored my common sense. Fiona may be inexperienced, I thought, but she is certainly thoughtful, and aside from the Maestro and Marshall Haines, she is the only one in the house I feel comfortable with.

Thank God I had stood my ground and chosen Fiona over the Signora's sly-faced Anna, who would probably have reported all my shortcomings to her supervisor.

Speaking of the devil, I thought as Fiona said, "Senior Grazziano said to tell you that she would like a word with you this morning, Mrs. Singleton."

"Thank you, Fiona," and then, because I didn't want the housekeeper to continue to find fault with her, I added, "I believe they pronounce it *Seen-ora,* Fiona. It doesn't come easy to me, either. I'm British, you know."

She smiled. "Oh, I knew that, Mrs. Singleton. I can understand you, and that's more than I can say about them Eyetalians. They talk gibberish, they do, but I'll try to remember. *Seen-ora.*" She repeated it softly. "Kinda sounds like *Begorra,* so that should make it easy. Thank you, Mrs. Singleton."

I sipped the hot tea, wishing I didn't have to face the others over breakfast. Would they think me rude if I didn't join them? I wondered. "Fiona," I said. "Is it acceptable at the villa to have breakfast in one's room?"

"Oh, yes, Mrs. Singleton. Mrs. Faro does it all the time. She calls it *brunch*. That's because she sleeps late and has two meals in one, I guess." She rolled her eyes. "Quite a feast it is, too, but then Mrs. Faro likes to eat, she does. And Mr. Nicky, he never eats breakfast a'tall, though he's the one what should."

"I need to write some letters," I said, "so I'll have breakfast up here."

I smiled to myself. If I skip lunch, I won't have to cope with any of them until this evening. Although I must admit, things had gone better at last night's meal, probably because Carla had not been present. She had taken the afternoon train to Baltimore, suddenly deciding she needed more time to rehearse with the accompanist.

I did write a letter to Maggie. She was my last tie to home, and the thought made me a little sad. Ours had been a small family and we had moved around so much that I had never formed any lasting friendships as a child.

I supposed that was the reason my parents and I had always been so close—the three of us against the world, more or less, because times had been hard when I was growing up. Mama and Papa had both been orphans. Their mutual loneliness had forged a bond between them that had blossomed into a beautiful and enduring love that was tragically short-lived.

My mother was only twenty-eight when she died and I was ten. After that, it was just Papa and me, and although I never had much in the way of material goods, I never lacked for love.

Papa was frequently out of work, but somehow we always managed and he made sure I stayed in school. In fact, he insisted that I continue my education, and the day I received my teacher's certificate, he was the proudest man in England.

Looking around me now, I wondered how he would feel about all this opulence and the woman who had left him behind to achieve it.

In his goodness, he would probably feel pity, I thought, but I had none to give. My gentle father had worked himself into an early grave while his selfish mother had been wallowing in luxury, and I could not forgive her for it.

Fiona returned with a tray, and I ate a leisurely breakfast of tea and warm buttered toast. Then I finished Maggie's letter and sealed it, smiling to myself as I pictured her reaction to the news of my marriage.

"Had your cap all set for him, didn't you, ducks," she would say.

Not really, I thought as I walked into the dressing room. It was all Forrest's idea and I can't imagine why.

One of my demons suddenly hissed, and poisoned thoughts shot through my mind like venom. *You're an heiress, Charlotte. That's why!*

I shook my head in denial. Forrest didn't even *know* I was an heiress when he married me!

My blood chilled. I could have sworn I heard someone laugh.

"Fiona," I called, and then louder, *"Fiona!"*

She came to the dressing room and stood in the doorway. "You be wantin' something, Mrs. Singleton?"

Thank God, I thought, and shrugged. "No, I just heard you laugh and I wanted to make sure you were still here."

"I'm still here, mum, but I ain't been laughing. This is a pretty scary house."

"What do you mean by that?"

She looked embarrassed. "Nothing, mum. Pay me no mind."

My voice rose. "I want to know, Fiona. What did you mean?"

Her face turned as red as her hair. "The other servants, they try to scare me, but it's only because I'm Irish and they know we're a superstitious lot."

"What do they say?" I insisted.

She sighed. "They say the villa's haunted, mum."

When I was calmer and dressed in a yellow sprigged morning gown that made me look even younger than my years, I went downstairs. I spotted Anna, and gave her Maggie's letter to post, and recalling Fiona's message, I said, "You may tell the Signora I can see her now."

"The Signora's waiting for you in her office," she said, and like a fool I let her lead me there, not realizing my mistake until I saw the smirk that passed between Anna and the housekeeper when I was shown into the room.

Of course, I thought, I should have requested that the housekeeper be brought to me instead of the other way around. Oh, Lord! Will I ever learn to be the mistress of the villa?

The housekeeper's office was a small room on the servants' side of the house. The Signora was seated behind a large desk and I was placed in the awkward position of having to stand before her like a recalcitrant child.

Seemingly absorbed in her account book, she let me stand there a moment before looking up. "Mr. DeSantis has suggested that the countess's costumes be donated to the Metropolitan's museum. Is that agreeable to you, Mrs. Singleton?"

Her black eyes bored into mine and I cursed myself for the stammer that suddenly erupted in my speech. "Of c-c-course . . . An ex—cellent suggestion."

"Good. Then, I will remove them in your presence."

She reached for a large ring of keys that lay on her desk and I suddenly had second thoughts about the whole thing. She was going to remove the costumes from the countess's room. Would Forrest approve? Suppose the missing will is hidden in the costumes!

Oh, why isn't he here to make these decisions? I thought as I docilely followed her out of the room. I am not equipped to be mistress of a mansion and she

81

knows it, but I can hardly back down now without appearing completely inadequate. What would I say? I have to ask my husband first?

The countess's suite was located on the far side of the west wing, the Signora informed me as I followed her up a back stairway and down a maze of winding corridors. Pausing to catch her breath, she said, "The countess had this wing added after she visited Patti's Welsh mansion."

I must have looked blank for Signora Grazziano gave me an impatient frown and said, "Adelina Patti, the opera singer. Have you never heard of her?"

"Yes, yes, of course. I believe she gave a farewell performance at Covent Garden several years ago."

The Signora sniffed. "Patti gave *six* farewell performaces. The screech owl didn't know when to retire." Her dark eyes flashed and she said, "Patti's voice could never compare to Gia's." Pausing outside a door at the end of the corridor, she leaned against it. Her èyes turned misty and I sensed that she had forgotten I was there. "Gia Gerardo was the greatest star that opera has ever known," she said in a voice that was almost reverent.

"Did you know her long?" I asked.

She regarded me contemptuously. "Forty-five years." Then she looked right through me and her eyes grew dreamy again, "So young we were, the youngest girls in the chorus. But it was the chorus at La Scala!" she shouted, raising her arm in a gesture of triumph.

Then she smiled a sickly smile and her eyes glittered insanely. I felt my skin begin to crawl, but an instant later she was herself again, waspish, but perfectly rational. "We had no secrets from each other, either, Signora Singleton. Tell that to your husband!" she said, turning her back on me.

I didn't know what to say. What did she mean by such a remark?

Unlocking the door, she flung it open and stepped back, allowing me to enter first.

The sitting room—at least that's what I supposed it to be—was very large and ornately decorated in gold and black. Delicate china ornaments graced all the tables and I pressed my hands to my sides, subconsciously fearful of breaking something.

The Signora was gazing upward, a rapt expression on her face, and following her gaze, I found myself staring at a portrait of a woman over the fireplace. I gasped, and the Signora said triumphantly, *"Sì,* that is the great Gia Gerardo!"

The face was the one I had seen Fiona wear through the mirror. I could not have imagined it, for the resemblance was too striking. Was it the countess's ghost that haunted this house? I wondered.

"That's Gia as Carmen, her greatest role," the Signora said as we both stared upward.

The portrait's dark, sultry eyes stared back at me, and I felt a shiver run down my spine.

"Gia was all fire and ice, and you . . ." The Signora paused and held me captive with eyes that scrutinized my face. "No, you are nothing like her," she added emphatically.

"I look like my English mother," I said, feeling myself cringe at the woman's relentless inspection.

She smiled. "You said that before, Mrs. Singleton." Then walking briskly across the room, she flung open another door. "The countess's bedroom," she said.

The room was done in gold, black, and a bright Chinese red. It was overpowering, and I felt myself growing nervous as I entered it.

Gold and white brocaded walls and a huge bed draped in red satin and lined in gold flashed before my eyes. The heavy matching drapes were pulled back and secured with gold silk tassels. I pictured Gia Gerardo (I can never think of her as my grandmother) receiving her lovers in this room that fairly reeked of sumptuous debauchery.

Every wall held a mirror, and catching a glimpse of myself, I thought that I looked small and insignificant, like a little brown wren lost in a brilliant tropical paradise.

The Signora was watching me, too, and I squirmed under her gaze, feeling frumpy and unfashionable in my childish little morning dress.

"The costumes are in the dressing room, but Gia's personal wardrobe is in here," she said, opening a sliding door to reveal a dazzling array of gowns.

There are more clothes here than in Madam's shop, I mused, wondering how one woman could possibly wear so many.

"Gia had beautiful gowns," the Signora said, reaching inside to bring out a handsome one beaded all over in silver and white. "She wore this when she was presented to your queen." The Signora's lips curled into a smirk and she added, "Gia said she was a dowdy little woman."

The remark offended me and I thought how shallow they both were to judge a great and gracious lady by her clothes rather than her accomplishments.

Returning the gown to its position on the rack, she brought out another, a shimmering green satin trimmed with feathers. "Carla tried to get her sticky fingers on this one," she murmured. "She fancies herself made to wear emerald green, but Gia wore it better even when she was old."

"What's to be done with these gowns?" I asked.

She gave me a disparaging look. "You could never do justice to them, and besides, Gia would not want anyone to wear them."

I felt my face catch fire. "I had no intention of . . . I mean, I only wondered what you planned to do about them."

I realized I had again dropped the reins, as Madam used to say, but I never wanted to hold them in the first place. I felt no kinship with Gia Gerardo and I wanted nothing that had been hers; not this accursed house,

84

nor anything in it, and certainly not her clothes!

Holding back tears of embarrassment and frustration, I met the Signora's gaze. "I think we should go over the costumes now," I said stiffly.

She didn't belabor the point and I think she might have realized that she had gone too far, but it wasn't in her nature to apologize.

We spent what was left of the morning, sorting and packing the elaborate costumes which had been stored in yet another large built-in closet. The Signora reminisced over each and every one:

"Gia shocked the world when she wore this as Aida." And slipping her hand under whisper-thin chiffon in a pale lavender hue, she challenged me with her eyes. Every vein and line in her hand showed clearly through the diaphanous material and I gasped, wondering what the countess had worn underneath the costume.

Evidently the Signora read my mind, for she smirked. "Only a woman with a perfect figure would dare to wear it. Gia was already thirty-seven, but her body was magnificent. Every man in the theater desired her and every woman there was jealous." Carefully folding the garment, she mused. "At the end, Aida and her lover are entombed alive. *O terra, addio.*" She spoke the words softly and added, "Their love duet reduced the audience to tears."

Bringing out a gorgeous peacock blue gown with a voluminous old-fashioned skirt, she spread it out before me and said, "Beautiful, isn't it?" I nodded and she continued. "From *Traviata*. What a wonderful Violetta she made! The role mirrored Gia's own vibrant personality," she explained.

The Signora shook her head slowly, and once again, I felt my presence forgotten. "Verdi fell in love with Gia when he heard her sing the difficult *"Amami, Alfredo"* passage. He was forty, married, and Gia was only nineteen." She shrugged. "Giuseppe Verdi was a powerful man, why shouldn't Gia accept his help?"

I gave her no answer. It would have been ludicrous to

speak of honor or morality. Evidently fame was an all-consuming obsession with Gia Gerardo.

Other costumes followed: a high priestess's robe from *Norma,* a maid's costume from *Martha,* and a slim, virginal white gown worn in *Roméo et Juliette.* There were wigs, headpieces, and crowns, and finally the famous Gypsy costume from *Carmen,* fiery red and dripping with spangles.

The Signora ran her hands lovingly over the full, brightly colored skirt. "She was a perfect Carmen, dark and sensuous. The opera was not a success when it was first presented in Paris. Did you know that?" she asked and then answered herself. "No, of course you didn't. Bizet himself was French, but the French can't do Carmen," she mused. "Solange was too cool and refined for the part, but Gia was *Italiano.* Ah, such fire, such *passione,*" she said, raising her fingers to her lips and blowing a kiss into the air. "Four years later when Gia sang it at the Metropolitan, she brought the house down. Six curtain calls she took that night. Did Patti or Jenny Lind ever have as many?" Then staring off into space, she added softly. "Poor Bizet! He died thinking his masterpiece was a failure. What a pity he couldn't have seen Gia as Carmen. He might have lived!"

I helped her fold and pack the garments in boxes, trying unobtrusively to check each and every one for the missing will. My heart leapt when I found a paper stuffed inside a pocket, but it was only a note written in Italian.

I handed it to the Signora and she smiled as she read it.

"From one of her admirers. He says he's madly in love with her. They all were," she said, crumbling it into a ball and stuffing it into her own pocket. "They filled her dressing room with flowers every night. They sent her presents, French perfume, diamonds and furs. One foolish young man even committed suicide over her."

"And did she care for any of them?" I asked.

"No. She laughed at them. We both did."

Their cruelty disgusted me. "Who was the father of her child?" The words suddenly tumbled out of my mouth, and the bold question took us both by surprise.

Her eyes widened and then just as quickly narrowed. "Didn't your husband tell you?"

"He doesn't know, but I thought perhaps you might since you knew her so well."

She smiled slowly. "*Sì*, I knew Gia well. I tell you before, we had no secrets from each other." Her eyes bored into mine for what seemed like an eternity and then she said, "Gia never once spoke to me of a child!"

The full meaning of her words suddenly penetrated my thick brain. She thinks me an imposter!

My heart was racing, but I stared her down. "Law firms don't make mistakes," I said. "The investigation was thorough."

She gave me a disinterested shrug and I wanted to shout that I wished it *could* be a mistake. I didn't want this vain, immoral woman's blood flowing in my veins, and the fact that the Signora admired her so much was only a reflection on her own character.

We returned to our task in silence and finally the last costume was folded and packed, the box tied with heavy cord.

The Signora walked over to the bed and tugged impatiently at the embroidered bell cord above it. "One of the male servants will carry the boxes out for you," she said. Then she swept her eyes around the room and a tortured expression suddenly appeared on her face. "Mr. Singleton instructed me to leave the keys with you," she informed me coldly, and wrenching them quickly off the ring, she slammed them down on a nearby table. "There were only two, Gia's and mine." And then with a toss of her head, she added, "Everything is as she left it, but keep the door locked or things will soon begin to disappear."

Without saying another word, she turned on her heel and left the room.

I heard the door close and my heart began to pound.

I was alone and I could feel the room closing in on me. This had been the countess's bedroom and her presence still dominated it.

I avoided looking into any of the mirrors, for I had an uncanny feeling that it would not be my own face I would see reflected there.

Why doesn't the servant come? Forrest will fault me for this, I told myself. *Why didn't you take that opportunity to search the room?* he would say. But how can I make him understand that I have no right to touch this woman's things? She is a stranger; I dislike her, and I know she would have been as contemptuous of me as the Signora is.

Why then had she made me her heir? I wondered. Was it only to salve her conscience, or had she expected that I would be a different kind of girl? Had she imagined me to be beautiful and sophisticated; a worthy successor to reign in her place?

Then she must be bitterly disappointed, I thought, for I am none of those things. And, to add insult to injury, I have already broken one of her prized possessions.

Ghosts return to rectify their mistakes, or so I had heard. Was the countess's spirit trying to tell me that I didn't belong here? I already knew that, but what was I to do about it?

A tremendous crash suddenly rent the air, making me jump.

The sound had come from the sitting room, and I had to force my shaking legs to take me there.

Peering cautiously around the corner first, I gasped. The countess's portrait lay staring up at me from the floor!

Chapter 7

"Tell me it ain't true, Mrs. Singleton."

Fiona stood over my bed wringing her hands, and I looked back at her in confusion. I had just awakened from an afternoon nap and my brain was like a fresh sheet of paper.

"What?" I mumbled, and before she could answer, the disturbing incident that had happened only this morning flashed before me.

The loud crash had sent servants racing to the scene, and when they discovered the portrait lying on the floor, they stopped in their tracks, too terrified to move. Evidently the superstition about pictures falling from walls was a universal one.

"Oh, mum, some of the servants say a picture fell off the wall. That means a death in the house. Even them Eyetalians know that." She crossed herself and wrung her hands again. "They say it happened before the countess died, too. Oh, Blessed Mother of God, it could be any one of us this time."

I wasn't usually a superstitious person, but I will admit I was as terrified as the servants when I saw the portrait had fallen off the wall. And now to hear that it had happened before!

"Perhaps the nail was loose," I said.

I think I was as anxious to convince myself as Fiona, but she was not easily swayed.

"Antonio said he hung that picture back up himself after the first time, and Antonio's a carpenter. He knows how to hammer a nail, he does."

What could I say? There should have been a logical explanation for it, but I certainly couldn't think of one.

"What time is it?" I asked, anxious to get her off the subject. It was late, I knew, because the room was in shadows.

"Seven o'clock, mum. Time to be getting dressed for dinner."

How could I have slept so long? Now I should never be able to get to sleep tonight, and the very thought of lying awake in this spooky, haunted house was unsettling, to say the least. Only one more night and Forrest will be home, I mused.

Looking at Fiona's frightened face, it suddenly dawned on me that should she leave, I would be forced to accept Anna as my personal maid.

"The east wing is a comparatively new addition," I heard myself say. "All building structures go through a settling process. I'm sure this is what caused the picture to fall."

I don't know where I got such a theory, but it sounded logical and Fiona embraced it with enthusiasm.

"I niver would have thought of that, mum, but it makes sense, it does." Shaking her head, and smiling with relief, she said, "It's lucky I am to have such a clever mistress. You've eased me mind, and I'll be giving a piece of it to them Eyetalians in the kitchen—like to scare a body to death with their caterwauling."

Now if I could just put my own mind at ease, I thought. But, there were other things I could find no logical explanation for—the strange dreams; the laughter I had heard when I wasn't asleep; and most terrifying of all, the face that had been superimposed over Fiona's in the mirror.

"Would ye be wantin to wear this one?" Fiona was

90

holding up a lace-trimmed teal blue gown. "It's ever so pretty." Running her rough little hand over the smooth, lustrous satin, she smiled wistfully. "So soft it is, like a rose petal."

Suddenly I was back in a London stockroom, my own eyes lingering just as wistfully over a beautiful pale pink gown. I had taken it over to the mirror and was holding it up in front of me.

"I don't pay you to daydream." The voice had startled and embarrassed me, and I'd turned to find Madam standing in the doorway.

Her sharp eyes had taken me in from head to toe and then dismissed me with an amused smile. "A little wren pretending to be a peacock, eh, Miss Stone?" The smile quickly turned into a scowl. "Get back on the floor and stop wasting time."

Fiona was waiting for an answer and impulsively I said, "The gown *is* lovely, but the shade's a little too dark for me. Why don't you take it, Fiona? It's only using up space in the closet."

Her eyes widened in astonishment. "Me, mum? You'd be giving such a fine gown to the likes of me?"

"Well, if you don't want it, Fiona . . ."

"Oh, mum, I want it. Niver in this world did I ever expect to have such a beautiful gown. I'll be packing it in me hope chest, mum, and saving it for me wedding day, I will. Oh, saints preserve us, but it's lucky I am to be working for such a fine mistress as yourself."

"Now don't be giving me so much credit," I said, imitating her brogue and sending her into peals of laughter.

"Ah, mum, sure and it's a miracle that brought me here. Probably the work of me guardian angel."

I thought the devil a more likely candidate, but I didn't dare suggest it.

*   *   *

91

Cocktails were served in the drawing room before dinner and as I hastened to join the others, I recalled with a touch of nostalgia the very first time I heard that peculiar American term.

It was our second night out on the crossing and I was trying my best to appear grown-up and worldly.

"Would you like a cocktail before dinner, Charlotte?"

"No, thank you. I don't think I could eat one. I'm a little squeamish about things like that."

His laughter had hurt my feelings, but his words filled my heart with unbelievable joy.

"Oh, Charlotte, I'm not making fun of you. I adore everything about you. Don't ever change."

But lately Forrest hadn't found my mistakes so endearing, I mused.

"You're the mistress of this house now, Charlotte. For God's sake act the part!"

Trying to do just that, I swept into the drawing room, masking my insecurity with what I hoped would pass for a self-confident smile.

"Charlotte, how lovely you look," Marshall said, and the Maestro, who was standing next to him, kissed my hand.

I accepted a glass of sherry from the waiter and took a sip for courage when I saw Nicky Faro heading toward me.

"Good evening, Charlotte. I hear you were present when Gia's portrait fell off the wall."

"That's right," I said. "The servants were rather upset, but we British are not superstitious."

I hadn't meant to sound supercilious, but as soon as the words left my mouth I wanted to take them back.

"Italianos are not superstitious either," a deep voice answered. "However, we have a healthy respect for the supernatural. Perhaps because our culture is older and a little wiser than yours."

The voice belonged to Victor DeSantis who had been standing behind me, and with the sharpness of a stiletto, he succeeded in ripping my self-confidence to shreds.

"I apologize," I said weakly. "I didn't mean to offend . . ."

"Offend?" He followed the word with a disparaging laugh. "*You* could never offend me, *cara mia.*"

He walked away and the group's embarrassed silence was finally broken by Nicky Faro. "Nice work, Charlotte. It takes me the better part of an hour to get under Victor's skin. You did it in five minutes."

"Nicky, that's enough," Marshall said. Then he gave me a sympathetic look. "Pay Victor no mind, Charlotte. He's been drinking all afternoon."

I smiled my gratitude and emptied the glass of sherry. So much for my pathetic attempt to appear sophisticated, I thought. Victor DeSantis may be drunk, but he will not forget my unfortunate remark.

We kept the same seating arrangement for dinner and I found that the Maestro's accent had grown on me and I could understand him a little better.

He had been a conductor in Italy, he told me, and then he had moved to England to teach. Gia had been one of his pupils, and years later she had persuaded him to come to America to teach the students she was sponsoring.

"Three of them are with the Metropolitan now and one is singing with an opera company in Milan. In six months Carla and Marshall will be ready," he said.

"I know nothing about music, but I enjoy it immensely," I confided.

"Of course, it is in your blood. Perhaps you have inherited more than an appreciation for music. Do you sing?"

I laughed. "Only when no one is listening."

"I should like to hear you. Come to the studio tomorrow."

"I'll come," I said. "Not to sing, but to learn. I helped the Signora pack the countess's costumes today and I would love to know more about opera."

"Good. You come. I tell you whatever you want to know."

Nicky joined in. "The Maestro knows secrets about all the great divas from Jenny Lind to Melba. Don't you, Maestro?"

The old man shrugged and smiled.

Victor, who was seated at the far end of the table, looked up and said, "Secrets? What secrets?"

"Nicky's teasing the Maestro about the prima donnas," Dorcas explained.

Victor laughed drunkenly. "Bitches, every one of them. Jenny Lind," he muttered, sloshing the wine around in his glass before drinking it. "A tight-assed, sanctimonious prude, but she wasn't above letting Barnum book her in every cow palace in America for an advance of a hundred and eighty thousand."

"Not bad money for those days," Nicky said. "What's the matter, Victor? Were you jealous?"

"Jealous of Barnum? He promoted freaks, for God's sake. You think I'd let Gia's name be mentioned in the same breath with Tom Thumb?"

Nicky shrugged. "So much for the Swedish Nightingale. She was a housecat anyway, compared to Gia and Patti." He turned to me with a smug expression. "Gia and Adelina Patti were rivals both in their professional and personal lives," he explained. "If Patti got a thousand pounds for a performance, Gia wanted two thousand. Patti married a marquis, so Gia had to have a title, too. And when Patti acquired her opulent Welsh mansion, Gia bought the Villa Montelano. Patti put in—"

"Shut up, you *castrato*," Victor shouted. "Gia never imitated Patti. It was Patti who imitated Gia! And as for your grandfather, Gia was ready to divorce that sniveling leech, but he saved her the trouble by conveniently dropping dead!"

Dorcas swelled up like a toad and her eyes fairly

94

bulged out of their sockets as she fixed them on Victor. "How dare you call my son a *castrato!*" she shrieked. "And how dare you tell him to shut up. Shut up yourself, you drunken fool!"

All three of them began talking at once, and Marshall tapped his spoon on the wineglass and spoke over the din. "Please, let's all calm down."

"Calm down," Dorcas answered. "He calls my son a *castrato* and my father a leech and I'm supposed to calm down!"

I didn't know what *castrato* meant, but calling one's father a leech was certainly an insult. Nevertheless, I was as shocked at Dorcas's behavior as I was at Victor's. The expression on her face was murderous, and I couldn't help thinking that if looks could kill, Victor DeSantis would already be dead!

At this point, the Maestro quietly intervened. Catching Victor's eye, he said something to him in Italian and they both got up and left the table.

Out of the corner of my eye, I saw the door leading to the small salon move. Someone had been listening! Small wonder, I thought. What servant could resist eavesdropping on such a shocking display of tempers.

I don't think anyone else noticed it, though, for all eyes were focused on Dorcas, who had slumped back in her chair and was loudly proclaiming that she was about to faint.

Servants were sent scurrying for spirits of ammonia while Nicky fanned her with his napkin. Dorcas had studiously avoided falling from the chair, I noticed, and seemed miraculously to recover after one whiff. "That's enough," she said sharply, pushing the maid aside and almost knocking the smelling salts out of the girl's hand.

Declaring herself better, she remained at the table to consume a generous slice of a rich chocolate torte.

We all retired then to the drawing room and were relieved to learn that Victor had gone to bed. "I shall say good-night, too, Charlotte," the Maestro said. "But, please come to the studio tomorrow." He looked to Marshall for support. "You'll sing for her, won't you, Marshall?"

"It will be a privilege."

The Maestro turned to me, "There, you can't refuse now. This young man is destined to become a famous tenor."

I promised to come and the Maestro bade us good-night.

"How about a stroll through the gardens," Marshall suggested. "It's a beautiful evening. You won't even need a wrap."

I was anxious to escape the Faros, whose disagreeable expressions effectively discouraged conversation, so I quickly took him up on the offer.

Passing through the small salon to the conservatory, I followed him outside to a moon-drenched garden whose flagstone walks were banked with lush flowering shrubs.

A gentle breeze filled the air with intoxicating scents, and I breathed them in deeply. "It even smells heavenly," I said.

"The countess took great pride in her garden," Marshall told me. Then he laughed. "She was determined to outdo Patti again."

"Then, they *were* rivals," I said.

"Oh, yes indeed. As to who copied whom, I'm inclined to believe Nicky was right, but DeSantis would never admit it." He took my arm and led me down the winding path. "Patti is eight or nine years younger than Gia and most prima donnas are jealous of their successors."

"What did you think of the countess?" I asked.

He paused before answering. "She had the most magnificent voice I have ever heard and I shall always be grateful for her patronage."

The voice, I thought. Was that all that mattered

to any of them?

We sat down on a stone bench overlooking a little pond and he said, "Art is a stern taskmaster and a jealous lover, Charlotte. Sometimes it leaves no room in an artist's life for anything else." He paused and bent down to pick up a pebble. He tossed it into the water and said, "It's a high price to pay," he added.

"Is it worth it?" I asked, for I honestly wanted to know.

"Once I thought it was, but lately I'm not so sure."

"I'm afraid I'm too mediocre to have such a problem," I said.

"You're not mediocre, Charlotte, and you have more common sense than any of us at the villa. I wonder if Forrest knows how very lucky he is."

I was vaguely uncomfortable with the remark, but his expression held no hint of impropriety, so I decided it would be silly to take offense. Turning the subject around, I said, "You don't speak the way Forrest does. Are you from another part of the country, Marshall?"

He laughed. "I'm surprised you noticed. There are so many different accents here at the villa, but you're right. I'm from the midwest—Clear Creek, Missouri, to be exact. My father was a small-town preacher, and I sang in the church choir. There was very little money, but we survived." His glance took in the carefully laid out gardens and the sprawling mansion they graced. "I didn't know places like this existed until I came to the villa," he said softly.

His confession astonished me. Marshall was so self-confident, so urbane. It was hard for me to believe he was not to the manor born.

I felt a sudden kinship with this kindly young man whose background was not unlike my own. I probably have more in common with him than I do with Forrest, I mused.

The thought disturbed me, for I loved Forrest desperately, but I had to admit that we were as different as calico and silk.

"You'll adjust to the villa and all its crazy occupants. I did," he confessed, reaching over and grasping my hand in a gesture that might have offended me had it not been so forthright and sincere.

Deeply touched by his perception, I did not draw away. "I appreciate your friendship, Marshall," I said, and on that note, we stood up and made our way back.

The house loomed before us, its mismatched architecture making it appear like some deformed monstrosity. My skin prickled, and glancing up I saw a curtain move in one of the windows. The figure quickly stepped back and I couldn't distinguish if it was a man or woman who had been watching us.

The house, when we entered it, was eerily silent and the only light left burning cast its amber glow over the great hall. We parted then, Marshall making his way to the west wing. I stood at the foot of the stairs and watched his retreat. The darkness swallowed him up and his muffled footsteps soon disappeared, leaving me completely alone. My feet took wings and I ran up the steps, dodging shadows through the long corridor to the safety of the Blue Room.

Gasping for breath, I ducked inside and closed the door. But, before I could reach for the lamp, a pair of strong arms encircled my waist. I tried to scream, but my throat was paralyzed. Low male laughter exploded in my ear, and with superhuman strength, I broke away.

"Charlotte, Charlotte!" Forrest's voice penetrated the confusion in my brain as I slumped to the floor. An instant later the room was flooded with light and my husband was kneeling beside me. "Oh, sweetheart, I'm sorry. I wanted to surprise you. I didn't mean to scare you to death!"

Gathering me up in his arms, he carried me over to the bed. I was trembling and crying with relief. "This is Thursday," I said. "You weren't supposed to come home until tomorrow. How was I to know it was you?"

Overcome with remorse, he rubbed my cold hands and dried my tears with the tenderness of a father ministering to a frightened child. "There, there, it's all right now. I had no idea you were so nervous. What did you think I was—a ghost?"

"That's not so farfetched," I said. "The servants say this house is haunted."

"Surely you don't believe that nonsense!"

His attitude was so condescending that I couldn't confide in him. What would he think if I said that I had seen a skull leaning over my bed and that when I looked at my maid through the mirror, she had turned into another person? Or that I heard voices humming and laughing when no one was there?

Perhaps my nerves were getting the better of me, I thought. I was never fanciful before. On the contrary, I have always prided myself on being a practical person.

"No, I don't believe in ghosts," I lied. "And I'm not superstitious, but popping out at me in the dark is no fair."

"You're right and I stand corrected. Am I forgiven?"

I laughed. "You're forgiven because I've missed you and I'm glad you're home early, but how did you manage it? I thought you were supposed to be in court."

"I was. I wrapped up the case early so I could come home and keep an eye on you. By the way, what were you doing out in the garden with Marshall Haines?"

Had it been Forrest I'd seen at the window?

"He offered to show me the gardens," I said. "Dorcas, Nicky, and Victor argued at the dinner table and the atmosphere was pretty strained in the house. I needed a breath of fresh air."

"What did they argue about?"

"I'm not sure." Pausing, I tried to reconstruct the conversation in my head. "I think it started when the Maestro asked me to come to the studio. I wanted to know about opera and Nicky made some remark about the Maestro knowing all the prima donnas' secrets. Then he and Victor got into a discussion about the countess and Adelina Patti. Victor had been drinking and one thing led to another. Victor called Nicky a *castrato* and his father a leech. What's a *castrato,* anyway?" I asked.

"A eunuch. Years ago in Italy they castrated young boys so they would keep their high singing voices."

"That's barbarous!" I said. "Wasn't it illegal?"

"Of course, but everybody looked the other way. They were mostly poor boys. Their parents needed the money and some of them, like Farinelli and Pacchierotti, did become rich and famous."

"But why? I don't understand," I said.

He shrugged. "Historians say the voices of the *castrati,* which are lost in antiquity now, were magnificent and strangely unique, neither tenor nor soprano. Some of them were homosexuals," he added matter-of-factly, "but others were not. Nevertheless, they were forbidden to marry."

The dark side of music suddenly revolted me. What could be more diabolical than to mutilate a child in the name of art?

"So, now you know why Dorcas was upset with Victor."

I sighed. "I suppose so, but to cause a scene like that!"

"That's the way they are, Charlotte. It'll all be forgotten tomorrow."

"Carla wasn't present," I said, thinking that she surely would have added fuel to the fire.

"I know."

"How do you know?"

"Because she was in Baltimore."

"You saw her?"

"She stopped by last night after her rehearsal."

I should have confronted him then, gotten everything out into the open, cleared the air! But I did nothing, coward that I was, and when he made love to me, I opened my body and my soul to him, overwhelmed with gratitude that Forrest was here with me now, and for this moment in time, he was mine and mine alone!

In the aftermath of passion, I slept like one who has been drugged, and the sun had long been up when I was jolted awake by the terrifying sound of an ear-splitting scream!

Chapter 8

We both sat bolt upright in the bed.

Forrest stared at me with sleep-drugged eyes. "What the hell was that?"

"Someone's screaming. Something terrible must have happened," I said, jumping up and reaching for my dressing gown.

My teeth were chattering and my hands shook so much I could scarcely tie the sash around my waist.

"Don't get yourself upset. You know how excitable they are." Forrest got up too and put on his own robe. "Stay here, I'll go see what's wrong. The cook probably burnt the toast," he said, trying to make me smile, but we could hear the sound of running feet along the corridor.

There was no way I was going to stay in the room alone, so I followed him out the door.

Looking down from the staircase into the great hall, we saw that servants were trying to calm a young maid who was seated in a chair, wailing in Italian. *"La manonera. La manonera,"* she sobbed.

"What's going on here?"

Forrest took the stairs as he spoke, but I remained behind, my teeth chattering and my legs like rubber.

"The Black Hand, Signore," one of the male servants said, "She keeps saying it, *The Black Hand!*"

All of the servants looked absolutely terrified and several hastily crossed themselves and turned their eyes to heaven. The girl stood up then and said something else in Italian. Forrest's expression changed immediately and he took off at a run leaving the great hall. Several male servants followed after him, and in the midst of the confusion Nicky and Marshall arrived on the scene followed by Victor DeSantis.

The servants all started speaking at once, again in Italian, and I had no idea what was going on until Marshall grabbed the young maid by the shoulders and shook her. "Stop it, you're hysterical. Are you saying he's dead? *Morto?*"

Then Marshall, Nicky, and DeSantis hurried off as Forrest had done, leaving the female servants to minister to the young maid and chatter among themselves.

My legs gave way and I slumped to the floor. Fiona was right. The fallen picture had predicted a death in the house and now somebody was dead. But who, and what, had the maid meant by *the Black Hand?*

I don't know how long I sat there, hugging my knees like a frightened child. The servants had dispersed, taking the crying maid with them, and still I sat, rocking back and forth, wondering what had happened and praying that somehow I had misunderstood, or better yet, that the maid had misunderstood and nothing shocking had happened at all.

In a little while Forrest came back, the others trailing behind him.

"I say we call the police," Nicky said.

"No!" Forrest's voice was like a command.

Victor DeSantis glared at Nicky. "Don't be more of a fool than you already are, Faro. Do you want the police here, sticking their big noses in the villa's affairs?"

"The girl was hysterical," Marshall said reasonably. "She may have imagined it."

Nicky looked subdued. "I doubt that, but perhaps you're right about the police. The servants heard her, though. What about them?"

"Let Sophia handle the servants," Victor answered.

Everyone was in their night clothes and Forrest said, "I suggest we get changed. The doctor will be here soon."

He started upstairs and the others turned and headed back to the west wing.

I stood up when Forrest reached the top of the stairs. "Oh, Forrest, I've been so frightened. What is it?"

He seemed surprised to see me. "Have you been here all along?" I nodded, and he put his arm around me. "You should have stayed in the room, Charlotte. Come along."

"But what was it?" I insisted. "What was that maid screaming about?"

"Wait till we get in the room," he said, guiding me down the long corridor.

The door was still open the way we had left it, and once we were inside, he said. "The Maestro is dead!"

"Oh, no," I said, dissolving into tears. I couldn't believe the Maestro was gone. Why, only last night he had seemed fine and I had been looking forward to visiting him in his studio today.

Forrest led me to the bed and covered my trembling body with the blanket. The Maestro had resided in a guesthouse on the grounds of the estate, he informed me, and it was there that the maid discovered his body when she came to bring him his morning coffee.

"It looks like a heart attack," he said, "but we'll know for certain after the doctor arrives."

Forrest dressed hurriedly and left. I had asked him to inform the housekeeper that I was not to be disturbed, for I didn't feel up to coping with Fiona, not yet, at least.

Several minutes later, I heard a carriage arrive, and looking out the window, I watched the gray-haired driver step down and open the door. The doctor emerged carrying the customary black bag and the two of them walked toward the back of the estate. The driver had looked familiar and I suddenly placed him. He was the groom whose inheritance had caused such an uproar when the will had been read.

It seemed such a long time ago and yet it had only been four days since all of our lives had been changed by the droning voice of Forrest's Uncle Henry reading The Last Will and Testament of Gia Gerardo.

I was grief-stricken and frightened by the Maestro's death. True, I had hardly known the man, but he had been kind to me and I had looked forward to becoming his friend. As for my fears, I had tried to convince myself they were foolish, but how could I challenge them now? The omen had foretold death twice—and twice it had come to pass.

Something else disturbed me, but I couldn't quite put my finger on it, and then my attention was again directed to the window. Victor DeSantis and the Signora were carrying on an animated conversation in the driveway. I couldn't tell if they were arguing or merely talking. All of the *Eyetalians,* as Fiona calls them, make use of dramatic facial expressions and much gesturing of hands.

The conversation abruptly halted and the Signora disappeared from my view. Someone was approaching and I saw that it was Nicky Faro. The two men then hurried off in the direction that Forrest had gone.

I dressed in an appropriately somber gray morning gown and waited for Forrest to return, and when he did, I suggested that we have breakfast brought up to the room.

I was not concerned about Fiona, knowing Forrest's presence would prevent her from discussing the morning's events.

He seemed preoccupied and readily agreed. I rang for Fiona and then asked, "Was it his heart?"

"What? Oh, yes, the doctor said it was a heart attack." I started to cry and he said, "Don't, Charlotte. We'll all miss the Maestro, but he was old and his heart had been weak for a long time."

"Did he have any relatives?"

"No, no one. We're going to bury him from the local church. Victor's making the arrangements."

"Is that how the countess was buried, too?" I asked.

"What? Oh, no, Gia was buried from the cathedral in Baltimore. A big, flamboyant funeral—she would have loved it," he added wryly.

Fiona arrived then with our breakfast. She looked pale and I noticed that her hands trembled as she set the tray down on the table, but she was in control, at least on the surface.

When we were alone again, I remembered something I had forgotten to ask Forrest. "What was all that about the black hand?"

He frowned slightly and methodically buttered a biscuit. "It's nothing for you to worry about."

"I heard what the maid said, Forrest. What did she mean by it?"

"I suppose you'll find out sooner or later." He reached across the table and patted my hand. "It's nothing, really. I just don't want you getting upset. Have you ever heard of the Mafia?"

"I don't think so."

"It's a secret society that was started centuries ago in Sicily. In the beginning it was good, something like your Robin Hood band, but it became corrupt, and for the past two hundred years it has terrorized Italians all over the world. In this country, they use a symbol, the Black Hand, and when an Italian sees that, he knows he's marked for death."

"But what has that to do with the Maestro?"

"Nothing, really. The maid thought she saw a paper lying beside the Maestro with a black hand on it, but the girl was hysterical. There was no paper. I think she imagined it."

"But you said he died of a heart attack."

"He did. The doctor confirmed it. Nicky wants to believe somebody sent him the Black Hand and scared him to death."

"Is that why Nicky wanted to call the police?"

He nodded his head and ran a hand through his hair. "Nicky's a damn fool. Can you imagine the publicity that would have generated? The newspapers would be accusing the Mafia of controlling the opera, no less. Thank God, Victor for once agreed with me!"

"But, if someone really did that . . ."

"Don't even think such a thing, Charlotte. He was an old man and his heart gave out. That's all there is to it!" He threw down his napkin and in a gentler tone said, "The servants here are like children, Charlotte. It's up to you as the mistress, to keep them on an even keel. If they say anything about this, reassure them and then drop the subject. You must set the tone for the servants. Do you understand?"

"Yes, I understand."

But what about me? I thought. How was I going to keep myself on an even keel? How was I going to explain away the picture and all the other strange things that were happening. And as for the Black Hand, how can Forrest be so sure the girl imagined it? He was the first person to get there, but maybe somebody had already removed it.

Or, maybe he *removed it himself!* my demon said.

"Charlotte, what's wrong?"

"Nothing."

He came around to my side of the little table and put his arms around me. "I thought for a minute there you were going to faint. Oh, sweetheart. What has happened to my brave little girl? You got by in London without family, without money, and you weren't afraid of anybody, not even that old dragon of a landlady. What's come over you, sweetheart?"

To keep from answering, I buried my head in his shoulder. This house and the spirit who dwells here have come over me, I mused. They are contaminating me from within, and if I am not careful, they will destroy me.

The Maestro's body was taken to the parish church to lie in state until the funeral on Monday. Although most of his contemporaries had preceded him into the next world, several important members of the opera community were expected to come down from New York to pay their respects.

The Signora made so many demands on the servants that they scarcely had time to think about the tragedy. The young maid who had discovered the body was not to be seen, and Fiona informed me that she had been dismissed.

"They say the Signora gave her a glowing recommendation and a big bonus. Now why would she do that?" Fiona asked, searching my face like she suspected I was keeping something from her.

"I imagine that was Mr. Singleton's idea," I said, effectively discouraging any further questions.

She knew nothing about the Black Hand, which did not surprise me. All of the servants were Italian with the exception of Fiona. They obviously considered her an outsider, and then too, the Signora had probably clamped a lid of silence on the whole episode.

As for myself, I tried not to think about it.

The New York guests and Forrest's Uncle Henry were to arrive on Sunday and spend the night at the villa. The funeral mass was scheduled for eleven the next morning.

"Since there are no performances on Mondays, those from the Met can stay for lunch and then catch the afternoon train back," Victor informed us.

How considerate of the Maestro, I thought. Even his

108

funeral shall not interfere with the opera!

Victor had then gone on to give us a thumbnail sketch of the expected guests:

Mario Vidici, assistant director of the Met, had not personally known the Maestro, but was acting as the company's representative.

Quiet and unassuming, the soft-spoken Mr. Vidici seemed out of place among his more loquacious countrymen, though all of them, I noticed, treated him with great respect.

The other man, Don Alberto Rinaldi, had been a promising singer in his youth. One of the Maestro's early students, he had come to America after losing his voice to diphtheria. He had corresponded with the Maestro over the years and was one of his greatest admirers, according to Victor.

Miss Simpson, the younger of the two women, had been one of Gia's protégés from the Peabody, but the older lady had sung in Italy when the Maestro had conducted at La Scala. Like Gia, "the Baroness" had acquired her title through marriage; hers to an Austrian nobleman. She had discarded the baron, but not the title, incongruously attaching it to her own name to become Baroness Greco. I met her for the first time over cocktails in the small salon before dinner.

"Our host, Mr. Singleton," Victor said. Then as an afterthought, "And Mrs. Singleton."

Forrest smiled and kissed the woman's plump hand. "My wife is Gia's granddaughter," he added.

Baroness Greco gave him a surprised look and reached for the lorgnette that rested on her ample bosom. *"Nipote?"* She turned and peered intently at me through the glass. "Gia was your grandmother?"

Forrest answered for me. "That's right, Baroness, Charlotte's father was Gia's son."

I felt myself blush as the woman held the glass closer and scanned my face with dark, piercing eyes. "You look nothing like Gia," she said.

109

Carla must have overheard and she sauntered over, glass in hand, to join the conversation. "That's what they all say, but what about me? I've been told I not only sound like a young Gia Gerardo, I look like her, too. What do you say to that, Baroness?"

"You have black hair, Gia had black hair, but Gia's voice was full, *perfetto*," she added with a smile, and Carla turned scarlet. Baroness Greco went on smiling, and ignoring Carla she turned to me. "Your *nonna's* voice was magnificent. I say that without jealousy," she confided, "for I was *mezzo*."

"Did you ever appear with Gia?" Forrest asked.

"Certainly not. She was notorious for upstaging her fellow performers."

I felt myself warming to this outspoken woman. Not only had she put Carla firmly in her place, but something in those dark, penetrating eyes told me that that enormous bosom hid an equally large heart.

Later that evening I was watching Forrest, who was on the other side of the room engaged in conversation with Victor. My face must have betrayed my feelings, for Baroness Greco, who was standing near me, said, "You love him very much, don't you, my dear?"

"Of course. He is my husband."

She laughed. "You are very young, Mrs. Singleton."

"Please call me Charlote, and may I just call you Baroness?"

"Of course."

"Why did you laugh? Isn't it natural for a wife to love her husband?"

"Not always, but then I am a jaded old woman, and you are a bride. I'm probably jealous. It's been a long time since I had a handsome young husband."

"Are you a widow?" I asked.

She hesitated and shrugged. "Perhaps. I don't know for sure. I divorced my first husband ages ago."

"I'm sorry."

"So am I," she answered. At that moment Carla

110

appeared beside Forrest and whispered something in his ear. Then she laughed and tapped him on the shoulder with her fan.

Baroness Greco's eyes followed mine. "That one has the ambition," she said, "but she doesn't have the voice. Giuseppe was soft-hearted. He shouldn't have wasted his time with her."

"Who is Giuseppe?"

"Giuseppe Barranco, your Maestro."

"Of course. I only heard his name once," I said. "It sounded unpronounceable to me, and I was glad everybody just called him Maestro."

She gave me a puzzled look. "You don't speak Italian and you have a British accent. Why is that?"

"My father was raised in an orphanage in England," I said. "He never even knew he was Italian."

"I see. I thought it strange that I'd never heard Gia had a child. Where is your father now?"

"He died over a year ago. Forrest came to England and told me about the countess. He brought me to America for the reading of the will."

"Oh? And when were you married?"

"A month ago on the crossing."

But, it's not like that, I wanted to say as the silence between us grew awkward.

We both continued to watch Carla flirt openly with my husband, and then Baroness Greco cleared her throat and said, "And now that the Maestro is gone, I suppose you'll be saying farewell to Carla Pinetti, too."

Of course, I thought. It hadn't even entered my mind, but there would be no reason for Carla or Marshall to go on living at the villa without their tutor.

I felt better, but I'd reckoned without Carla. She was way ahead of me, as I would soon discover.

We left for the church in four carriages; a landau and two victorias from the villa in addition to Mr. Wilson's

111

ancient coach, which had been recruited to assist in getting all of us to the funeral at one time. I was relieved that Forrest, his uncle, and I would be using one of the private carriages, for I didn't relish another reckless ride with the surly Mr. Wilson.

Cal Marcus, the groom who had inherited Gia's racehorse, was our driver, and when we were seated, he said to Forrest, "If you don't mind, Signore Singleton, I come inside. Is all right with you?"

"Of course, Cal. You knew the Maestro. You have as much right as any of us to come to his funeral."

"*Grazie, signore.* I sit in last pew. Don't bother nobody."

"Don't worry about it. Cal. Sit wherever you want," Forrest said.

The funeral marked my first attendance at a Roman Catholic mass. The service, almost entirely in Latin, was incomprehensible to me, but I was deeply moved by the pomp and pageantry of it.

Never had I heard such music. I felt as if I was listening to an opera, or what I in my ignorance imagined an opera to be, but later I learned that the music was The Requiem in D minor and that Mozart had composed it for the funeral of an Austrian nobleman—a fitting tribute, I felt, to an *Italian* nobleman like the Maestro.

It also marked the first time I was to hear Carla and Marshall sing, and although untrained in music appreciation, I instinctively knew that Marshall's voice was far superior to Carla's. The countess's words, written in her will, came back to me as I listened. *His voice will take him to whatever heights he cares to climb.*

When the service was over, the casket was placed on a cart and taken to the little cemetery behind the church for burial. I was reminded of my parents' funerals and it saddened me to think that their graves would now remain forever unvisited and uncared for.

My thoughts turned then to the countess. Does she rest in peace? I wondered. Or does her restless spirit still walk, manipulating and controlling the Villa Montelano and all who dwell within its walls?

We returned to the churchyard and stood in a group, all of us sobered by the stark reality of death.

Mr. Vidici broke the silence. "The music world has lost a great master in Giuseppe Barranco," he said.

Don Alberto nodded solemnly. "The Maestro taught me everything I know, and I shall pass all of it on in his memory."

Carla pressed a dainty handkerchief to each dry eye and looked beseechingly at Mario Vidici. "The Maestro loved my Carmen," she said, and both the Signora and Victor DeSantis gave her astonished looks.

"He has written a letter requesting that the Met schedule a production of *Carmen* for my debut." She paused dramatically and sighed. "Poor Maestro, he didn't have time to mail it."

The Signore and Victor exchanged impatient glances and Baroness Greco rolled her eyes.

"I just remembered, I have a copy of that letter," Carla added. "Shall I send it to you, Mr. Vidici?"

"By all means, Miss Pinetti."

"Poppycock!"

The unexpected exclamation caused us all to jerk our heads toward the speaker, who turned out to be Wilson, the disagreeable old coachman. Nicky Faro stood beside him and it was obvious that they had been arguing.

Bestowing a glare on the rest of us, the short-tempered cabbie climbed up on his perch and took off in a cloud of dust.

Victor chuckled. "From the mouths of bambinos and imbeciles comes the truth."

Carla's face caught fire and she said, "That horrible old man." Then she turned to Nicky, who was walking toward us. "What's wrong with that fool? He's supposed to take us back to the villa."

Nicky shrugged. "He didn't want to wait. Said he was missing fares standing around here. Don't worry about it. Some of us men will walk back."

Forrest and Marshall said they could use the exercise and the three younger men took off on foot. I would have preferred the walk myself, for it was a beautiful September day, but I didn't think Forrest would appreciate my deserting our guests. Carla, of course, made sure she rode with Mr. Vidici, and to her obvious annoyance, Victor handed Miss Simpson into the same carriage and then squeezed in himself.

The short ride brought us back to the villa only slightly ahead of the walkers. The ladies took advantage of the time to freshen up, and when I returned from my room, Anna informed me that luncheon was to be served on the terrace.

Round tables with colorful yellow and white striped umbrellas had been set up and guests stood below in the gardens chatting and admiring the late-blooming roses.

"Here's Charlotte now," Forrest said, coming forward to take my hand as I walked down the flagstone steps from the terrace.

I took in the scene before me and for the first time since coming to the villa felt a measure of peace. In a matter of days now Carla would be gone, and the thought gave me confidence. I looked forward to a pleasant afternoon free from the nagging insinuations of my demons.

"Come and welcome Don Alberto to the villa," Forrest was saying. "He'll be staying to take over for the Maestro."

"You mean Carla and Marshall are going to keep right on studying here at the villa?"

"Yes. Carla spoke to Vidici and he persuaded Don Alberto to accept the position. Don Alberto himself studied under the Maestro, so he's familiar with his methods. It seemed like the right thing to do," he added as an afterthought. Then he winked and nodded his head in the direction of the others. "Maybe they'll be on their good behavior with Vidici's friend living here?"

I smiled woodenly and, wanting to avoid his eyes, gazed beyond him to the fringes of the garden. A woman stood lounging against a tree and my blood chilled when I recognized her face as the one I had seen Fiona wear in the mirror.

"What's wrong?" Forrest said, holding my hand a little tighter.

My gaze automatically shifted to him, and when I looked back, the countess's ghost was fading. As I watched, it evaporated before my eyes like a dewdrop in the sun.

Chapter 9

All of my self-confidence evaporated along with my grandmother's ghost. Why did I keep seeing this woman's face, hearing her hum in the dead of night? What did she want from me?

Or had it really happened? I asked myself. Perhaps these manifestations were only figments of my imagination, hallucinations brought on by the knowledge that I am unable to fulfill my husband's expectations.

The wife of Forrest Singleton and the woman who presides over the Villa Montelano should be accomplished and charming, I mused. Such a woman would have no problem competing with Carla or coping with the servants. She would be a delightful conversationalist, a gracious hostess . . .

"Charlotte, did you hear me?"

Forrest's words brought me up short, and still feeling disoriented, I said, "I'm sorry. What did you say?"

"I said, I think it would be polite if you welcomed Don Alberto to the villa."

Why should you? my demon whispered. You weren't even consulted about it.

I ignored the vicious voice inside my head and smiled at Don Alberto. "I understand you'll be staying with us," I said. "Please allow me to welcome you to the Villa Montelano."

116

He kissed my hand. "Thank you, gracious lady. I am overjoyed to be of assistance."

I was definitely not overjoyed, but I tried not to show it. After all, none of this was poor Don Alberto's fault.

Luncheon was announced then and the group returned to the terrace. The seating arrangement was informal, guests seating themselves where they pleased at one of the four round tables.

Forrest and I were joined by Don Alberto and Baroness Greco, who opened the conversation by saying, "Now that I shall be living in Baltimore, I hope to see all three of you frequently."

I was surprised and instantly pleased. "You're moving to Baltimore, Baroness?"

"Actually, I have already moved, but I've been spending the past month in New York. I keep an apartment there," she added.

"Wonderful," Forrest said. "Did you purchase a house?"

"As a matter of fact, I did. It's on Charles Street, not far from the Washington Monument. Are you familiar with the area?"

Forrest smiled. "Very much so, I have a townhouse in Mount Vernon Square."

"Then we're neighbors," she exclaimed with a smile in my direction. "You must come to town with Forrest one day soon, Charlotte. We'll go shopping and I'll take you to the Women's Exchange."

Forrest feigned surprise. "Good heavens, Baroness, I don't want to exchange her."

"Silly man, the Women's Exchange is a delightful little shop with a restaurant attached. Ladies like to meet there for lunch."

Her suggestion appealed to me, for the incident in the garden had left me badly shaken. Words tumbled out of my mouth like a gushing stream. "I would love to come. Why don't we make it this week? Forrest will be going back tomorrow and I could come with him."

117

The baroness looked surprised and my cheeks flamed. I sound like Carla, I thought. "I'm sorry, that's rather soon, isn't it? We can make it another time."

Forrest looked relieved. "Perhaps next month," he said jovially.

The baroness ignored him. "Nonsense. Whenever Charlotte wants to come will be fine." She patted my hand. "We shall have a lovely time, my dear." Then glancing sidewise at Forrest, she gave him a coquettish smile and turned back to me. "We can even take in the opera, Charlotte, if you think your handsome husband will escort us."

"I would be honored," Forrest said, "but I must insist that you ladies postpone this excursion until next week. I expect to be tied up in Washington for the next several days."

It was agreed, and later as we stood outside the villa, waving to our departing guests, Forrest pointed out that now was not the most auspicious time for the two of us to be away from the villa.

"They're all still hoping to find a second will. Had you forgotten about that, Charlotte?"

"But your uncle said there was no second will."

"There isn't, but I just don't like the idea of those vultures snooping around looking for one."

"But won't they have the same opportunity next week?"

"Not exactly, and I'm glad you brought that up. I almost forgot to tell you, the local locksmith will be here tomorrow to change some of the locks."

"Does the Signora know?"

"Forget about the Signora, Charlotte. You are the mistress here. The man will report to you."

I didn't feel up to assuming any responsibility and my face must have shown my concern, for he planted a playful kiss on the tip of my nose and said, "Relax, sweetheart. All you have to do is accept the keys when the job's done. Tom's familiar with the villa," he

118

explained. "Gia was always changing the locks." He chuckled to himself. "When she was alive, this house was bulging with guests. Gia would give them all keys, and then when she fell out with them, she'd change the locks." He shook his head. "Your grandmother was quite a character, Charlotte. Sometimes it's hard for me to believe that you two are related."

My sentiments exactly, I thought. "So, the locksmith will take care of everything then," I said.

"Yes. He's to change the locks on the countess's room, on the Maestro's cottage, and the hunting lodge. Just impress on Tom that we want only one key per lock. And Charlotte, hide those keys, and make doubly sure after you've gone over the countess's room that you lock the door."

The very thought of entering that room again terrified me, but something else bothered me more. "Suppose there is another will," I said. "What are we going to do about it?"

"Challenge it in court, of course."

His words made my heart sing, and overcome with relief, I vowed never again to allow the demon of suspicion to poison my mind.

"That's why I want you to go over the room as soon as possible," he was saying. "I don't trust Dorcas and Nicky, and if we have to go to court, I want to be prepared."

My fears suddenly seemed childish in the face of such logic, and I promised to go over the room as soon as the locksmith had finished.

When we entered the house, one of the servants informed Forrest that his uncle wished to see him in the library.

"I'll probably be tied up for the rest of the afternoon," Forrest confided. "The Maestro left everything to charity, but some of his holdings are in Italy and sorting it all out is a complicated process."

119

"Don't worry. I'll be fine. It's a beautiful day for a walk."

We parted and I stepped outside again. Following the driveway, I came to the carriage house, and slipping through a wide board fence I headed toward the stable and the woods beyond.

A magnificent view of gently rolling hills stretched before me to the east, and stealing a glance back at the villa, I was appalled anew by its ugliness. The house seemed to mock me, and in the glare of the sun it blurred before my eyes like yet another figment of my distorted imagination. Turning my back on it, I cast my eyes over the beautiful terrain, finding it inconceivable that all this land now belonged to me.

As I approached the stable, I saw the elderly groom who had inherited the race horse. Spotting me, he smiled and tipped his cap. *"Buona sera, Signora."*

"Good afternoon," I said. "Isn't this a beautiful day?"

"Sì, Signora."

"It's very warm for September," I said.

"Sì. They call it Indian summer."

"Does it get cold in the winter here?" I asked.

He nodded and smiled. *"Sì Signora.* When winter comes, these hills will be covered with snow. *Bella!* But I like the sunshine better."

"Have you been in America long?" I asked him.

He hunched his shoulders in a shrug. "Twenty years, but I traveled around, worked in different places, mostly out west. I only been here coupa years."

"You *are* from Italy?" I asked, for I had assumed he was, but then I was certainly no expert on accents.

"Sì, from Calagirone. That's in Sicily," he explained. "First job I get over here, my English it ain't so good. I say I'm from Calagirone and the other hands, they think I'm saying my name. So, they call me Cal and I've been Cal ever since."

We laughed over the story and then he said, "Do you

ride, Signora?"

"No, I'm afraid I never learned."

"Is nice. I teach you sometime."

I pictured myself riding on horseback over this beautiful, rolling countryside and the thought pleased me. "I'd be ever so grateful if you would. I always thought it would be something I'd enjoy."

"I show you. You come to stable whenever you're ready."

"Thank you, Mr. Marcus, I will."

He corrected me. "Everybody here calls me *Cal,*" he said shyly.

He was an elderly man and I was the daughter of working-class people. Uncomfortable with *Mrs. Singleton* and *Cal,* I said, "Everybody here calls me *Charlotte.*"

He laughed. "I call you *Miss* Charlotte and you call me Cal. Okay?"

"Okay," I said, and on that friendly note, we parted.

I wondered why he stayed on. Surely now with his pension, he could afford to leave, but then I supposed working at the villa had become a habit with him as it had with Signora Grazziano.

Of course the Signora is obsessed with the villa *and* its former mistress, I thought. No doubt she, along with all the displaced heirs, will stay put for the entire grace period.

"October, November, December, January, February, March." I counted the months aloud on my fingers and sighed. It was going to be a long winter.

The woods were beautiful. A narrow stream ran through the center with cliffs jutting from the opposite side and I could see what looked like a little house at the top. I wanted to pick my way across and climb up to see it, but my thin slippers were not made for hiking.

That must be the hunting lodge, I decided, shielding

my eyes with my hand for a better view. I wondered what it was used for and why Forrest would have its lock changed.

The estate's geographical location was really quite beautiful, I thought, finding it almost sacrilegious for the villa to be situated in such a spot. An architectural horror, it was a blemish on the landscape with its showiness and bad taste, and for the hundredth time I wondered how my father could have come from a woman with such distorted values.

Could it be possible that this was a mistake—that my father was not this woman's son? The Signora does not believe it to be true, I reasoned, and she has known the countess since her youth.

Victor DeSantis had openly expressed those same sentiments in the law office. *"Gia never had a child,"* he said, his face purple with rage.

But Forrest believes it to be true. *"Beyond a shadow of a doubt,"* he had said. Then it must be so, I told myself, throwing a pebble into the little stream. It sank to the bottom with a thud and I walked on, drinking in the beauty that surrounded me.

The trees were just starting to turn and I thought that in another few weeks they would be even more glorious, all crimson and gold. They'd drift gently down like big, colorful snowflakes and cover Mother Nature's floor with a bright handsome carpet.

Looking up toward the cliff, I caught another glimpse of the little house. Something about it intrigued me and I thought of Mayerling. A Hungarian prince and his mistress had committed suicide in a hunting lodge there about ten years ago. I had been a child at the time, but the tragic love story had fascinated me and fired my imagination.

Perhaps this one has a romantic history, too, I thought, and wanting to see more of it, I very foolishly climbed up on a large boulder and stood on tiptoe for a better view.

Of course, I lost my balance and tumbled off, twisting my body to break my fall. Luckily I wasn't hurt, but I'd be stiff in the morning, and brushing the dirt from my clothes, I decided to explore the woods another time.

Spying a well-worn path to my left, I picked up a stout stick and used it like a cane, hoisting myself slowly up the rather steep hill. It brought me out on a dirt road, and looking around, I decided that it was the same road we had traveled this morning on our way to the funeral.

Complimenting myself on having a sense of direction, I walked slowly along the narrow winding road. Trees were thick on either side blocking out the sun, and in the distance I heard a rumbling noise. I wondered if we were in for a storm. The day had been unseasonably warm, I reasoned, increasing my pace, for I didn't fancy getting soaked in a cloudburst.

The thought brought back memories of another storm when I had gotten soaked on my way home from work. That was the day I had met Forrest. What a wet, miserable little creature I must have presented in my sodden clothes, while Forrest, as always, had been impeccable. What had possessed him to take me out to dinner? I mused. He could just as easily have presented his case to me in Mrs. Hill's parlor.

The rumbling noise became suddenly deafening and I jumped back just in time to avoid being struck by a coach that rose like a charging bull over the crest of the hill. Grabbing hold of a low-hanging branch, I held on for dear life as it thundered past me.

Once the danger was over, I became angry. I could have lost my footing and plunged over the steep embankment that ran alongside the roadway. I recognized both the coach and the driver. That man Wilson is completely reckless, I thought, and should not be allowed to drive so much as a bicycle.

I was sitting in a hot tub, soaking away the road dust and relaxing my tired muscles, when Forrest poked his head in the bathroom. "That looks inviting," he said. "Mind if I join you?"

"I've been walking and the water's full of road dust," I warned him.

"I don't mind a little road dust," he said, peeling off his clothes and stepping into the tub with me.

The first time Forrest had done this, I had been shocked. We had been on our honeymoon and it had seemed a little depraved. I have always been extremely modest, but Forrest has no inhibitions and I was fast losing mine.

Lovemaking followed as a natural consequence of our frolic in the bathtub and we were still in bed when one of the servants knocked on the door.

I threw the covers over my head, mortified lest the servant suspect what we'd been up to.

"Tell him I'll be right down." I heard Forrest say.

As soon as the door closed, I poked my head out. "What is it?" I asked.

He was throwing his clothes on. "Oh, I don't know, some urgent matter that Uncle Henry wants to discuss. He thinks we're still in the office and I should be at his beck and call."

I fell asleep after he left, and when I awakened, it was seven o'clock. Poor Forrest, I thought, still closeted with Uncle Henry and it's almost dinnertime.

Jerking the bell cord, I rang for Fiona. If I was to be dressed and downstairs in time for cocktails, I would need her help.

In a matter of minutes she arrived, breathless and flushed with excitement. "Such commotion downstairs, mum. A body needs good nerves to work in this house, and that's a fact."

"What's wrong now?" I said.

"You mean you don't know? You haven't heard?"

I was losing patience. She wasn't really frightened, so I didn't think this latest catastrophe could be anything serious, but it was obvious that Fiona was thrilled by it and she wanted to prolong the suspense.

Still wrapped in the glow of lovemaking, I was happy, and I didn't want to hear any more bad news. "Just tell me what it is," I said, giving her a look that would have rivaled one of Signora's scowls.

"Mr. Forrest was attacked!"

"What?"

"Oh, he ain't hurt, mum, just a bump on the head. Mr. Singleton had Cal go for the doctor. A body can get a concussion sometimes from even a little tap on the head and I guess they wanted to be sure."

"But who? How?" I asked, feeling my nerves begin to tighten up again.

She shrugged. "Mr. Forrest never saw who did it."

"How did it happen?" I asked, trying to be calm, but a crazy thought kept buzzing around in my head. *Could a ghost physically strike someone?*

"Mr. Singleton gave Mr. Forrest the key to the Maestro's cottage on the edge of the woods. I guess he needed some of the Maestro's papers for something," she added. Her eyes grew large and it was plain she relished the telling of it. "Anyway, Mr. Forrest went to the cottage and somebody was already in there, hiding behind the door, mind ye." Raising her arm dramatically, she brought it down. "Whack! He hit Mr. Forrest over the head and ran back out the door. Knocked Mr. Forrest out, it did, and when the poor soul came to, there weren't nobody there."

"Poor Uncle Henry," I murmured.

"Oh, Mr. Forrest was calm as you please, mum. They say he went right on doing what he come for and when he finds the paper he needs, he goes back to the house and mentions it kinda casual like to the Signora.

125

'Looks like you got a poacher in the woods,' he says, and then he tells her what happened."

I rode to the station with Uncle Henry and Forrest. Uncle Henry still had a bump on his head, but otherwise he was none the worse for wear. He hated being fussed over and dismissed the incident as the work of some young ruffian in the area. "He probably thought there were valuables there and he could just help himself to them," he said.

Cal Marcus drove us to the station. When he assisted me from the carriage, I said, "Thank you, Cal," emphasizing his name.

Remembering our conversation, he smiled. "Have a safe trip, Miss Charlotte."

I felt we were friends now, and I was glad. He was someone I could relate to. Not talented or grand, to the others he was an object of scorn, as was I.

While we waited for the train, the old coach pulled into the station. "That man Wilson almost ran me off the road yesterday," I said.

Forrest gave me a surprised look. "What were you doing in the road?"

"I went for a walk in the woods. The ground was rough, and I didn't have on the proper shoes, so I took that narrow road leading back to the house. That old coach came charging over the hill and almost tumbled me down an embankment."

Forrest looked angry. "I'm going over there right now and give him a piece of my mind. He's a menace to the community."

"Please don't," I said. "It won't do any good, and besides, Cal is going to teach me to ride, so I won't be walking in the road anymore."

The shriek of the train whistle drowned out my voice and I forgot about the disreputable old coachman as the train came into view and the small group on the platform moved forward eagerly to board. We exchanged hurried kisses and then Forrest and his uncle were gone and I was alone again.

Cal was standing by the waiting carriage and he must have sensed my mood, for he said, "I teach you how to ride this week, Miss Charlotte. Give you nize little filly. Her name's Angelina. You talk, she listen—listen everything you say." He laughed then. "But, she no tell. *Cavallos,* they make good friends, *sì?*"

I supposed he meant the horses and I nodded.

He helped me into the carriage and then studied me with his gentle grown eyes. "Trust the horses here at the villa, Signora, but not the peoples."

Chapter 10

About an hour after I got back from the station, Anna came into the morning room to say that Tom Atkins, the locksmith, had arrived.

I was reminded of a ferret as she stared at me through black eyes narrowed to slits. "He says he's to report to you. Why you send for him?" she asked.

I ignored the question. "Just show him in, please."

She was back almost immediately, a lanky young man following behind her. "Name's Tom, ma'am," he said. "Mr. Singleton asked me to come up here and change some locks."

I acknowledged the man's greeting and Anna closed the door. Of course, I was positive that like my old landlady, she had her ear pressed to it from the other side. It hardly mattered, though. This sort of thing could certainly not be kept secret.

He knew what was to be done, and recalling Forrest's words, I instructed Mr. Atkins about the number of keys and stressed the fact that he should leave them with me when the locks were installed.

Then I showed him to the west wing and waited inside the countess's room while he worked on the door.

I was relieved to see that Gia's portrait had not been rehung, and looking about the room, I felt nothing, no ghostly presence, no sense of foreboding. It was just an ugly, overdone room.

"This makes the fourth or fifth time I've changed the lock on this door," Mr. Atkins said. "Pretty near three times for the cottage, but the lodge, I ain't never changed the lock on it before."

"Is the lodge that house I see from the woods, the one that sits on a high precipice?" I asked.

"Yes, ma'am."

"How does one reach the lodge? I've seen it from the woods, but there must be a road."

"Oh, there's a road all right," he answered, "but that's the long way round. There's a swinging rope bridge down yonder on this side of the villa connects right to it. The bridge's safe. A little scary to cross on a windy day, though. I recollect it was your husband's family built the first one."

He must be confused, I thought. "My husband's family?"

"Yes, ma'am. First bridge was built 'bout thirty years ago."

"But you said my husband's family built it. What do you mean?"

"I mean when the Singletons lived here. When the villa was called Lauraland. I was knee-high to a grasshopper in them days, so I don't remember much about it, but the old folks do."

Dear God, I thought. This was once Lauraland, the home Forrest could never forget! Why hadn't he told me? I tried to act casual. "I understand it looked very different then."

"So they say. I don't recall. You know how young'uns are, ma'am. We was kinda scared to come this far into the woods after what happened here."

I waited for him to go on, but he didn't, and I couldn't show my ignorance by asking. He assumed that as Forrest's wife, I knew what he was talking about. And I should have known, only my husband hadn't seen fit to confide in me.

"All done," he said, handing me a key. "I'll just get on

over to the lodge now."

I locked the door and put the key in my pocket. The room could wait. I didn't feel up to going over it now. I was confused and hurt by this newest revelation and I couldn't shunt it aside like I had so many other things.

Tom Aikins tipped his cap. "I'll just use the back stairs, ma'am, and when both locks are done, I'll bring you the keys."

"Fine," I said in a tight voice.

I'm supposed to be the mistress here, I thought, and I don't even know where the back stairs are located!

Pretending to examine the new lock, I lingered, letting him get ahead of me. His long strides took him quickly to the corner, and when he turned it, I followed, my soft slippers making no sound on the thick carpet.

He had vanished, but I found the stairway and took it down thinking that it probably ended in the servants' quarters. There was a door leading outside from the landing, though, and when I opened it, I found myself on high ground.

Walking up a slight incline, I could see the lodge and the rope bridge, which was swaying. Tom Atkins had obviously just crossed it.

I didn't want the locksmith to see me, so I turned and entered the house again, but I would be back, I told myself. If I am to be mistress here, I have a right to get to know this wretched villa *and* its secrets.

I continued on down the stairs and found that they did lead to the servants' quarters. The Signora looked up with surprise when I passed her office.

"Can I help you?" she said, getting up from behind her desk and hurrying toward me.

"No, thank you," I answered, continuing on my way.

She caught up to me and said, "Anna tells me the locksmith is here." She jangled the ring of keys at her waist and regarded me with hostile eyes. "How many locks is he replacing?"

"Only three."

130

"I'll pick up the keys from him myself."

"That won't be necessary," I said. "There will only be one key for each lock and Mr. Atkins will turn them over to me before he leaves."

Jangling the keys again, she glared at me. We stood there, eyes locked in mortal combat for what seemed like an eternity, and then the Signora turned and headed back to her office.

I returned to the east wing, and a short while later Mr. Atkins reported back to say that he was finished. Handing me two more keys, he said, "You tell Mr. Singleton he won't have no trouble with break-ins now. Them locks on the lodge and the little cottage were old, but I replaced them with Yale locks."

When he had gone, Anna poked her head in the door to say that luncheon was being served buffet-style on the terrace again. Slipping the keys in the pocket of my shirtwaist, I joined the others who were all present, probably in deference to the newcomer, Don Alberto.

Dorcas buttonholed me as soon as I walked outside. "I hear Baroness Greco has offered to show you the shops. When are you going?"

I decided to be evasive. "I'm not sure. It depends on Forrest's commitments."

"I hope you're not disappointed," she said. "What shops did you favor in London?"

The question was so ludicrous that I couldn't help smiling. "I'm afraid I only patronized the shop where I worked."

Her eyebrow shot upward. "You worked in a shop? I thought you were a teacher."

"I have a teacher's certificate," I explained. "And I was waiting for an opening in a private school when Forrest contacted me."

"Making you a much more lucrative offer," she added with a vicious sneer.

"I beg your pardon?"

Her face contorted in an ugly scowl. "The two of you aren't going to get away with this," she said. "And if

131

you have any sense, you'll get out while you still can."

Shocked, I stared up at her. Her beady little black eyes met mine and the broad nostrils flared, reminding me of a pig snorting in anger. A chill ran down my spine and instinctively I backed away.

"Oops," Marshall said, steadying me. "Sorry, Charlotte, I shouldn't have been standing so close."

I wondered if he had overheard any of the conversation, but his face betrayed nothing. "I think the buffet is ready, ladies," he said.

Dorcas turned away and gratefully I took the arm that Marshall extended to me.

It was another warm Indian summer day, and the cold buffet consisting of lobster and chicken salads, an arrangement of luscious-looking fresh fruit, and an array of mouth-watering pastries was tempting, but I had lost my appetite.

Dorcas's verbal attack had shaken me more than I cared to admit even to myself. This was the second time I had been accused of being an imposter. I had scoffed at the accusation before, but I hadn't known then that the Villa Montelano and Forrest's beloved Lauraland were one and the same.

"Is that all you're going to eat, Charlotte?" Marshall shook his head and stared at the thimbleful of chicken salad I had placed on my plate.

"I'm not very hungry," I answered.

Carla, who had come up behind Marshall and was heaping her plate with generous portions from each dish, said, "English women eat like birds. I noticed that when I was in London. They all have small diaphragms," she added, expanding her own chest and drawing attention to full breasts with jutting nipples that strained the confines of her bodice. "That's why England has so few great divas and Italy has so many. Her eyes never left Marshall's as she took a ripe strawberry off his plate and plopped it whole into her mouth. "Delicious," she said, chewing it slowly and running her tongue suggestively over beestung lips.

Victor was watching the performance and he clapped. "Practicing for *Carmen,* eh, Carla?"

"Bestia," she hissed under her breath. Then in an aside to Marshall she said, "Victor thinks they should have buried Carmen with Gia, but Vidici's all but promised me the role. Let's sit over there," she said, ignoring me and jerking her head toward a table well out of Victor's earshot.

Don Alberto made his appearance then and she gushed, "Come, Maestro. Sit over here with us."

Marshall took his plate and mine to the table and presently Don Alberto joined us.

A portly man in his fifties, the new tutor was mild-mannered like the mentor he so admired. I think he felt it his duty to launch the careers of his old Maestro's last pupils, for it couldn't have been easy for him to pick up stakes and leave New York on such short notice.

"This," he said, gesturing with his hands to take in the terrace and surrounding gardens, "reminds me of Craig-y-nos."

"Really," Carla said. "Then you've been there, Don Alberto?"

He nodded and Marshall looked at me and explained, "Craig-y-nos is Adelina Patti's estate in Wales." He winked his eye at me and turned to the older man. "Which would you say is more grand, Maestro, Craig-y-nos or the Villa Montelano?"

"I would say both are *equally* grand."

Marshall laughed. "You are a diplomat, sir. Già's ghost would have haunted you if you'd said Craig-y-nos."

Startled, I said, "Gia's ghost!"

"Just a joke, Charlotte," Marshall answered.

I colored. "Of course, but some people say the villa is haunted."

He shrugged. "The locals perhaps. Something about the people who lived here before."

The conversation turned to music then and my mind began to wander. Absentmindedly, I reached into the pocket of my skirt and felt the three keys. Now would be the perfect time to explore, I thought. They'll be out here for hours, consuming wine and discussing music, and I won't have to worry about any of them watching me.

Pleading what was fast becoming my standard excuse, a headache, I went back inside. To avoid running into the Signora or any of the servants, I used the front staircase and crossed over into the west wing by way of the second floor.

I passed the studio, which was locked, and wandered down the deserted corridor toward the countess's suite, but I did not stop there.

An unseen force seemed to be propelling me on down the long corridor to the end, making me turn the corner and walk a few more steps until I was standing at the top of the back stairway, looking down.

I was going to the lodge, but I could not have told anyone why.

A brisk wind almost tore the door from my hands as I stepped outside, and I wished I had worn a shawl. The gardens and the house had shielded the terrace, making the day seem balmy, but up here on higher ground the air was cool and only a few steadfast leaves quivered on branches already stripped for winter.

Using Mr. Atkins's heavy bootprints as a guide, I climbed the steep incline that led to the rope bridge. He had said it was safe, but looking at it up close, I had second thoughts about crossing it.

A short bridge, it had a wood-plank floor, but the sides were open, with nothing but ropes for the crosser to cling to. It connected two cliffs which were only about eighteen or twenty feet apart, yet the drop in between was easily forty feet down to the rock-strewn stream.

I drew courage from looking at the boards, which appeared to be thick. If it could take Mr. Atkins's weight, it should certainly take mine, and stepping gingerly out, I stood upon it.

Before I realized it, I had taken several steps, and looking back I saw that I was well away from the other side. Forward or back? Again, something propelled me forward, and holding on to the ropes, I made my way cautiously.

When I got to the middle, the bridge started to sway. The wind had picked up and I had visions of sliding through the ropes and crashing on the rocks below.

What had possessed me to do this? I wondered, but the strange compulsion that had brought me here moved my feet forward and carried me to the other side.

Looking back, the bridge seemed longer and much more fragile as it swayed against the wind. How will I ever bring myself to cross it again? I thought, and then I remembered that Tom Atkins had said there was a road.

Looking up at the sky, I saw with a sinking feeling that it had darkened. Please don't let it storm, I prayed, but in the next instant, I heard the distant rumble of thunder.

I'll never cross that bridge again, so I might as well see the lodge now, I decided, taking all three keys out of my pocket and looking at them. The locksmith had marked them, *BR* for bedroom, *C* for cottage, and *L* for lodge.

I inserted the proper key and the door creaked open. When my eyes had adjusted to the darkness inside, I saw that I was standing in a completely furnished room.

A comfortable-looking couch, sturdy chairs, and rag rugs gave the little sitting room a homey air, but a chill pervaded it and I had an irrational feeling that there was something evil here.

A blast of wind slammed the door shut and I jumped, rushing over and opening it again to assure myself that I could leave whenever I wanted.

It was foolish of me. I had the key, but I just didn't like the door being closed, so I went outside, and picking up a rock, I lodged it under the sill to keep the door ajar.

Pine paneling and a gun collection mounted over the fireplace added to the rustic atmosphere, but I didn't think this had been used as a hunting lodge—leastways, not for a long time.

My suspicions were confirmed when I opened a closet in the bedroom and found a man's dressing gown and a woman's red velvet robe hanging side by side. Why did she need a trysting place? I thought with disgust. She made no secret of her lovers.

I came back to the sitting room and found that the wind had blown the door wide open. A loud clap of thunder made me jump, and streaks of lightening zigzagged across a black sky. Then rain and hail the size of marbles poured from the heavens and sent me scurrying to close the door.

I leaned against it, shutting out the storm, but I did not feel safe. The evil that I had sensed when first I entered this house was stronger now. I was afraid to stay, but I could hardly wander around looking for a road in a raging storm.

As soon as it lets up, I'll leave, I decided. Peering out the window, I watched the rope bridge swaying in the wind, and, shuddering, I thought that no power on earth could ever get me to set foot on that thing again.

If only it wasn't so cold in here, I thought. Rubbing my arms, I starting walking around the room to keep warm. It was then that my eye fell on a large brass chest; I raised the lid eagerly.

I could not believe my good fortune, for it was filled with logs. Now if I can just find some matches, I'll be able to wait out this storm in comfort, I thought.

Luck was with me again, for a box of matches lay on the mantel piece and in no time at all I was basking in the warmth of a crackling fire.

Scanning the room more carefully this time, I spied a small desk that I hadn't noticed before. I felt like an intruder, but nevertheless I walked over to it and pulled down the lid. The little cubbyholes insides were stuffed haphazardly with papers and I pulled them out and examined them.

They were mostly bills and receipts. Several were from Tom Atkins, and glancing over them, I could well understand why he knew his way around the villa.

Every lock on every door in the house must have been changed at least once, according to the receipts. What a suspicious woman, I thought, and suddenly wondered if that wasn't like the pot calling the kettle black.

But I hadn't always been cynical. And I wondered, Was my grandmother gradually shaping me into her own image?

Never! I vowed. Forrest owed me an explanation, but I would not judge him until I had heard him out.

I stuffed the papers back in the cubbyholes and opened one of the drawers. A large portfolio was on top. I lifted it out and read, *Bloodlines and All Papers Pertaining to Race Horse Registered As Lady Baltimore*. Replacing the portfolio, I brought out the large pink satin box that had been underneath it. It contained writing paper and a few letters.

I lifted out one yellowed with age. It read:

10 February, 1874
Dear Gia,
    There was a bracelet inside the flowers I sent. Did you see it? Please do not ignore me. My heart is aching for you. I am your slave and I adore you. If you don't meet me tonight I shall kill myself.

I wondered if the young man the Signora had told me about had written it. Hadn't she said one of Gia's admirers had committed suicide over her? Dear God, I thought. Why would she keep the letter? Did she think of it as a trophy?

There was one from Victor DeSantis proposing a tour and others that I merely glanced over, but I had

137

lost the taste for delving into my grandmother's shallow life and putting the box back I closed the drawer.

I got up and looked out the window. The warmth from the fire had steamed up the glass, so I went into the bedroom to look outside.

The bedroom was cold, so I assumed the window would be clear. Reaching up, I pulled back the drape and what I saw *was* clear—so clear and so hideous that I froze.

A silent scream rose in my throat, for outside the window stood a tall tree and from it hung the body of a man. I watched in fascinated horror as the grotesque figure swayed eerily back and forth in the wind.

The scene emblazoned itself on my mind and I can see it still, the thick knotted rope, the head tilted to one side and the feet dangling in midair.

I gasped and pulled the curtain shut. The evil was *outside* the house, *not inside*. Dear God, I thought. Should I leave or stay?

I was about to go back to the sitting room when I heard a noise. I had forgotten to lock the front door and again I froze, my ears alert to even the smallest sound. A moment later, I heard a creak that told me the door was slowly being opened.

Adrenaline shot through my blood and a primitive instinct took possession of my body. Like a cat I moved swiftly and silently across the room to the closet. My hand reached for the knob and turned it slowly. Then when I heard the unmistakable sound of approaching footsteps, I stepped inside and pulled the door carefully shut.

Imprisoned in total darkness, my terror was so great that I feared I might lose contol and scream, giving myself away. The poacher, I thought, for I was convinced it was he. Hadn't he been hiding in the cottage? Hadn't he attacked Uncle Henry. Oh, God, what will he do to me?

If only there were more clothes in here, I thought,

moving behind the two dressing gowns that hung in the closet.

Time passed and I heard no sound. Had he left, I wondered. Was it safe to come out now? Perhaps I could hear something if I opened the door just a crack.

My hand closed around the cold metal knob and an instant later it was wrenched from my grasp. I saw the rifle before I saw the man, and then I fainted.

When I came to, I was lying on the bed and Cal Marcus was rubbing my hands. "Miss Charlotte, please. I no mean to scare you. I see the smoke coming from the chimney. I think that poacher, he coma back."

"Oh, Cal," I said. "I thought you were the poacher."

He smiled. "We both maka mistake. Okay, now, *sì?*"

I grabbed his arm. "No, listen, Cal. Something terrible has happened. Oh, thank God, you're here."

He looked at me with concern. "Wassa wrong, *figlia mia?*"

"Open the curtain and see for yourself," I said, pointing to the window.

Giving me a puzzled look, he stood up and crossed the room.

I turned my head while he pulled the drapes.

"Wassa wrong?"

"Look at the tree," I said. "Don't you see it?"

"See what?"

"The man," I shouted. "There's a man hanging from that tree!"

"No, Signora. No man. Come see for yourself."

Chapter 11

I forced myself to get up and look out the window. "But, it was there," I said. "I saw it."

I started to shake and Cal put a big arm about my shoulder. "This was when it was storming?"

I nodded and he said, "Something mebbe got caught on tree, *cara mia*. Mebbe it looka like something else to you. It was bad storm, Miss Charlotte."

"Could—could someone have t-taken it down?"

He shrugged. "Why they do that, Signora?"

"Oh, I don't know. I guess I'm just crazy."

His brown eyes softened and he smiled. "No crazy, Miss Charlotte, just scared, and you couldn't see good in the storm."

But I *could* see good, I thought. And never as long as I lived would I forget what I had seen.

Cal was watching me and he said, "Let me takka you home now, Miss Charlotte."

"I won't cross the rope bridge," I said emphatically.

"Naw, no bridge, *cara mia*. I came on horseback. We ride home together. Okay?"

I decided to tell no one about my harrowing experience in the lodge. I still hadn't discounted the theory that someone had cut down the body, but there were other alternatives to be considered.

Cal thought that the storm had distorted my vision, but that explanation didn't hold water with me, for the scene I had witnessed had been crystal clear. That in itself seemed strange, I had to admit, for shouldn't the window have at least been rain-splattered?

I didn't want to think it had been another supernatural manifestation and I refused to dwell on that possibility.

Could it have been a hoax? The more I considered that theory, the more logical it became. Any number of people did not want me here; that was certainly obvious. Nicky's sly insinuations, Carla's insults, and the other three's outright accusations all came back to me.

Victor had expressed his doubts as soon as the will had been read and the Signora and Dorcas had called me an imposter to my face. I would not put it past any one of them to have arranged a mock hanging for my benefit, and so I watched them all with a jaundiced eye.

The week passed. I was surprised how quickly, for I had taken Cal up on his offer. "You're a natural," he told me with a grin after our first lesson. "This is horse country, *cara mia,* and you gonna be the best horsewoman in the county."

I was amazed, both with my progress and with how much the sport fascinated me. In the saddle every day, I retired early at night, and drugged with exhaustion, slid effortlessly into a deep and dreamless sleep.

Forrest had asked me to go over the countess's effects, but I hadn't done it. The man's robe hanging in the closet along with the pitiful letter she had kept as a souvenir sickened me and I had no stomach for more of the same.

I didn't care about finding another will. He's the one who wants this accursed house, I thought. Let him be the one to look for the will.

The day before Forrest was expected home, Victor

surprised me by appearing on the second floor of the east wing.

I had just left the stable and was still in my riding habit when I saw him standing in front of my room.

"I was about to leave you a note," he said by way of explanation. "I'd like to meet in private with you tonight.'

Remembering the Black Hand, I wondered if he was in the habit of slipping notes under doors. "Can't we talk now?"

"I don't discuss business standing up in hallways." He scowled down on me from his great height, making me feel incredibly small, and then his sensuous mouth curved in a nasty smirk. "Surely, you weren't suggesting . . ." he said, then shook his head. "No, *cara mia,* I wouldn't think of soiling your impeccable reputation by entering your boudoir."

As if I would invite you, I thought, hating him for the lewd interpretation he put on everything.

"I won't take too much of your time," he was saying. "Meet me in the conservatory at twelve o'clock."

"Midnight!"

Again, that smirk. "Is there something wrong with midnight, Miss Stone?"

"Miss Stone?" I repeated.

He shook his head. "I apologize. A slip of the tongue. I meant to say, *Miss Charlotte.* That's what the groom calls you, isn't it? Miss Charlotte," he mimicked, raising an eyebrow. "It *sounds* British."

"It *is* British," I answered, and moving quickly past him I placed my hand on the doorknob, and drew myself up to my full five feet. "I can't meet you. I always retire before midnight."

He laughed. "You always retire before midnight? Why? Are you afraid your carriage will change into a pumpkin, and your new clothes will turn into rags?"

Placing his hands on either side of the door, he leaned over me. His face showed vestiges of the coarse peasant stock he'd sprung from, and Forrest's description of the Mafia leapt to mind. "What I have to say will be of interest to you," he murmured.

I didn't like having him so close to me and I said, "All right, I'll come. Now, if you'll excuse me, I have to change."

I wondered what he had to say and why he wanted to make such a secret out of it, but artistic people seemed to thrive on drama, as I had discovered of late, and although Victor was certainly not an artiste, his whole life had revolved around the stage.

I put in my usual appearance for cocktails and dinner, but then as had been my habit since riding, I excused myself and retired to my room.

I was exhausted and it annoyed me that I would have to stay awake until after midnight just to safisfy a disagreeable old man's whim.

I dismissed Fiona with a thin excuse. There was no point in getting undressed only to have to dress again in another two hours, so after winding the alarm, I stretched out fully clothed on the bed.

I was beginning to have second thoughts about this. Why had I agreed to be a party to it? A secret meeting, and at midnight yet! The whole thing smacked of cheap melodrama. He had probably lifted it straight out of some opera, I thought with disgust.

I must have drifted off to sleep, for the next thing I knew the alarm clock was ringing in my ear, and reaching over, I shut it off.

Wishing the disagreeable meeting was over, I splashed cold water on my face, smoothed my hair, and left the room.

The corridor was in semidarkness and with an omnious sense of déjà vu, I leaned over the banister and looked down into the great hall. The silence, the tilting armor, the eerie amber glow—all was as before, and as I slowly descended the staircase, I heard it again, the low, ghostly hum.

143

The sound followed me as I raced through the great hall, but when I reached the conservatory, it abruptly stopped.

"Come in," a disembodied voice called.

I stood poised in the doorway, my heart beating wildly, and after a dramatic pause, Victor emerged from the shadows. "Come in and sit down," he said, indicating a stone bench.

The room was hot and the cloying scent of gardenias filled the air. In the dimly lit conservatory, the dead white blooms appeared luminous and a little ghostly.

I walked over to the bench and sat down, but he remained standing. "I don't believe, any more than the others do, that you are Gia's granddaughter."

I opened my mouth to protest, but he waved his hand. "I don't care anything about that," he said impatiently. "I only want one thing . . ."

I waited, and after a long, pregnant pause, he added, "This house."

Again, I tried to speak, but he cut me off. "I don't give a damn about protesting the will, or finding another one." His black eyes glittered with an almost-insane zeal and his voice rose. "You can keep everything else, but the Villa Montelano belongs to me!"

I wanted to leave. His presence and the intoxicating odor of the gardenias was making me sick. "I'm sorry," I said, rising. "I'm tired and this conversation is pointless."

His eyes flashed, but he quickly brought his anger under control. "I'm prepared to make you a handsome offer, Charlotte. That is your name, isn't it, *cara mia?*"

I started to leave, but he took hold of my arm. "Don't be a fool. I don't know what Singleton's told you, but you hold the reins, *cara*. The house is in your name. You sell it secretly to me, and when the year's up, I take possession and you're off the hook."

"I wouldn't dream of signing anything without my

husband's advice," I said haughtily, and holding my head high, I turned and walked out of the room.

Long after this night had passed, the dead-sweet smell of gardenias would haunt me and make me remember his parting words.

"What makes you think you can trust your husband?"

We were all gathered in the small salon having cocktails when Forrest swept into the room. As always after a separation, his handsome face and the startling blueness of his eyes made my heart skip a beat.

Accepting a drink from the waiter's tray, he crossed the room to brush my lips with a husbandly kiss. "Missed you," he said in an undertone, and slipping an arm about my waist, he greeted the others and then gracefully eased himself into the conversation. "You say the storm was bad up here?"

"It caused a lot of damage," Don Alberto said.

"Knocked huge limbs off some of the trees in the woods and blew them down into the stream," Marshall added.

I gasped. Could that be the answer? Are the dead man and the broken branch lying in the stream?

"We had hail big as marbles," Don Alberto was saying. "It came up suddenly, too. We were all out on the terrace eating lunch."

"Ripped the umbrellas to shreds," Marshall added.

If a body is found, I thought, then that will establish a perfectly natural explanation for what I saw. Did I wish some poor soul dead? I didn't like to think so, but neither did I like to think that I was mad. Or that somebody was trying to drive me mad.

Dinner was announced, and as Forrest was leading me into the dining room, he said quietly, "Are the locks changed?" I nodded and he said, "Good. I hope you put the keys in a safe place."

"Of course," I answered, and then a feeling of panic

washed over me. I hadn't put them anywhere. In my agitated state, I had forgotten all about the keys. They must still be in the pocket of my skirt.

"Now that that little problem is settled, we can go to Baltimore with our minds at ease," he said.

I made a mental note to transfer the keys to my jewelry box, but I had more important things on my mind. Now that Forrest was here, I was reluctant to bring up Lauraland. I have always hated confrontations and now I found myself reverting to form and having second thoughts about initiating one. Perhaps it would be a mistake. He may be planning to tell me in his own good time. It would spoil our trip to Baltimore and I need so desperately to get away from here, I thought.

Looking down the long table at his animated, handsome face, my heart swelled with pride. I loved him and I knew he loved me. We can discuss it some other time, I decided. It's not all that important and maybe it would be better if he was the one to bring it up.

After an interminable time, the heavy, four-course meal finally ended and we all retired to the drawing room. Don Alberto asked Carla and Marshall to sing, and the impromptu little concert lasted for over an hour.

I found Carla's voice reedy, but Marshall's was magnificent. Of course at that time the technicalities were beyond my grasp, but I was nevertheless interested in hearing about them and so I listened with attention to the lively discussion that followed the concert.

Don Alberto commented that very little about the singing voice is fully understood because it is impossible to observe a throat in action.

"Didn't the great García invent a mirror apparatus for that purpose?" Forrest asked.

"*Sì*, but it cannot reflect the underside of the vocal cords," Don Alberto explained. "We know only that singing is accomplished by expelling air through the vocal cords. Then resonators such as the larynx pick up the sound and amplify it."

"Training is everything," Carla said, giving Don Alberto a coquettish smile. "We're so fortunate to have you, Maestro."

Victor fixed himself a drink and joined the group. After complimenting Carla on her selection from *Carmen,* he pointed out that in the opera the aria must be sung while dancing. "Very strenuous, and hard for a light voice to handle," he said.

She shrugged, but her eyes were murderous. "Vidici doesn't anticpate a problem."

Victor sat down and addressed Don Alberto. "Did you ever hear Gia float top D, Maestro?"

"I don't believe I did."

"Too bad," he said, studying the drink in his glass. "It was like nothing that's ever been heard before. She called it her 'fourth voice.'" He leaned forward confidentially and explained. "It was a method she learned from an aged *castrato* in the Sistine Chapel choir. It involved keeping the mouth virtually closed as in humming. Gia practiced it all the time."

"How well I remember," Dorcas exclaimed sarcastically "That incessant humming. It got on my nerves."

Nicky looked amused. "They say Emma Calvé goes around chanting a mantra. Some swami gave it to her."

Victor eyed him coldly. "There's no comparison there."

Don Alberto effectively soothed Victor's ruffled feathers. "It's a well-known fact that humming nurtures the voice," he said.

So, now I know, I thought. But why am I the only one who hears her?

"Alone at last," Forrest said, closing the door and taking me in his arms. He kissed me hungrily, and I

147

knew I would not bring up Lauraland or Gia's ghost or anything else unpleasant.

You're a coward, my demon said.

Maybe tomorrow, I answered, giving in to the honeyed kisses and practiced hands that were driving me wild with desire.

"Get undressed," he whispered, and I shed my clothes like his wanton slave, letting them drop in a pile at my feet.

He picked me up and carried me to bed. Our coming together was urgent and a little violent. "Oh, Charlotte, I'm sorry," he said afterward.

But I reached out to him, and pressed his head to my breast, I murmured in a voice still husky with passion, "Don't be. I wanted you the same way."

We made love again, slowly and more gently this time, and then, spent, we collapsed in each other's arms. Warmed by the embers of love, we drifted off to a deep and contented sleep.

I awoke to the sound of running water and a hearty male voice raised in song. Glancing casually at the closed bathroom door, I got up out of bed and reached into the closet for my robe.

I slipped it on and stood staring vaguely into the closet, when suddenly I remembered the keys. Thank God, Fiona hadn't washed the shirtwaist, I thought, pulling it out and thrusting my hand in the pocket. I pulled out two keys, but where was the third?

Feeling a sudden panic, I turned the garment upside down and shook it, but nothing fell out. I looked at the two keys in my hand. One was marked *BR* and the other, *C.* The key to the lodge was missing!

I knelt down and started feeling around the closet floor.

"What are you looking for?"

Forrest's voice made me jump. "Nothing," I said, staring up at him with sudden panic.

He regarded me with an amused smile and offered

148

me his hand. "You're crawling around the floor for fun?"

"I thought I heard something drop," I said, "but I guess it was nothing."

God forgive me, but I didn't have the nerve to tell him I'd already lost one of the keys.

Slipping the other two into the pocket of my robe, I took his outstretched hand and let him help me to my feet. Later, when Forrest wasn't looking, I transferred the keys to my jewelry box.

Had it fallen out of my pocket on the ride through the woods? I wondered. If so, I would never find it, but on the other hand, if someone should pick it up, they wouldn't know what it was for.

I still couldn't bring myself to tell Forrest. It seemed so stupid, as if I couldn't be trusted to do even the simplest thing.

No, I decided, the door is locked, and if I can't find the key, neither can the others. I'll just have Mr. Atkins make me another one when I get back from Baltimore.

"You're looking very serious," Forrest said. "Like a little girl who's been naughty and fears a spanking."

Good Lord, I thought, but I smiled and said, "I'm not a little girl."

"Oh, yes, you are." He came up behind me and took the brush from my hand. Drawing it gently through my hair, he said, "Cal tells me you can ride."

"Yes," I said. "He's a wonderful teacher, and such a nice man, Forrest. I really enjoyed our lessons."

"Cal knows horses," he said. "I was as surprised as the rest of them that Gia left him Lady Baltimore. She probably did it to spite Victor and Nicky," he added, "because Gia was hardly a compassionate woman, but it's still a nice thing for old Cal."

"Can we ride this morning?" I asked.

"You bet. I want to see this superior horsewoman that Cal is raving about."

We dressed in our riding habits and after a quick

breakfast headed for the stable. Cal was not about, but one of the hands saddled our horses.

"Let's ride through the woods," I said.

He nodded his head. "You're the equestrienne. I'll follow your lead."

Wanting to show off, I spurred the little filly to a gallop and raced through the clearing that stretched to the woods. At the entry, I pulled the mare up short, shocked at the sight that met my eyes.

Several huge trees had been felled; their exposed roots giving a mute and almost obscene testimony to the violence that had been done.

Forrest rode up beside me. "I thought they were exaggerating yesterday, but you had quite a storm up here, didn't you?"

I said, "Yes, it was terrible."

"Where were you, sweetheart? Hiding in a closet?"

I must have looked startled, for he laughed and said, "Well, as I recall, you're pretty terrified of storms. At least you gave me that impression when we rode through these woods in old Wilson's coach."

Why didn't I tell him his little joke was more truth than fiction? Why didn't I tell him that I had seen a man hanging from a tree outside the lodge? And why didn't I admit that I was here today hoping to find proof that what I had seen was not a figment of my imagination?

My reasons were obscure, but I didn't want to probe them. Perhaps I was afraid of opening a Pandora's box, but as I would later discover, secrets, like neglected wounds, tend to fester with time.

"Smile. I was only teasing," he said.

"I know," I answered, and changing the subject, I added more cheerfully, "Let's walk around a bit."

We dismounted and, holding hands, strolled down to the stream. It was swollen and clogged with debris, but there was no sign of the macabre evidence I was seeking.

The woods suddenly depressed me and I wanted to

leave. Turning to Forrest, I saw that he was staring up at the lodge. There was a far-away look in his eyes, and when I spoke I got the feeling I had jolted him back from another world.

"Huh? Sorry, darling. What did you say?"

"I said, let's go back. It's damp and depressing here."

"You're right," he said, taking my arm and silently leading me back to our mounts.

As we rode out of the wood, I spotted two men on the other side of the stream. One of them was Nicky Faro and the other man looked like Wilson, the disreputable old coachman. I was about to mention it to Forrest, but when I looked again, they had disappeared.

Chapter 12

We sat facing each other in the train as it sped through the rolling Maryland countryside and Forrest playfully snapped his fingers. "You can come out of your trance now, Trilby."

"Sorry. I was daydreaming."

He gave me a mock frown. "That's not very flattering, Mrs. Singleton."

"Oh, but it is. I was daydreaming about us."

"And?"

"And, thinking about the wonderful week we're going to have in Baltimore."

"I'll have to spend time in the office, too, Charlotte," he cautioned me.

"I know, but you'll be home every evening and in the daytime, I'll have the baroness to keep me company."

Eyeing me with amusement, he said, "I'm surprised you approve of the baroness."

"Why is that?"

He shrugged. "She's crazy, she's Italian, and she's every inch a prima donna."

I knew he was poking fun at me. "Perhaps you're right," I said, "but at least she treats me like a human being."

His eyes softened and he reached over and took my hand. "I know it hasn't been easy for you, Charlotte, but in a few more months they'll all be gone and we'll have the house to ourselves. Then we can make changes."

A far-away look came into his eyes and I knew he was remembering the house as it once had been. "Trust me," he said. "The villa can be made a truly elegant home." His blue eyes sparkled with enthusiasm and he added, "We'll send those damn domes back to Persia, or wherever they came from. We'll transform the gingerbread house. Get rid of all its gaudy red and pretentious gold."

I nodded.

But can we get rid of its ghost?

Forrest picked up his briefcase. "Mind if I look over some briefs, sweetheart?"

"Not at all. I'm going to read."

I opened the book, but I was more interested in watching my husband. I was enormously proud of Forrest. In the working-class world that I had been born to, members of the legal profession were set apart from other men and were accorded the respect and admiration usually reserved for the artistocracy. A barrister, I mused. It hardly seemed possible that I was married to one.

Peering out the train window, I thought that I might have been back in England. The whitewashed cottages we passed reminded me of a little town in Devonshire.

Papa's job in the mill there had only lasted a year, but it had been a prosperous, pleasant place. Had we stayed, I might have married a postman or a clerk from the mill, I mused. Perhaps I might be living in a house like the one we just passed.

The thought distressed me, for I suddenly realized that without the villa and its possessive ghost, Forrest and I would never have met at all.

I must have nodded off, for the next thing I knew, the train had slowed to a halt and the conductor was marching down the aisle bellowing, "Bal-ti-more. All off for Bal-ti-more."

We disembarked and in no time at all were

comfortably seated in a hack and on our way to Mount Vernon Square.

The streets were filled with carriages and drays and they clattered over the cobblestones making a sort of music that was pleasant to my ears. The whole hectic, busy scene filled me with joy. It's so good to be home, I thought and almost said, but I didn't think Forrest would appreciate the remark.

Before ever we reached it, General Washington's monument loomed before us like a welcoming beacon. It dominated not only the square, but the whole upper section of town, and although my forebears must have considered him the enemy, I found the general's presence rather reassuring.

Once home, I walked through every room, taking in the soft, muted colors and the understated elegance of the furnishings. A kind of peace settled over me and I wondered how I could ever return to the villa with its vivid hues and curlicues.

Oh, how happy I would be to hear Forrest say, *We'll sell the villa when the year's up and come back here.*

I turned to find him smiling, a little smugly, I thought. "Makes you feel like you've stepped into a matchbox, doesn't it?"

I must have looked puzzled, for he added, "The house—I mean, it seems so small after the villa."

I felt a stab of disappointment. I saw a house that I wanted to call home and he saw only that it was small.

The following morning I surprised Forrest by appearing in the cozy little dining room to have breakfast with him.

"You didn't have to get up," he said, putting down his paper and rising to greet me.

"I wanted to see you off, and besides, I always get up early. I know it's not fashionable," I added. "But then neither am I."

"I'd say you look very fashionable this morning," he

said, taking in my bottle green suit with its slim skirt and Zouave jacket trimmed in braid. "Nevertheless I wouldn't call on the baroness before ten, darling."

"Don't worry. I won't make a social blunder."

He laughed. "Believe me, darling, the baroness wouldn't know it if you did. The only thing aristocratic about the old girl is her title."

"I thought you liked her," I said.

"I do like her. I just wanted you to relax and stop worrying about social blunders. Now ring for Nancy. I've already ordered," he added, pulling out my chair.

When we were seated next to each other, he handed me the women's section of the *Baltimore Sun*. "Since you're going shopping, you might want to look over the ads," he said.

I knew he was anxious to resume his reading, so I rang for the maid, and after asking Nancy to bring me some toast and tea, I opened the paper he had given me.

Hutzler's was offering ladies' kidskin gloves for a dollar and a quarter, and O'Neil's had a sale on winter coats. *Six dollars and fifty cents,* the ad read, *These stylish coats in an assortment of colors usually sell for ten to twelve dollars.* I skimmed over an article about two young women, who wearing bloomers, had bicycled through a small town called Sweetwater. Some of the townfolk were so scandalized that they had thrown stones at them.

Nancy brought our breakfasts up from the kitchen by means of the dumbwaiter. I had never seen one before coming to Mount Vernon Square, though I supposed English houses with servants had them as well.

Forrest had told me that once as a small lad he had frightened one of the kitchen maids to death when she hauled it down and found him hiding inside.

I was sure he had been a mischievous little boy, but probably adorable, I thought, stealing a glance at him as he pored over his newspaper.

He caught me looking at him and said, "Now, what

are you thinking about?"

"I was thinking that you were probably adorable as a lad."

"I was a hellion," he said, "while you were probably a perfectly proper little English girl."

We finished breakfast and Forrest kissed me goodbye.

"Have a great day," he said. "And by the way, we'll be going to the opera Thursday evening, so get the baroness to help you select a new gown. Something daring and sophisticated," he added.

I waited until I heard the clock strike ten and then I put on my hat and left the house.

Another gorgeous September day, the weather was ideal for walking, which was what I intended to do. The baroness lived only a short distance away, and if I took my time, I should not arrive so early as to appear gauche.

Mount Vernon Place is bounded by four squares, or parks, which provide a cruciform setting for the Washington Monument. They are handsome squares, one guarded by the sculpture of a majestic seated lion who looks out over his domain like a king.

Strolling through the south square, I passed the Lily Fountain. Forrest said that last summer after a ball, a celebrated Baltimore belle and her escort had walked through it on a dare. Soaked to the skin, they had frolicked under the monument in their evening clothes, causing quite a sensation.

Forrest had added that once this same young man invited guests to a dinner party in honor of a Prince del Drago. The prince turned out to be a monkey who sat at the table and threw champagne glasses at the other guests. Forrest thought it was hilarious, but I was horrified.

The baroness's house, which shouldn't have surprised me, was a châteauesque curiosity that had been squeezed onto a townhouse lot. Three stories high, it had been built to resemble a French château with long narrow windows and a pointed tower.

Completely out of place with the other houses on the block, it caught the eye and dominated the scene like the baroness herself.

A very stately butler answered my ring and ushered me into the drawing room. Handsomely done in green and gold, the room had a regal air, but the effect was one of quiet elegance rather than ostentation.

"Charlotte, *cara mia,* but it is good to see you again." The baroness swept into the room and embraced me warmly. "Beppino is giving me trouble," she said. "The little *castrato* won't do his scales and I have told him there will be no treat until he performs."

The baroness gave no explanation as to what she was talking about, although she was referring to a pupil. That the boy was a *castrato* was a complete shock to me and I could only nod when she said, "Let me give him another five minutes. That's all, five minutes, then we'll leave, *sì?*"

She swept out of the room and a second later, I heard her strong voice trilling a scale, "Do, Re, Me, Fa, So, La, Ci, Do. Take the high C, Beppino, like a good boy," she coaxed.

All of a sudden, a shrill, high note filled the air. Like no sound I have ever heard, it was strange, almost inhuman. So that is a *castrato,* I thought.

"Wonderful, Beppino. Good boy, good boy." She shouted, and then lapsed into Italian, no doubt heaping more praise on the unfortunate child. "Now we must go see our friend, Charlotte," she said.

The door opened and I stared in amazement at the baroness, who was holding the biggest, fattest black and white cat I have ever seen.

"This is Beppino," she said. "Doesn't he sing magnificently?"

I smiled in relief and patted the cat on his head.

"Sometimes I can get him to go all the way up the scale," the baroness said. "I told Vidici he should sign him with the Met."

Plopping the cat down on a big satin pillow, she put on her hat and, linking her arm in mine, said, "Let us be off to the shops, Charlotte."

Recalling Forrest's words, I smiled to myself. *She's crazy, she's Italian, and she's every inch a prima donna.*

But I like her, I thought, feeling lighthearted for the first time in many days.

Catching the stern-faced butler's eye, the baroness said, "Harcourt, have the carriage brought around front."

With no change of expression, he held the door open and answered, "Your carriage awaits, Baroness."

"Thank you," she mumbled, sweeping grandly out the door. I followed in her wake, and once we were seated in the carriage, she said, "The man is so efficient, he knows what I want before I ask for it. Are all British butlers like that?"

I laughed. "I wouldn't know, Baroness. I never had a butler."

"Neither did I," she said, dismissing the subject. "Take us to O'Neil's," she told her driver, and then turned to me. "What are you looking for?" she asked.

"Forrest wants me to get something new for the opera tomorrow night, but if we don't see anything it's fine," I added.

"Nonsense, we have two days," she said. "We'll find something fabulous. I know several little boutiques we can try."

We tried them all and finally settled on an elegant white lace.

"White is in fashion," the baroness said. "But, Baltimore doesn't know it yet. They're a little slower than New York," she explained. "But, that's good. You'll set a trend, Charlotte."

We went to the Women's Exchange for lunch. I had thought it a strange name, but the tearoom was only a convenience for the exchange, which handled beautiful handmade items on consignment. It offered women an opportunity to display their handiwork and contribute

158

to charity, since a portion of the proceeds went to the famous Johns Hopkins Hospital.

The shop was staffed by volunteers, well-to-do ladies who gave their services freely to assist the hospital and to help other women attain a degree of independence.

The little tearoom located in the rear of the shop was doing a brisk business when we entered. Unpretentious and almost spartan with its plain wooden tables and chairs, it reminded me of church suppers at the little Anglican church in Devonshire.

The baroness was recognized immediately and we were shown to a table. It was obvious that she was a frequent customer and most likely a generous contributor, I thought.

We placed our orders for the house speciality, chicken salad, which the baroness informed me was the best in town, and the waitress brought us steaming cups of tea.

Removing her gloves, she regarded me slyly. "So, how are you getting along out at the villa?"

I hesitated, and she coaxed me. "No so good, eh?"

Wanting desperately to unburden myself, I blurted out the truth. "Some of them think me an imposter."

"Are you?"

"If I am, I don't know it," I said honestly. "I really can't help it that my grandmother made a secret of my father's birth."

She smiled. "You are not an imposter. They are the imposters."

"What do you mean?"

"They fell over Gia, all of them, pretending to be so grateful, pretending to be so loving, but she was not fooled, as they have now discovered to their sorrow."

"How well did you know Gia—and the rest of them?" I added.

She shrugged. "In our profession, we all know one another. We do not always like one another, but there are few real secrets among us. Gia was unique, in that she managed to hide this one indiscretion extremely well."

"Did you like my grandmother?"

"Certainly not," she answered bluntly. "Gia was a devil. Egotistical—well, we all are," she admitted. "But Gia was vicious and fiercely possessive. She used people. I'm sorry, *cara mia,*" she added, "but you asked me, so I tell you the truth."

"She's haunting the villa," I heard myself say.

The baroness didn't gasp, but neither did she smile, and her reaction encouraged me to go on.

"I've seen her twice—once in my bedroom and once in the garden—and I've heard her humming," I added.

"Have you discussed this with anyone else?"

"No, not even Forrest."

"Why not?"

"I'm not sure. Perhaps because he doesn't believe in the supernatural."

"Such things can happen," she said. "But, there is another possibility. Someone might be trying to frighten you, trying to make you leave the villa."

"I know, but who, and how? I heard the humming, I saw . . ."

"Perhaps Carla, or Sophia," she said. "They could both project their voices in a hum."

"But I *saw* her," I insisted.

"Illusions can seem very real, *cara mia.*"

I thought of the hanging man, but I didn't mention it. It would have proven her point, and right now I wanted to convince someone that I had seen Gia's ghost.

"It would be something Gia would do," the baroness said, looking thoughtful as she tapped her finger on the table. "As I said before, Gia was very possessive. She might not want you to have the house for some reason." Her expression suddenly changed, as if something had just caught her fancy, but she didn't pursue the subject.

"Tell me about Gia," I said.

She stirred her tea and toyed with the chicken salad, which had just arrived.

"I met Gia and Sophia Grazziano when the three of us sang in the chorus at La Scala. Gia was a poor ignorant country girl then, but she had a gorgeous natural voice."

"Were you friends in those days?"

"Gia was nobody's friend," the baroness said. Then she shrugged and added, "Well, maybe Sophia's. Anyway, the opera was Verdi's *Rigoletto*. We were rehearsing for the opening and the composer was at the theater every day. Verdi was probably forty and Gia was eighteen or nineteen, but she flirted outrageously with him." She shrugged again. "Verdi would not have been adverse to dallying with an ambitious young girl like Gia."

"When was this?" I asked.

"1851 or 1852, I can't remember exactly, but when we closed, Gia moved to England. She told Sophia she'd had an offer to study there."

"My father was born in 1853," I said.

"Don't jump to conclusions, *cara mia*. I only tell you because you ask. This may be only a coincidence, and besides, it hardly matters anymore, does it?"

"No, it doesn't," I said. "Please go on, Baroness."

"The next time we met, Gia was a rising star. She was being managed by DeSantis and had just acquired the first of three husbands. I can't remember his name. He was a German, and quite wealthy."

"What happened to him?"

"They were divorced after a few years. Gia was having an affair with a very handsome tenor, Luigi Sommbalani. He became her second husband." She rolled her eyes. "It was quite a tempestuous marriage. They finally divorced and Gia went on to become the reigning diva of Europe, until Adelina Patti appeared on the scene, that is. They became arch rivals, you know," she added, and I told her I had heard quite a bit about that.

The baroness then suggested that we continue the conversation back at the château. "It's time for Beppino to practice his scales," she said with a perfectly straight face, and then added, "Cats have short memories, you know, so I go over them with him twice a day."

We left the exchange and, on the short ride back, the baroness continued her narrative. Gia married Dorcas's father, Count Igor Belinski, in the early eighties and he died about ten years later. It was then that Dorcas and Nicky came to the villa to live.

"What about Victor DeSantis?" I asked. "When did he come to the villa?"

"As far as I know, Victor has lived at the villa from the beginning."

"Were they lovers?" I asked.

"I don't think so. Victor was Gia's manager and the arrangement was a profitable one for them both," she added.

I declined her invitation to return to the château as I expected Forrest home around four. She gave me a bawdy wink. "Ah, youth. Ah, love," she said. "I understand perfectly, *cara mia*. If I had a virile young husband in my bed, I wouldn't be practicing scales with Beppino."

Chapter 13

The white lace gown was by Worth. Designed to herald the new century, the *art nouveau* fashion was daring in its very simplicity. The tight skirt molded my hips, revealing the contours of my body to a degree that could be considered indecent. The train was extremely long and when brought forward formed a swirling spiral at my feet.

Now, standing before the full-length mirror, I was having second thoughts. Did I look like a child dressed up in her mother's clothes?

Forrest's tall figure suddenly appeared behind mine. "Very nice," he said, wrapping his arms around me.

Seeing us together in the mirror made me more conscious than ever that I was no match for my husband, who cut a dashing figure in his white tie and tails.

"Something's missing, though," he said, studying me in the mirror, and self-consciously, I averted my eyes.

His hands moved swiftly over my head and I felt the coldness of metal on my bare skin. Looking quickly back to the mirror, I gasped. A glittering diamond necklace hung like stars around my neck.

"How do you like it?" he asked, hooking the clasp.

I was not accustomed to opulence and would have been more comfortable wearing a simple string of pearls. Furthermore, my background made it difficult for me to justify extravagance, but I didn't want to appear ungrateful.

"I'm speechless," I said. "I've never seen anything so magnificent."

"It belonged to my grandmother. The only piece left out of a sizable jewelry collection. She just couldn't bear to part with it, I guess."

"Then I shall treasure it all the more," I said, feeling suddenly sentimental because it was an heirloom and had belonged to a woman who obviously meant a great deal to my husband.

The baroness had invited us for cocktails before the performance; afterward we were to dine as her guests at the Stafford Hotel.

We took a hack to the baroness's odd-looking house, and when Forrest handed me out of the carriage, I saw that a red carpet had been laid on the pavement from the curb all the way up the steps to the entrance.

Harcourt, the ever-efficient butler, was already waiting at the open door, and after taking our wraps, he ushered us in to the drawing room.

Resplendent in purple velvet, the baroness greeted us warmly. Her heavy black hair shot with silver was arranged in an elaborate pompadour and her ears and neck sparkled with diamonds.

I thought as I looked at her that age had added interest to a face that had probably never been pretty. The nose was a little too long and the jaw too square, but the baroness's dark expressive eyes sparkled with warmth and little crinkling laugh lines were etched in the corners.

She introduced us to her escort, Owen McRae, a distinguished-looking man in his sixties who told us he was the architect who had designed the baroness's unusual townhouse.

He called her *Josephine* and I remembered then that Victor had introduced her in Italian as *Giuseppina*. I thought the Anglicized version of the name suited her better—or perhaps it merely suited me better, since I could pronounce it.

Before we left, Mr. McRae persuaded the baroness to sing for us. An accomplished pianist, he accompanied her and it was obvious that this was something they both enjoyed doing.

Her voice was rich and still strong, though she was nearly seventy.

"Could we hear something from *Traviata?*" I asked.

She hesitated a moment and Owen McRae said, "You can do the *'Addio del passato,'* Josephine."

"All right. But remember, it was written in a higher key."

Although I did not understand the Italian words, the hauntingly beautiful aria was so touching that I was moved to tears. When it was over, I self-consciously dabbed at my eyes, and overcome with emotion, managed to say, "Thank you, Baroness. That was absolutely beautiful."

Crossing the room, she swallowed me up in a warm embrace and whispered in my ear, "Music is definitely in your blood, *cara mia.*" Then she patted me on the shoulder and added, "Like it or not, Charlotte. That means you're Gia's granddaughter. Trust me, I can tell."

Before leaving for the opera, the baroness insisted that we hear Beppino do his scales, and to the amazement of us all, the cat stood up on his hind legs and executed a series of sounds that could have passed for notes on a scale.

We arrived at the Academy of Music in the baroness's handsome carriage. The Academy, an imposing structure in the Romanesque style, topped the skyline at a hundred feet or so, Mr. McRae informed us.

He seemed particularly proud of the edifice, and the baroness said, "Owen was one of the architects who worked on the Academy."

"Oh, is it new?" I asked.

Owen McRae laughed. "New for a building, but old

for you young people, I'm afraid. That was in the early seventies," he explained. "I was a young man about your husband's age then and working for a very famous architect by the name of Neilson. It's been said that the Academy compares favorably with Covent Garden," he added. "So, I'll be interested in your opinion, Mrs. Singleton."

I merely smiled. I'd never been to Covent Garden, but I didn't want to embarrass Forrest by saying so.

The evening was one I shall never forget. The theater was indeed magnificent. Mr. McRae informed us that the enormous chandelier that hung from the center dome held 240 candle-shaped burners and almost a thousand chains of crystals.

The high ceiling was frescoed and the pale colored walls were traced in gilt. Our private box was curtained with green velvet drapes, and upholstered armchairs allowed us to view the performance in absolute comfort.

Feeling very young and gauche, I looked out over a sea of faces: important-looking men, beautiful, sophisticated women. I would have given anything at that moment to have been older, taller, plumper, and with hair any color at all but brown.

Suddenly the house lights dimmed, and a hush settled over the auditorium as the conductor raised his baton. I leaned forward and stared down into the pit, my eyes darting from one musician to the other as their instruments blended together to produce the loveliest sound I had ever heard, so poignant and beautiful.

The curtain rose, and still leaning forward, I gazed down on the beautifully staged opening scene. Realistically set in an elegant drawing room, the colorful costumes and the gay, party atmosphere all combined to make even more moving the bittersweet love story of Violetta and Alfredo.

The music evoked such pathos in my heart, that I couldn't help wondering about the composer. Could my father be the son of Giusseppe Verdi?

"Traviata has a new fan," the baroness remarked as she watched me applaud every curtain call with renewed enthusiasm.

Later that evening when we were having a late supper at the Stafford Hotel, I asked her, "Did Gia ever sing *Traviata?*"

"*Sì,* many times. It was one of her favorites."

"Did she ever see the composer again?"

"I don't know, though Gia liked to say that Verdi had been passionately in love with her. Your grandmother thought no man could ever forget her, but what they couldn't forget was her voice," she added.

"Was it so unusual?"

Her eyes grew dreamy and she spoke almost reverently. "Once I heard Gia float a high C out over the stage. It left her body and soared like a shooting star, passing over the world in a blaze of glory and then going out into infinity. *Madonna mia,* but it was perfect, like a note from heaven."

Once again I was saying good-bye to Forrest, only this time our positions were reversed. I was the one who was taking the train and he was seeing me off, for it was Sunday afternoon and I was going back to the villa.

The station was crowded and we stood on the platform waiting for the train to arrive.

"You will go through Gia's things and clear out the room when you get back, won't you, darling?"

We'd just spent a wonderful week together and I didn't want to think about the villa, but I nodded and said, "Yes, I promise I'll get to it this week."

"Good. I wouldn't mention it to Sophia, though. The old girl would only get upset. It's none of her business, of course, but the Signora worshiped Gia. She probably thinks the room should be turned into some kind of a shrine," he added with a laugh.

I saw nothing humorous about it. "Forrest, that woman is unbalanced. If you could have seen her when we were going over the costumes . . ."

"Hero worship," he said. "Underachievers often latch on to someone they admire and turn them into gods. It happens all the time in the theater, Charlotte. Believe me, old Sophia is as sane as a judge about everything else. The villa runs smooth as glass, right?"

I couldn't deny it, and feeling like a puppet on a string, I nodded.

"Well, that's Sophia's doing, and while we're on the subject," he added, sounding like an adult lecturing a child, "if you don't learn to take over, sweetheart, we might be forced to ask the Signora to stay on."

His words stung, and tears of frustration welled up in my eyes. "I'm sorry I'm so incompetent," I mumbled.

"I didn't say you were incompetent—*you* did—and until you get that silly notion out of your head, you'll never be able to deal with the Signora or any other bully." Then his expression softened and he gave me an indulgent smile. "Here's a handkerchief. Now blow your nose."

I felt like a fool, and overcome with embarrassment, I held the handkerchief up to my face. "Did anybody see me?"

"Only the whole depot. I'll probably be arrested for child abuse." Then he laughed and held up his hand. "Just kidding. I swear."

I handed him back the handkerchief and he shook his head and smiled at me. "What am I going to do with you?" he said.

People started to leave the waiting room then and Forrest grabbed my hand. "Come on, the train must be in."

We exchanged hurried kisses and in a matter of minutes I was on the inside looking out at Forrest standing below. I tapped on the window and he looked up and waved, but just then the train lurched forward and a blast of smoke momentarily obscured him from my view. When it cleared, the train had picked up speed and I could just barely make his figure out in the distance when something bright and green beside him caught my eye.

It might have been a woman wearing a green dress, but I couldn't be sure because the station had disappeared behind a clump of trees.

Chiding myself for being suspicious, I leaned back in the seat and closed my eyes, but my demons would give me no rest. Carla, Carla, Carla, they taunted.

The train's grinding wheels picked up the mantra and repeated it over and over again inside my head.

"Mind if I sit here, miss?"

I jumped at the sound of a human voice and looked up to see a woman standing in the aisle.

"No, of course I don't mind. Please sit down," I said.

She was a plump, countrified-looking woman in her sixties, wearing an old-fashioned black bonnet that tied under her chin, and what was probably her best dress, also black and shiny from years of wear.

"I was sitting in that seat up there," she said, nodding her head toward an empty seat on the aisle. Then cupping her hand next to her mouth, she leaned toward me confidentially. "I ain't sitting next to no drinking man, though. Smelled it on him," she added.

"It's best you moved, then," I said, not knowing what else to say.

"Excuse me, miss, but you talk different. Where would you be from, if you don't mind my asking?"

"I'm from London," I said.

"Mercy sakes, all the way from London, England. You sure are a long way from home."

In more ways than one, I thought, and hoping to discourage further conversation, I opened my book and started to read, but the relentless wheels kept repeating, *Carla, Carla,* until I wanted to scream.

"Carla's at the villa," I said out loud like a crazy person.

"Did you say something, miss?"

"Not really. I guess I was reading out loud."

"That's all right, dear. I do that often when I read my

169

Bible. A body won't forget what he reads out loud."

"I hope you're right," I said.

Eager to resume the conversation, she beamed at me. "I'll just bet you were a teacher in London."

"No. I worked in a dress shop, but I did study to be a teacher."

"There, I knew it. And where would you be headed for now?"

"The Villa Montelano," I said mechanically. "I mean, it's about a mile from—"

"I know where it is," she said. "And I wouldn't go there if I were you." The words had hardly left her mouth when the whole car was plunged into total darkness. Her words hung suspended in the void like harbingers of doom and I panicked and would have screamed, but a second later it was light again and I realized we had just gone through a tunnel.

"Why not?" I said, anxious to continue where we had left off.

"'Taint no place for a nice young woman to work, that's why. There's a lot of drinking goes on up there, and other things I won't mention."

"Do you live nearby?" I asked cautiously.

"No, but my sister does and she told me there's a bunch of theater people living up there—opry singers and furriners they are, too." Her face turned red. "I don't mean you're a furriner, child. You speak English good as I do myself, but nobody can understand them Eyetalians. 'Sides that, folks say there's a ghost up there." Suddenly looking past me, she peered anxiously out the window. "Mercy me, we're coming into my station."

She started gathering up parcels as the train ground to a halt. "Nice talking to you, miss. You take my advice, and find a job someplace else."

She hurried down the aisle, her short figure disappearing as other passengers followed her off the train.

Something Tom Atkins had said suddenly clicked in

170

my brain and I got up and ran after her.

"Who is the ghost?" I shouted.

She was just stepping off the train and she turned and looked up at me with surprise. "A man," she said. "He hung himself in the woods a long time ago."

I went back to my seat and the train pulled out of the little station. Now I knew why the locals were afraid of the woods. But who was the man? I wondered, and why would his spirit appear to me?

When I got back to the villa, I learned that Carla had gone to New York to pressure Vidici about her debut. Refusing to engage in any more farfetched conclusions, I thanked God for small favors. At least I would not have to contend with Carla for a while.

Lured by the gorgeous autumn weather, I put off going over my grandmother's effects, preferring instead to spend my time riding. Forrest's admonitions to the contrary, the truth of the matter was that I still feared risking a confrontation with the Signora.

And so it seemed like fate when Dorcas announced for my benefit that the state fair would open on Friday.

"Gia turned it into an annual holiday," she said. "The servants look forward to it, so I hope you'll allow the custom to continue."

It was an offhanded acknowledgment of my position, but coming from Dorcas, even that took me by surprise. "Of course," I mumbled, and Marshall quickly joined in.

"It's a holiday for all of us. You'll enjoy it, too, Charlotte."

"There's a race track," Nicky said. "That's all that interests me."

I didn't tell anyone I wasn't going to the fair until Thursday morning. I knew Victor and both the Faros couldn't care less, but Marshall would be disappointed.

Pleading another headache, I relayed the excuse through Fiona.

171

She was overly solicitous and even offered to stay behind to take care of me.

"I wouldn't think of it," I said. "You go and have a good time. I'll be just fine."

Like a parade, they rumbled out of the drive, the carriages and several wagons loaded down with laughing servants.

I turned away from the window and started to get dressed. The house was eerily quiet and I almost wished I'd gone with the others. But, I had promised Forrest, and this was too good an opportunity to miss.

I put on a plain black skirt and a white shirtwaist and when I absentmindedly slid my hand into the pocket, I pulled out the missing key marked *L* for lodge.

It must have gotten caught in a seam, I thought, relieved that now I wouldn't have to ask Tom Atkins to make me another one. Dropping it in the jewelry box, I picked up the key marked *BR* and left the room.

Knowing that I was alone in the house gave me a creepy feeling, although, in truth, I seldom encountered others in the corridors.

I crossed over into the west wing, and walked down the long hall to Gia's room. My courage almost deserted me and I paused uncertainly before the door like an uninvited guest.

As I stared at the shiny new lock I took a step back, for it had suddenly turned into the face of a gargoyle, it's bolts becoming hooded eyes and its keyhole a gaping mouth.

The illusion unnerved me and I dropped the key, which was immediately swallowed up in the thick multipatterned carpet. I had to get down on my hands and knees to find it, and when I stood up again, a perfectly ordinary lock with brass bolts and a long, narrow keyhole met my gaze.

Chiding myself for being a fool, I unlocked the door, and as I did so, I thought I heard a noise, not from inside the room, but from behind me at the other end of the long corridor. Could somebody else be in the house?

Suddenly, entering the room seemed preferable to remaining in the corridor, and I quickly stepped inside and shut the door. The poacher, I thought. He could have been watching the house, and if he had seen them all leave . . .

I didn't want to pursue the thought, and placing my ear to the closed door, I listened, but the house was cloaked in silence and I had to assume my nerves had been playing tricks on me again.

Turning my attention to the job at hand, I marched purposefully into my grandmother's boudoir. I was anxious to get this over with as soon as possible, and to keep my fertile imagination from running away with me, I went first to the huge closet and slid the door all the way back.

No surprises awaited me, and breathing a little easier I did the same thing with the other closet, which the Signora and I had emptied when we'd packed away the costumes.

Neither ghost nor human was hiding inside, and feeling a little easier, I went to the long dresser and opened the top drawer. The glittering collection of diamonds, emeralds, and rubies made me gasp. There were bracelets, necklaces, and brooches, jewelry of every shape and kind resting in the drawer's velvet-lined compartments.

The huge stones set in shimmering gold seemed to wink a mocking salute to me. I knew I could never do justice to them, neither did I care to, I told myself.

Overwhelmed, I absentmindedly picked up a small heart-shaped locket that seemed out of place in such elegant company. One tiny pearl set in the center was its only adornment, and turning it over, I saw the words, *Amore, Roberto* engraved on the back.

Poor Roberto, I thought. This insignificant little heart would hardly have appealed to Gia with her expensive taste, and acting on a sudden impulse, I put the necklace on.

It was the kind of piece I liked, dainty and elegant in its very simplicity. It's mine. I can wear it, I thought, but all the while my hands were reaching to unhook the clasp.

The tiny safety catch would not budge, though, and I gave up trying. She probably never wore it anyway. I told myself.

I hurried through the other drawers, which contained mostly lingerie; marabou bedjackets, embroidered gowns and petticoats in satin and lace. All were neatly folded and stacked in colors.

This meticulous arrangement was obviously the Signora's work and the thought made me nervous. I turned around quickly, half-expecting to see her behind me.

There was no one there, of course, but the feeling persisted and then I heard the faint but unmistakable sound of a tuneless hum.

The room turned icy cold and I watched in fascinated horror as a wavy, ghostlike figure slowly began to materialize in the air. The apparition kept fading in and out as if it wasn't strong enough to stay, and I couldn't distinguish what it was.

Finally, it faded altogether, and I had to wonder if in my nervous state I had merely imagined it.

Returning to the task at hand, I carefully patted the stacks of lingerie into place before closing the drawer. All of these things will have to be packed up and given to some charity, I mused, for I shall certainly never wear them.

Again, I felt a presence behind me. My skin tingled and the hairs on the back of my neck bristled as though charged with electricity. I whirled around and what I saw turned me to stone.

Fully developed now, the apparition stood but a foot away from me. Her feet were bare and she was dressed in peasant clothes, but I recognized it immediately as being Gia, although she appeared to be a much younger woman.

The angelic face was beautiful beyond description, and like a statue I stood mesmerized, never taking my eyes away from her.

Then my admiration slowly turned to horror as the beautiful face began to change. Innocence disappeared and sensuality took its place. The eyes glittered and turned hard and then she smiled, that evil, creepy smile that turned my blood to ice water.

Terrified now, I wanted to run, but my body had turned into stone and I could only stand there, my panic rising as the figure floated slowly toward me.

The apparition was now wearing a ball gown and her neck and arm were covered with jewels, but I stared in horror at the face, which was disintegrating before my eyes.

Mutely, I watched the rosebud lips crumble into dust and a skull's grin replace the sensuous smile. Ugly black sockets appeared where the eyes and nose had been and I gasped as the skeleton, still wearing its jewels and ball gown, advanced on me.

Self-preservation brought me sharply back to life, and an instant later I had the door open and was running down the corridor toward the back stairway.

I didn't stop running and never looked back until I had reached the top step. Not wanting to trip, I paused to lift my skirt, and then I felt the sudden impact of a powerful shove that sent me plunging headfirst down the steep staircase.

Chapter 14

"Charlotte, can you hear me?"

Forrest's familiar voice jolted me back to consciousness and slowly my bruised brain began to function. I had been in Gia's room and her ghost had appeared to me again. I had watched her face turn into a hideous skull, her body become a skeleton.

"She's in a coma," a woman's voice said. "You go for the doctor. I'll stay with her."

That syrupy voice could belong to no one but Carla, and suddenly I remembered being shoved. Someone had pushed me down the stairs! Had it been Carla?

No, no, don't leave me. I tried to say the words, but my mouth was stiff and I could only moan.

"She's coming around now," Forrest said.

"But aren't you going for the doctor?"

"I sent Cal. He should be back any minute now."

Thank God, I thought, drifting back into unconsciousness again. Their voices grew faint, but the voices inside my head clamored to be heard.

Isn't it strange that Carla and Forrest should both arrive home on the very same day? And didn't you see a flash of green from the window of the train?

The next time I woke up, I was in my own bed. Forrest was holding my hand and a strange man was bending over me. "I'm Dr. Matthews," he said. "How do you feel, Mrs. Singleton?"

"My head hurts."

He nodded sympathetically. "I'm not surprised. You had a nasty fall." Then he smiled and glanced at Forrest. "Gave your husband quite a scare you did."

"You're sure she's all right?" Forrest insisted.

"Just keep her quiet for the next twenty-four hours. If she gets sick to her stomach or has any more fainting spells, send for me, but your wife's a healthy young woman. She'll probably be fine." He gave me an indulgent smile. "You'll be sore and stiff tomorrow, Mrs. Singleton, but nothing is broken."

"Thank God for that," Forrest said, giving my hand a squeeze.

"I'll leave something for her headache," Dr. Matthews said, and then he patted me on the arm. "Just take it easy, young lady, and don't go tripping down any more stairs. You could have broken your neck."

Forrest patted my hand. "I'll only be a minute, darling."

Then he stood up and walked out into the hall with Dr. Matthews.

You could have broken your neck. The doctor's words made me shudder and I tried to relive that split-second interval at the top of the stairs, but my mind was blank.

I could only remember that hideous apparition. It had come closer and closer and I had been running away from it. The next thing I knew, I had heard voices, Forrest's and someone else's.

Had it been Carla's? No, that's impossible, I thought. Carla was in New York.

Forrest came back then and I asked him, "Did Carla come home?"

He hesitated a moment. "Yes, as a matter of fact, she did. Why do you ask?"

"I thought I heard her voice."

"You did. Carla was the one who found you lying at the bottom of the stairs. How did it happen, Charlotte? Do you remember?"

177

"I was searching Gia's room."

He looked surprised. "Did you find anything?"

"No, I didn't finish because—because . . ."

"Because what, sweetheart?"

"Because I saw a ghost and I got frightened and ran out of the room." It sounded childish even to me.

An exasperated look crossed his face and he said, "Oh, for God's sake, Charlotte. There are no ghosts." Then he paused and added, "That's how you fell down the steps, isn't it?"

"I suppose so."

"Charlotte, this nonsense has got to stop. You could have been seriously injured." He paused again. "The room—did you lock the door when you left it?"

"No, of course not. I was terrified, Forrest. I just ran and then I guess I tripped and fell down the stairs . . ."

"You left the room unlocked?"

"I'm afraid so."

"I'll have to go back and lock it," he said. "Will you be all right for a couple of minutes? Carla's right downstairs. I could have her come up and sit with you," he added.

"No, not Carla. I'll be fine."

He kissed me gently. "She can be irritating, I know, sweetheart, but I am grateful to her for finding you."

"How did that happen?" I asked.

"She was in the kitchen, fixing herself something to eat. She said she heard this tremendous crash and ran out to find you at the bottom of the stairs."

"And then she alerted you?"

"That's right and I sent Cal for the doctor."

"Cal didn't go to the fair?"

"No, he never goes, too many buggies on the road, he says. Course he got run off the road right here. Almost didn't get to the doctor at all because of that damn coachman. Cal said Wilson came tearing out of the woods like a crazy man and forced him into a ditch."

Forrest's eyes darkened in anger. "Cal unhitched the wagon and left it in the road. That bastard Wilson never even stopped, and Cal rode to the doctor's house on horseback. I'm filing a complaint with the constable tomorrow and I'm also going to bring up the time he almost ran over you. The man's a menace and I want him off the road."

None of it made any sense then, but later all these unrelated incidents would fit together and I was to wish I had not been so timid about trusting my own instincts.

It took several days for the huge, bulging lump on my forehead to go down and for my two black eyes to heal, and by that time, Forrest had returned to Baltimore and another long week without him stretched before me.

I was anticipating his return with double pleasure, though, because the baroness and Owen McRae were coming back with him to spend the weekend at the Villa Montelano.

Forrest wanted Mr. McRae to look over the villa with an eye to dismantling some of the more absurd embellishments that Gia had added to the house, like the Moorish temple domes.

He had yet to confide in me that the villa was really Lauraland in disguise, and because I was afraid of what I might discover, I had shied away from bringing the matter up.

I was anxious to see the baroness, however, for I wanted to tell her about my latest confrontation with Gia's ghost. I also planned on asking her to help me finish going over my grandmother's room, for I just couldn't bring myself to go back there alone.

Forrest had locked up and returned the key to my jewelry box, but I knew he still expected me to finish the task I had begun.

I fingered the little locket which I still wore around my neck. I had shown it to Forrest and he had smiled and said, "What a funny little girl you are, Charlotte.

You mean to say that out of all Gia's jewelry, you picked this little piece?"

"I like it," I said defensively. "And besides, I'm not a little girl."

He'd lifted me off my feet and brought me up to his own eye level. "You're twelve years younger than me. You'll always be a *little* girl as far as I'm concerned." His kiss ignited sparks between us and we'd wound up in bed making very gentle love in deference to my bruises and stiff muscles.

But the next day, Forrest had to take the early morning train back to Baltimore—and I decided it was time for me to resume the duties of a hostess.

Fiona carefully arranged my hair so that the small bump that remained on my forehead was covered over by a fringe, and, wearing a high-necked gown that concealed what was left of my bruises, I went downstairs to have cocktails and dinner with the other residents of the villa.

Spotting the Signora coming out of the dining room, I took the opportunity to inform her that the baroness and Mr. McRae would be coming for the weekend.

"I'll have Anna prepare their rooms," she said. "And what about the menu? Is there anything in particular you would like served, Mrs. Singleton?"

I knew she was taunting me and I hedged. "What do you suggest?"

"How about *zuppa del mare?*"

I gave her the anticipated blank stare and she smiled smugly. "That's mussels, clams, shrimp, scallops, and calamari over linguini in a fresh tomato sauce."

"Very nice," I said.

"Followed of course by *Frutta del mare,*—filet of sole, and baked clams *oreganato* with lemon."

"Fine," I said.

"Then I would suggest broccoli, plum tomatoes and mozzarella with basil, and perhaps strufoli for dessert.

Is that also fine, Mrs. Singleton?"

"Yes, it sounds very nice."

"I'd say it was *excellent* compared to boardinghouse fare, wouldn't you say so, Mrs. Singleton?"

I ignored the sarcasm and she stared back at me with hateful eyes. "I hear you had an accident. You must be more careful, Mrs. Singleton."

Her words jogged my memory and I suddenly recalled those hands at my back.

"I shall be very careful from now on," I said.

She merely smiled and in a supreme gesture of contempt simply walked away, leaving me standing there alone.

I blinked back tears. The dinner would be perfect and the villa would go on running smoothly, for the Signora wanted to stay on and now I knew why.

This was her way of exacting revenge on the imposter for Gia's sake. But how far would she go beyond merely humiliating me? Somebody had pushed me down a flight of stairs. Had it been the Signora?

Voices drifted out to me from the small salon and I knew I had to gain control of myself. All the servants in the dining room, not to mention the Signora, had seen me downstairs, so I would have to join the others for cocktails and dinner, but I couldn't shake the memory of those hands on my back.

Had it been Carla, Dorcas, Nicky, Victor? I knew my jaundiced eye would look askance at every smiling face in that room. Even Don Alberto and Marshall, I thought. What did I really know about them? Or about any of them, for that matter.

And that includes your husband, my demon said.

The brass door handle was cold to my touch, and when I opened the door a sea of leering faces stared back at me.

"Charlotte, isn't this a nice surprise," Marshall said, and as he came forward to greet me, I thought I detected a craftiness about him that I had never noticed before.

181

"This calls for a toast," Don Alberto said, and somebody thrust a glass of champagne into my hand. "To our gracious hostess, Charlotte. Health, wealth, and a long life."

All the leering faces were staring at me and the glass slipped through my sweaty hands and hit the floor, splintering into a thousand pieces.

Anna suddenly appeared, and after handing me another glass, she stooped down to pick up the fragments.

"To Charlotte," Don Alberto said smoothly, and we all raised our glasses and drank.

Anna deposited the fragments in her apron and stood up. Meeting my eyes, she said in an undertone. "It's bad luck to break a toast."

"Charlotte, are you all right?" Marshall looked concerned, but he was also an actor, I recalled. Did he only pretend to be a friend? Unless another will was discovered, I was heir to a fortune. Perhaps he thought to make me his patron.

"I'm fine," I said.

Carla sauntered over and stood close to Marshall. "Poor little thing. She does look pale, doesn't she?"

A host of ugly thoughts whirled around in my head as I looked at the two of them standing there together. Gia had accused Carla of sharing her lovers. Had she meant Marshall?

Perhaps, but who else? Gia said lovers, meaning more than one, my demon reminded me.

I shall go mad if I pursue this line of thought, I told myself, and feeling suddenly weak, I was grateful for the steadying hand Don Alberto placed on my elbow. "Come, sit by the fire, Charlotte. You look cold," he said.

I let him lead me over to the large wing chair. The crackling fire was inviting, for the October night was cool.

"Can I get you another glass of champagne?" he asked.

"No, thank you. I'm fine, and the fire does feel good."

"You were trembling and you looked like you'd seen a ghost," he said with a laugh.

Ah, but I have, many times, I thought, but didn't say.

Dorcas was seated across from us and she joined the conversation. "That's not so farfetched, Don Alberto. There's supposed to be a ghost in the woods."

"Have you seen it?" I asked.

"No. I gather it hadn't appeared for a long time, but the locals claim there was one."

Don Alberto laughed. "There are no such things," he said.

Dorcas shrugged. "Not all the dead rest easy." Then she looked pointedly at me. "Gia probably doesn't."

Dinner was announced and we all took our accustomed places in the dining room. The elaborate meal which I later learned consisted of antipasto, a veal piccata, manicotti with basil, and a colorful medley of fresh vegetables in the chef's own secret sauce was delicious, but it only served to make me conscious of my inadequacies.

The Signora had been cruel, but her cutting words had been right on target. Boardinghouse fare was all I knew. How could I ever expect to plan and oversee culinary masterpieces like those offered on a daily basis at the Villa Montelano?

The conversation during dinner revolved around the county fair. The Faros, it appeared, were the only ones who had stayed together. They had spent the entire time at the racetrack, or so they said, while the others had apparently separated and wandered off on their own.

Any one of them could have left the fair and returned to the house, even Nicky, for Dorcas would surely lie for him.

Had I been pushed down the stairs? I couldn't

absolutely swear to it, but I could almost feel again those strong hands at my back. Dorcas is stronger than Nicky, I mused, staring at her hands as she toyed with her water goblet.

After dinner, we retired to the music room and Don Alberto persuaded Carla and Marshall to sing for us again. I had the uncomfortable feeling that I was being watched, and when I turned around, I saw that the Signora was standing in the doorway.

Victor saw her too and he said, "Sophia, come join us. Our protégés are about to perform."

She took a seat next to him and directly behind me. Their conversation, conducted in Italian, was punctuated by intermittent snorts of laughter from Victor, and my cheeks burned, for I sensed myself to be the object of their ridicule.

Carla sang first. Comparing her voice to the young soprano who had sung the lead in *Traviata,* I was more convinced than ever that Carla's voice had little to do with her success.

I could see her as Carmen, though, for she looked the part of a dark and voluptuous Gypsy girl and her every movement was calculated to suggest raw sensuality.

Stealing a glance at Marshall, I saw that he, too, was watching Carla, and on his face was etched a strange mixture of desire and hate.

Sophia slipped quietly out of the room after the concert had ended, and I was about to make my escape when Victor detained me.

"Have you given any thought to my proposition?" he asked.

Not wanting to antagonize him, I said, "I haven't had a chance to discuss it with Forrest, Victor, but why don't you ask him yourself when he comes back this weekend?"

"Because the house so far belongs to you, *cara mia.*"

"But Forrest is my husband. What is mine is also his."

"That depends on whether or not you and Forrest

184

Singleton are legally married."

I gave him an indignant look. "We were married by the captain of an ocean liner. Of course we are."

He put up his hand and chuckled. "If you say so, *cara mia*. For my part, I don't care if you are married or not, but I'll tell you something. Dorcas and Nicky are having you investigated. A poor little shop girl like you could go back to London and live in luxury for the rest of your life if you sell me this house. Just think, Charlotte, no more boardinghouses, and you wouldn't have to worry about being prosecuted no matter what Dorcas and Nicky's investigation might turn up."

I was so outraged, I didn't trust myself to speak without stammering, so I simply stood up and walked away. Holding my head high, I managed to say goodnight to the group in general, but once out of their sight, I burst into tears and ran blindly upstairs to my room.

Flinging myself down on the bed, I sobbed out my frustrations. Like wolves closing in for the kill, I saw my adversaries banding together against me. Time was running out and soon they'd all be forced to leave the villa. Had they decided to pool their resources and make me leave instead?

Dorcas and Nicky's investigation must have turned up the boardinghouse, for how else would the Signora and Victor have known about it? I hadn't mentioned it and Forrest certainly wouldn't.

Unless he is one of the wolves.

No, I protested, but the demon inside my head would not be stilled.

Forrest wants this house, and if something happened to you, he could marry Carla and make her the mistress. They were both here when you fell down the stairs. Either one of them could have pushed you.

The vile thought was instantly followed by remorse and I wondered if I could ever forgive myself for entertaining such a notion.

Slowly I undressed and got myself ready for bed. I

brushed my hair, but never once glanced at myself in the mirror. If I see Gia's face, I told myself, it will be because I am becoming just like her: suspicious, jealous, and possessive.

When I opened the drawer to put my jewelry away, a large brown envelope caught my eye. It hadn't been there before and an eerie feeling washed over me as I broke the seal.

Bringing out the single sheet of paper, I unfolded it and my blood ran cold as a large crudely drawn black hand leapt out at me from the center of the page.

My first reaction was one of alarm. I knew nothing about the Black Hand and had only just recently learned of its existence, but I had seen the raw terror it evoked. The servant who had found it lying beside the Maestro's body had been paralyzed with fear, and to seal her lips, the girl had been paid off and dismissed.

The message was clear. I was being asked to leave. But what will happen if I don't? Did the Maestro die of natural causes? Or did he die of fright? And if so, why? What possible threat could such a docile old man pose that someone would deliberately frighten him to death?

My teeth began to chatter and my whole body trembled with outrage. How dare they invade my privacy and threaten me with their ugly symbols. Did they think to frighten me to death, too?

Slowly, I let my eyes travel the room. Was I truly alone? Or was my unknown enemy even now hiding and observing my reaction to his or her warning?

The thought was terrifying and I dropped the note as if it were on fire. It fluttered to the floor and I left it there and walked purposefully across the room.

First I flung open the closet. I think if someone had been standing there, I would have dropped dead on the spot, but nothing was disturbed, not even my slippers which were lined up neatly in a row on the floor.

Feeling braver, I marched into the dressing room and then the bathroom, opening even the smallest closet, but all was in place.

Satisfied at last that I was indeed alone, I reached down and picked up the drawing. Wanting to hide it until the room was secured, I placed it in the cedar chest underneath the blankets. Tomorrow I would have Tom Atkins put a lock on the door.

I got into bed and closed my eyes. Mentally retracing my steps, I saw myself leaving the room and walking down the long empty corridor. Had it really been empty? Or had someone been watching, ready to slip into the room as soon as I was safely out of sight?

The Signora had been downstairs then, for I had encountered her in the hallway, and all of the guests were already in the drawing room when I entered it.

We had gone in to dinner and the Signora would have had an opportunity then to slip upstairs and enter my room. Was that why she and Victor had been laughing behind my back during the concert?

If anyone had disappeared after the concert was over I wouldn't have noticed, for that was when Victor had cornered me and delivered his scathing attack on my honor. And afterward, I'd been too shocked and upset to make coherent observations.

At any rate, I thought, Forrest cannot be considered a suspect this time, for he isn't even here.

Perhaps he planned it that way. Maybe he and Carla are working together.

Oh, God, deliver me from this demon of suspicion, I prayed. Forrest is my husband. I love him, and more than anything in the world, I want to trust him.

Chapter 15

I had Cal drive me into town first thing in the morning. I didn't mention that I had received the Black Hand, but I did ask him if he had ever heard of it.

He looked a little startled and then said, "Black Hand isa bad business, Miss Charlotte. Why you ask?"

"I don't know. I heard something about it once and I was just wondering if it was a joke or something."

He shook his head. "No joke. *Mamma mia,* not the Black Hand! Where I come from, Black Hand is called Costa Nostra. They do bad things to peoples, cut off their fingers, tear out their tongues. Everybody in Sicily is afraid of them. Over here they use Black Hand as a warning. The one who gets it, is marked for death."

I thought about the Maestro and I said, "Didn't the old Maestro come from Sicily, too?"

"*Sì,* but he came from Messina. Thassa big city on the northern tip. I come from the south."

"But he would have known about the . . ." I paused because I couldn't remember what it was called, but he understood.

"About the Costa Nostra? *Sì,* every Italiano know about that, Signora, but the Maestro, he know better than most. Costa Nostra had a vendetta against the Barranco family. They murdered the Maestro's father and brother."

"How horrible!" I said, understanding now how seeing the Black Hand could have brought on the Maestro's heart attack. "Did you know the Maestro's family in Sicily?"

"No, Signora. I waza poor farm boy. They were all rich, educated peoples. The Maestro, he told me about it himself one day when I was driving him into town."

"I see."

If he told it to Cal, he would have told it to others, I rationalized. Poor Maestro, he might have had a heart attack, but I was convinced now that it had been brought on deliberately.

We arrived in the little town and I thought that it reminded me of our villages in England. The business section consisted of a post office, a livery stable, a barber shop, and a general store where Cal informed me I could find Tom Atkins.

"The Atkins family owns the store, too," he explained.

Cal waited in the buggy and I walked up onto the wooden platform and entered the store.

It was dark inside and I almost stumbled over a bag of grain in the aisle.

"Careful," a cheerful female voice called out, and following the sound I saw a plump middle-aged woman walking toward me. "I keep telling them men to keep the aisles clear." She lifted the bag and hefted it over on top of several others. "Goin' for November now and the days are getting darker." She smiled then and said, "What can I do for you, miss?"

"I'm looking for Tom Atkins. I need him to install a lock."

Her smile broadened. "Why, you're the young lady from England. My sister told me about you. She met you on the train coming up from Baltimore."

Of course, the lady who told me about the ghost, I thought. "I remember her well. She was ever so friendly and we had an interesting little chat."

189

"Oh, you do talk nice. My sister said you did. 'Speaks the King's English,' she told me. 'Not like them . . .'" She paused and her face reddened. "Are you working up at the villa now?" she asked.

The door banged shut then and we both looked up to see Tom coming in the store.

"Here's my son now. Tom, this young lady is wanting to see you about locks," she told him.

He recognized me as he approached and smiled. "Mornin', Miz Singleton. Ain't havin' no trouble with them locks I installed up at the villa, are you?"

"No, but I need another one installed."

I could feel Mrs. Atkins's eyes on me and then she said, "Miz Singleton?"

"This here's my ma," Tom said, and then turned to his mother. "Miz Singleton's the mistress of the villa now, Ma. She's the countess's granddaughter come over from England."

Tom's mother was plainly surprised and a little flustered. "I'll be apologizing for my sister, Miz Singleton. She didn't know who you were."

"There's no need to apologize, Mrs. Atkins. We didn't exchange names."

I was sorry Tom had come in when he did. I had hoped to glean some information about the ghost from his mother, but this was obviously not the right time.

"I can get up there later on this afternoon," Tom was saying. "Gotta deliver some feed out in that direction."

"That will be fine," I said, and then stretching out my hand to his mother, I added, "It's been a pleasure meeting you, Mrs. Atkins. Please give your sister my regards."

On the way home, I asked Cal if he had ever heard about there being a ghost in the woods.

"Naw," he said, and thinking I'd probably heard about it in the store, he added, "Peoples in this town got funny ideas about the villa, Miss Charlotte. They don't like foreigners, tha's all."

I didn't belabor the point. Cal, with his heavy accent and dark, swarthy looks probably hasn't received much acceptance here, I mused, recalling the lady on the train's distrust of the *Eyetalians*. I wondered again why he stayed. He could go back to Italy now and live like a king on what Gia had left him. "Do you think you might ever go back to Italy?" I asked.

"No, Signora."

His ready answer surprised me and I would probably have pursued the subject, but he quickly changed it.

"You like I should drive through the woods or stay on the road?" he asked.

"Drive through the woods," I said. "I want to see how it looks with the trees stripped bare."

The conversation turned to the weather then, with Cal explaining how it differed in this part of the country from the southwest.

"This a big country," he said, "Italy, and England too, looka like li'l teeny specks 'longside it. I worked ranches all over from Texas to California," he added. "Saw lots of this big country."

"Didn't you ever want to settle down?" I asked.

"Sure. I'm settled down now. Too old to rope cattle and break horses no more."

"I meant, didn't you ever want to settle down with a wife and family."

"Had a wife once, but she left me."

He said the words in an offhanded, almost casual way, but I saw the pain in his dark expressive eyes and chided myself for being insensitive.

"I'm sorry, Cal. I shouldn't have asked."

"Tha's awright, Signora. It was a long time ago. Anyway, she's dead now." He crossed himself quickly and we resumed discussing the climate.

I'd never ask, but I couldn't help wondering what kind of woman would leave a man like Cal. Perhaps she didn't want to come to America, I mused. Or perhaps she came and then returned.

191

There are women who value their homelands more than their husbands, I supposed. But, I am certainly not one of them. I might hate the villa and long for England, but nothing on earth could make me leave my husband. No, not even the Black Hand, I told myself.

True to his word, Tom Atkins arrived that afternoon to put a lock on the bedroom door, and I rested a lot easier after that.

The week passed slowly and I found myself looking forward to Friday like a child anticipating a party. Forrest had promised to leave early and we planned on taking our guests riding and showing them around the estate in the afternoon. I was looking forward to spending time with congenial companions and for a little while I almost forgot about the Black Hand.

Fiona had cleaned and brushed my riding habit and Friday morning it hung in the closet ready to be put on. It wasn't a particularly stylish riding habit. I had purchased it hurriedly in Baltimore before moving up to the villa, but it was serviceable.

"Didn't they have anything in another color?" Forrest had said when I showed it to him.

"Yes, but brown is practical."

Practical, but dull, I thought, looking at it now and associating it with the image that Madam had planted in my mind. *Little Brown Wren.*

I pushed my moody thoughts away and slipped into the becoming apricot morning dress that Fiona held out to me.

Glancing at my reflection in the long mirror, I thought that happiness has a way of transforming even a plain woman into a beauty, for a rosy glow added sparkle to my eyes and a becoming color to my cheeks. In another two or three hours Forrest would be home and all would be right with my world again.

Hearing Mr. Wilson's noisy old coach rattling down

the road, I jumped up and ran to the window. Watching it career around the bend, I closed my eyes, not daring to open them until I heard it screech safely, if not sanely, to a halt in our driveway.

That coachman has to be insane, I thought, suddenly concerned for the baroness and Mr. McRae, who must have been terrified by the wild ride they had just been subjected to. As for Forrest, he would be furious, and I didn't know what my quick-tempered husband might do.

Hoping to defuse an explosive situation, I hurried outside just in time to see Forrest grab the coachman by his collar and slam him up against the carriage. "I've had just about enough of you," he shouted.

"Forrest, please, you're choking him," I said, running up and grabbing my husband's sleeve.

At that point, Mr. McRae suddenly emerged from the carriage and pulled Forrest away. "Take it easy, old man, You'll upset the ladies," he said calmly.

The baroness poked her head outside the carriage then. Her elegant hat was askew, but she was smiling and composed. "Tell the driver, he's no match for Italian cabbies," she said. "They'd have made it in half the time."

Mr. McRae hurried over and assisted her out of the carriage and I embraced her warmly. "I'm terribly sorry about the ride," I told her.

She dismissed my concern with a wave of her hand. "There's an idiot in every village," she said, and then added in an undertone, "Frankly, I rather enjoyed it. At my age, one doesn't get too many thrills."

Forrest was still glaring at Wilson, though. "I've a score to settle with you, Wilson, and you'd better hope we're not alone the next time we meet."

A young manservant from the villa had already retrieved the luggage from the top of the carriage, and Wilson lost no time climbing back on his perch.

Once out of Forrest's reach, his arrogance returned

and he looked down on him and said, "I know some secrets even you don't know, shyster. Make me an offer and I might sing for you." Then he laughed and, laying the whip on the horse, roared out of the driveway.

"As I said before, there's an idiot in every village," the baroness remarked, and Forrest laughed along with the rest of us.

I was grateful to the baroness for making light of an embarrassing situation, and much to my relief, Forrest's good humor returned and the unpleasant incident was forgotten.

None of our other guests appeared for lunch, which pleased me immensely, and the four of us enjoyed a congenial meal.

"I thought you promised us a horseback ride," the baroness remarked after dessert had been served.

"I thought you might be too tired," Forrest answered.

She turned to McRae. "Listen to him. I'm not so old that I can't look forward to a brisk ride on a glorious October day. Of course I'm not too tired. Opera singers have stamina, young man."

Forrest smiled and with his hands made a comical gesture of obsolescence. "A thousand pardons, Baroness. I am a fool, but then you already know that."

She laughed. "You are an actor and should have chosen the stage. But then, lawyers have to be actors, too, don't they?"

Mr. McRae looked at his watch. "If we're going riding, I think we'd best get started."

We retired to our rooms then to change and Forrest took me in his arms and kissed me.

"I was hoping the baroness would be too tired for riding. Then we could have taken a 'nap'" he added with a wicked grin.

I laughed. "They'll both be tired after the ride. We can take a 'nap' before dinner."

I laid my riding habit on the bed and started to

undress, but Forrest said, "Wait. I have a surprise for you." He disappeared into the dressing room and I could hear him fumbling around with the luggage in there. "Now close your eyes and don't peek," he called.

"They're closed," I said, and sensed he'd returned and was standing beside me, I held out my hand, but nothing was placed inside it.

"Now," he commanded, turning me around and directing my gaze to the bed. When I opened my eyes, the brown riding habit had disappeared and in its place lay a handsome one in green velvet. Next to it lay a matching riding hat lavishly trimmed with ostrich plumes in shades of green and gold.

It was an elegant outfit, something I might have admired, but known I could never wear. Forrest was looking at me and I felt a little sorry for him. He should be married to a handsome woman, I thought, someone who could complement his own good looks and make him proud.

"Do you like it?" he asked.

"Of course I like it," I said, throwing my arms around his neck. "It's gorgeous, but not very practical."

"My grandfather used to say it's not exciting to be practical. Now throw that other habit away and get yourself dressed."

He went into the bathroom and I tried the habit on. It was too long, but I had seen Madam turn over a waistband and very cleverly pin it in place. "This ees how it weel look after we alter it," she would say.

I went to work with my pins, and when Forrest came back I had the riding habit on.

"I was afraid it might be too long, but it's a perfect fit," he said.

Thank God for Madam and the American safety pin, I thought.

He was looking at me the way a man looks at a beautiful woman and my heart quickened. Could it be that he sees me in a different way?

Beauty is in the eye of the beholder, I thought as our lips met in a very sweet and tender kiss.

Have you forgotten that lawyers are actors? my demon whispered. *Even the baroness says it is so.*

Charlotte! Why didn't you tell me the shoes hurt? My father's voice came to me across the years.

I was five and Papa had bought me my first pair of brand-new shoes. Up until then I'd worn hand-me-downs from the mill foreman's children, but Papa had spotted me looking longingly at a pair of high-topped black kid shoes in a store window one day.

"You like them shoes?" he's said, and when I'd nodded he'd taken me inside and bought them for me. I don't know how I knew, but I was aware even then that Papa couldn't afford to buy me new shoes.

He was as proud and happy about them as I was, though, and later when the shoes raised blisters on my feet, I didn't want to spoil things by complaining.

I felt the same way now. The weekend had been so pleasant. And even the presence of all the greedy heirs had failed to tarnish it. In fact, much to my surprise, they had been charming, and not even once had they acted their usual obnoxious selves.

Friday night Don Alberto persuaded the baroness to join Carla and Marshall in an impromptu concert, and this time, with no undercurrent of malice to mar the evening for me, I was able to relax and enjoy the music.

The baroness's rich voice was liquid silver after Carla's thin, tinny notes, and servants who had probably not heard a real prima donna since the countess congregated in the corridor to listen.

Running the gauntlet of audience emotions, the baroness stirred her listeners with several powerful renditions and then reduced them to tears with the hauntingly beautiful *"Liebestod"* from *Tristan und Isolde.*

196

Saturday Don Alberto joined us for an early-morning ride over golden autumn hills that would soon turn white under winter's first snowfall. The land was beautiful no matter the season, and I found myself reluctantly drawn to it. Perhaps after Mr. McRae's renovations I can learn to accept the house as well, I told myself.

I had planned to ask the baroness to go over Gia's room with me, but it was an unpleasant task and I just didn't want to spoil the weekend with it.

Then there was the matter of the Black Hand. I had put off telling Forrest about that for the very same reason, but Saturday night he brought up the lock and I was suddenly jolted out of my apathy and plunged into a nightmare of doubt.

Forrest and Owen McRae were going on a duck shoot early in the morning, and Forrest was getting his equipment together and moving into one of the guest rooms so he wouldn't disturb me when he left.

Propping an enormous rifle up against the wall, he turned to me and said, "I lost that key you gave me, so don't lock this door when you and the baroness go riding tomorrow."

His words filled me with apprehension. "You didn't tell anybody you lost it, did you?"

"No, but I want to know why you're so paranoid about it."

I thought the remark an accusatory one, and I said, "I'm not paranoid. You had locks put on yourself and—"

He interrupted me with, "I had good reason for putting locks on both Gia's room and the lodge. Those are the first places they'd look for another will, but nobody is going to look in here."

His impatience suddenly evaporated and he kissed me on the forehead like an adult dismissing a child and said, "You've been so gay and charming this weekend, Charlotte, like your old self. I don't want to see you getting fanciful again."

"Fanciful," I said. "What do you mean by that?"

"I mean the ghosts and all your other irrational fears." He seemed a little disconcerted by my reaction and hastened to add, "I know it isn't easy living with our unwanted guests, but they'll be gone by the spring and then we'll let McRae get to work restoring the house. He has some wonderful ideas, Charlotte, and I promise you, when he's finished, you'll fall in love with the villa."

I twisted away from him, appalled by his condescending attitude. "You think I've been imagining things, don't you?"

Brushing a stray lock of hair out of my face, he continued in a calm, even-tempered voice, "Charlotte, I think you're still adjusting to some very radical changes in your life. Marriage, for instance," he said, and in a futile attempt to make me smile added, "Especially to a rogue like me. Then there was—"

I interrupted him before he could offer any further reasons for my so-called *irrational* fears. "Stop patronizing me, Forrest. I'm not a child," I said, and then without thinking stamped my foot like a frustrated three-year-old.

Hot tears stung my eyes and I pulled away when he tried to embrace me. I ran to the cedar chest and felt around blindly for the drawing. I'll show him, I thought.

When I didn't find it right away, I haphazardly tossed blankets, quilts, the whole contents, onto the floor in a disordered pile, and when it was empty, I picked up the discarded pieces and violently shook them out. Then I sat down on the floor and rested my head against the chest in defeat.

It was gone! But how? I had checked after Tom had installed the lock and it was there then, right where I had put it. Not once had I left the door unlocked, so how—

"What are you looking for, Charlotte?"

Forrest stood looking down at me, and in the shadows, his face took on a sinister guise. Holding out his hand, he said, "Get into bed, my dear. I'm going downstairs to fix you a warm drink. It'll help you have a nice, long sleep."

Chapter 16

I don't know what time I woke up or why, but my
first reaction was one of relief that I hadn't died in my
sleep!

My second reaction was a guilty one. How could I
ever have entertained the thought that my husband, the
man I loved more than life itself, had meant to kill me?

Surely, I must be losing my mind, I decided as I
recalled with sickening remorse how I had forced
myself to drink the nightcap Forrest had brought me,
all the while telling myself I'd rather be dead than
unloved.

Moonlight streamed across the room, and reaching
out my hand, I groped for the little alarm clock on the
bedside table. It was four o'clock. Forrest would be
leaving soon for the duck blind. I missed him already
and my conscience tormented me for last night's
disloyalty.

Unable to sleep, I got out of bed and stood by the
window. A harvest moon cast an amber glow over
fields dotted with haystacks, and gazing out over this
pastoral scene, I was struck by the irony of it. Outside,
peace and tranquility reigned, but inside the villa was
seething with jealousy and hatred.

My thoughts turned then to the Black Hand. The
drawing couldn't have just disappeared in thin air. I
must have misplaced it. By the light of the moon I went

through that cedar chest again piece by piece, but the drawing was just not there.

I checked the drawer where I had found it. I checked the floor and even looked under the bed. Finally, in a last, desperate attempt to prove I hadn't imagined it, I went into the dressing room to check the closet and froze in my tracks as the unmistakable sound of a woman's laughter suddenly erupted out of nowhere and rang in my ears.

Several seconds of silence followed before my stunned brain began to function again, and hurrying back to the bedroom, I unlocked the door and peeped outside. The long, dimly lit corridor was deathly still and completely devoid of any human presence.

I wanted to run across the hall, pound on the door, and beg Forrest to let me crawl into bed with him and stay until morning, but what could I say? My grandmother's ghost is laughing at me?

He already thinks me fanciful. Do I want him to think me insane?

Forcing myself back to bed, I eventually drifted off to sleep and when I awakened it was after eight. Forrest and Owen McRae were long gone, and the baroness and I had a hearty breakfast and then took off on our morning ride.

Several hours later, we had tethered our horses and were seated on a huge boulder by the stream. The sun was still warm, but it was almost November, and days like these would soon pass into memory.

"Your woodland paradise reminds me of a place I visited once in Austria," the baroness was saying, and looking up to the ridge, she added, "There was a hunting lodge there, too."

"When I first saw it, I thought of Mayerling," I said.

"Ah, yes, Mayerling. An illicit love that satisfied society by ending in tragedy. Fortunately, none of mine did," she added dryly, and then nodding her head toward the little house, she smiled. "Hunting lodges are notorious as trysting places and I'm sure Gia made good use of that one."

Recalling the two dressing gowns in the closet, I blushed.

"I'm sorry, *cara mia*. I've shocked you," she said, and reaching over, grasped my hand. "*Santa Maria,* how I envy you!"

"Whatever for?"

"For your youth and innocence, for your great capacity to love, and for your loyalty to that love."

Her words shamed me and filled me with guilt, but she was too deep in her own remorse to notice.

"Women like us, your grandmother and me, we chose fame over love. It was a bad bargain, but we were too selfish to know it," she added with a shrug.

I recalled something she had said the first night we had met. "You're talking about your first husband, aren't you?" I asked.

Her eyes grew dreamy. "*Sì.* I loved him, but I left him behind. You wouldn't have done it, and that's why I envy you."

No, I wouldn't have done that, I thought, but in my heart I have accused my husband of everything under the sun and last night I even imagined him capable of murder.

"Cherish what you have," she said, rising and brushing off her riding habit. The gesture reminded me that we should be heading back to the villa, for Forrest and our guests would be departing on the afternoon train.

I toyed briefly with the thought of confiding in her, but decided against it. Last night had made that impossible, for I could not risk having the baroness suspect that Forrest might have been the one who had removed the Black Hand.

We headed back then and arrived at the villa just in time to change for lunch.

I was surprised when I entered the bedroom and found Forrest still in his hunting clothes.

"When did you get back?" I asked him.

"Just a few minutes ago."

"You've been shooting ducks all this time!"

"Of course not," he said. "McRae's been back for hours. I had some business in town."

I thought it odd that he would conduct business in his hunting clothes and on a Sunday morning yet, but I made no comment.

Guns make me nervous, and noticing the rifle propped up against the wall, I eyed it cautiously. "Is that thing loaded?"

"Not anymore," he answered curtly. "But if it'll make you feel better, I'll take it with me. I'm going to use the room across the hall," he explained. "I need to shave and take a bath."

"That would help. We're running late."

I started to walk into the dressing room, but his tall figure barred my way. Mumbling something about being in a hurry, I tried to pass, but he would not budge and I was forced to look up at him.

A rough-looking man with a day's growth of beard stared back at me. He looked vulnerable and so unlike my self-confident, immaculately-groomed husband that for the first time in our relationship, I felt Forrest needed me as much as I needed him.

"I love you," I said impetuously, and missing his mouth, I grazed his chin with a timid kiss.

He bent down and expertly captured my lips with his. Then swooping me up in his arms, he laughed and said, "The hell with the other bathtub. I'll share yours."

"Forrest, we haven't time," I protested, but it was a weak protest, for we both understood that we needed to be one in body if not in soul.

Later, when this day had turned into a nightmare, I would torture myself with questions, but for the moment I reveled in my fool's paradise.

"How many ducks did you bag?" Victor asked, and Owen McRae held up six fingers.

"Forrest got most of them," McRae said. "He's an excellent shot."

"I prefer hunting bigger game," Victor said.

"Like what?" Dorcas asked.

"Like tigers in Delhi. I did that once. It was in 'Seventy-seven. That was when Victoria was declared Empress of India," he explained. "Gia was invited to perform during the festivities and before we left, the governor arranged a hunt for us."

"And did you shoot yourself a tiger?" Nicky asked.

"Unfortunately, no. One of the water boys got in the way and I shot him instead."

"Good heavens," I heard myself exclaim. "Did you kill the boy?"

Victor looked at me with snide contempt. "Save your outrage, *cara mia*. I just nicked him in the leg." Then he looked at Nicky and smiled. "He probably didn't run so good no more, but I'll bet in the future he stayed out of range."

"The unfortunate thing was that the tiger didn't get Victor," the baroness remarked in an undertone to the three of us who were seated far enough away from the others not to be overheard.

"Did Gia go, too?" Carla asked.

"No. Women are bad luck on safari."

Carla pursed her lips. "Pooh, men just don't want to be shown up. Women are natural hunters. Look at the animal kingdom if you don't believe me."

"They believe you," Dorcas said. "Everybody knows the female is more deadly than the male."

The conversation was making me uncomfortable. Dorcas and Carla's claims took on insidious overtones, and an icy chill ran down my spine when, as if on cue, the Signora entered the room to announce that luncheon was being served.

Looking from one woman to the other, my stomach contracted with fear. Which one of the three is the deadliest? I wondered, as we followed the Signora into the dining room.

Lavish gourmet dishes were served and since most of our guests were connoisseurs of the table, more attention was paid to the food than to spicing the conversation with disturbing innuendos.

Since the latter activity had diminished my appetite, I was relieved when Forrest looked at his watch and said, "If we're to catch the train, we'd better leave right away."

We had said our good-byes in private, but I decided to ride along when Cal drove Forrest and our guests to the station.

The weekend had been delightful, and would have been perfect but for the missing Black Hand. In order to keep the lid tightly shut on that Pandora's box, I had convinced myself that the drawing had been mislaid. Nevertheless, I felt a strong premonition that something even more terrible had yet to occur.

"I have so enjoyed the visit," the baroness said on entering the carriage. "You must come to town next month, Charlotte. The Baltimore Civic Opera Company will be doing *Carmen* and that you simply must see."

I promised I would, but my apprehension persisted and a terrifying thought suddenly popped into my head. Would I still be here next month?

Owen McRae seemed anxious to claim my attention before the baroness could do so again. "I want to thank you for your hospitality, too. And I want to say that you have inherited a magnificent house." Then, shaking his head, he smiled. "Forrest is right, though. The villa does not reflect the personality of his charming young wife. When I have completed my drawings, I'll bring them up for your approval, Charlotte. I think you'll be pleased with what I have in mind."

For some absurd reason, I thought of the inkblot castle. If the appearance of the house was altered, would that break the spell?

"We're both anxious to have the work completed as soon as possible," I said, and Forrest enthusiastically agreed.

The train was on time, and after hurried hugs and fond farewells, I was once again left at the station to smile and wave my handkerchief until the last car was out of sight.

I wasn't anxious to return to the villa, so I asked Cal if he knew where the Atkins family lived.

"Back of the store," he answered, confirming my guess.

"I need to see Tom about some work," I told him. "It's a beautiful day, so you can just drop me off and I'll walk home."

I really wanted to see Mrs. Atkins. Our conversation in the store had been interrupted, but I still wanted to hear what she had to say about the ghost in the woods.

The house was of white clapboard with a big, old-fashioned porch across the front. It looked like a farmhouse and had probably been one before the town grew up around it.

As I got closer, I saw that two women were sitting outside. One was Tom's mother and the other one, who was older, I took to be his grandmother.

Mrs. Atkins seemed genuinely pleased at the prospect of having company. "Come and set a spell," she said. "Ma and me, we was just fixin' to have ourselves a cup of tea. We'd be proud to have you join us, Mrs. Singleton."

Without waiting for an answer, she turned to the older woman and said, "This young woman's the new mistress up at the villa. She's related to that countess, but she ain't Eyetalian, she's English. This here's my mother-in-law, Mrs. Bessie Atkins," she said to me. "Folks just call her Miz Bessie."

Mrs. Atkins disappeared into the house for the tea and Miz Bessie squinted at me and pointed to the swing. "Sit over there, missy. I can see you better."

Something about the house and even the people, though their speech was far different, reminded me of the little English village I had loved. "This is a charming house," I remarked.

"My husband built it just before the war," she said.

I gathered she meant the American Civil War, and her next words confirmed my guess.

"Maryland was a divided state back in them days. My husband was for the South, and once we even hid two Confederate soldiers in the barn. It was dangerous, and I don't mind tellin' you I was scared, 'specially since the Singletons up at the big house were dyed-in-the-wool Yankees."

She paused as if to gauge my reaction and then continued. "Folks even thought the Singletons were part of the underground railroad. Some said there were secret passageways in that house and that's where the runaway slaves hid when they was travelin' north."

"Is that a fact?" I said, letting my eyes stray to the door for Mrs. Atkins. I really wasn't interested in politics. I wanted to hear about the ghost.

Tom's mother came outside then with the tea tray. "Brought us some cookies," she said, and then looked at me and smiled. "Ma been bending your ear, Miz Singleton?"

"Been talkin' about the war," Miz Bessie said.

"Young people don't want to hear about the past, Ma."

"Oh, but I do," I insisted. "I want to hear about the ghost. Your sister mentioned it when we were on the train."

"The ghost in the woods?" Mrs. Atkins asked.

"Yes. Your sister said it was the ghost of a hanging man."

She looked embarrassed. "That's mostly hearsay, honey. After Mr. Singleton died, folks started sayin' mean things, but they had no proof."

She looked extremely uncomfortable and I said, "Please tell me what they said, Mrs. Atkins. I'd really like to know."

"They said Singleton lost his money and then he

207

committed suicide," Miz Bessie retorted.

Mrs. Atkins's face turned beet-red. "Ma, for pity sakes!" She turned horrified eyes to me. "I apologize for her, miss. She's still fighting the war."

"Please, there's no need," I said. "It all happened a long time ago. It's of no importance now."

"I ain't sayin' it's true," Miz Bessie said. "I was only repeatin' what I heard."

The poor woman looked upset and I certainly didn't want to be the cause of a family argument. "It's my fault for asking, but like I said, it all happened a long time ago. My husband was a mere child then."

"Poor lad," Miz Bessie said. "They lost the house and that's when them Eye—" she was about to make another faux pas, but caught herself in time. "That's when your grandmother bought the house and changed it to the Villa Montelano," she said.

I stayed longer than I had planned, partially because I wanted to assure them that I harbored no resentment for Miz Bessie's remarks and partially because it was nice to sit on a shady porch and converse with homey, down-to-earth people for a change.

The sun was going down when I left the Atkins house, and a chill in the air reminded me that it was now the end of October. Lights were being lit in the houses and, in this working-class community of five o'clock suppers, mothers were calling their children in from play.

I'll have to take the short cut through the woods if I'm to make it home before dark, I decided, picking up my pace. The cold air hurt my throat and I stopped to catch my breath, but the dry leaves I had walked through continued to crunch.

Someone's behind me, I thought, spinning suddenly around. No one was there, but the pile of leaves had been scattered as though footsteps had zigzagged through them to reach a clump of bushes by the side of the road.

I resumed walking, every once in a while turning quickly to see if I was being followed, but I saw no one.

I was almost out of town, and looking back at the twinkling lights in the windows, I had a strong urge to run to the last house and seek refuge there.

The roadway was lined with clumps of the same thick bushes, and this time there was no mistaking the shrill laughter that pealed out from behind them.

I started to run, scattering leaves in my wake, and the laughter followed me, growing louder and more raucous as if my pursuer were playing some kind of macabre game with me.

My foot struck a leaf-covered rock and I sprawled in the roadway, unhurt but numb with terror as I turned my head and looked up into the face of a hideous, leering skull!

I could not move. I could not scream and my confused brain could not comprehend what was happening when two more hideous apparitions joined the first one.

"All Hallows' Eve. All Hallows' Eve," they shouted in unison, tearing off their masks and exposing my pursuers to be nothing more than three grinning boys playing a Halloween prank.

They ran off laughing and I picked myself up. My heart was pounding and my legs felt as brittle as the leaves I brushed from my clothes.

I must hurry, I reminded myself as panic threatened to overwhelm me. Surely, I will not allow myself to become undone by a group of giggling children.

But the vague premonition of doom persisted, and I found my thoughts harking back to the startling revelation that Forrest's grandfather was presumed to be the ghost in the woods.

Had he really committed suicide? Or was it all just village gossip?

The wind picked up and I wished I had worn a coat over my suit. Bitterly regretting my casual decision to walk home, I hurried up the winding dirt road as twilight settled in. I was having second thoughts about taking the short cut through the woods, but keeping to the road would mean I'd still be walking when night fell.

My thoughts again returned to the apparition I'd seen from the lodge. Had it indeed been Forrest's grandfather? And if so, why would it appear to me? Was I some sort of catalyst? What could these two spirits from the past want from me? I wondered.

The woods loomed before me and I forced myself to cross the road and enter it. An eerie stillness hung over the area and I jumped as an owl hooted from a tree.

Stepping carefully, I kept my eyes glued to the uneven ground, but something large and black crossed the periphery of my vision and I turned in surprise to see Mr. Wilson's old coach parked underneath a tree.

For the first time in my life, I was glad to see the thing. A ride, even a wild one, was suddenly preferable to a walk through the ever-darkening wood and I ran with relief toward the carriage.

"Mr. Wilson," I shouted, but he didn't answer, and when I approached the front of the coach, I didn't see him. "Mr. Wilson," I shouted again, and then I saw that he was lying down. "Wake up. You have a fare," I cried, climbing up beside him.

His eyes were wide open and death had captured and held intact the startled look he wore on his face. Dried blood and flies surrounded the gaping bullet hole in his forehead, and it was several seconds before I heard myself scream.

Chapter 17

My scream startled the horse, making him bolt, and I was thrown on top of Wilson's dead body. But hysteria and loathing gave way to instinct when I felt the coach move, and grabbing the reins, I managed to halt the frightened animal in his tracks.

Jumping out of the coach, I hit the ground hard. The stench of death and the thought of the stiff, cold body I had touched made me gag, and I lay there retching until I thought my insides would surely burst.

I must go for help, I told myself. I must summon the constable. A startled gasp escaped my lips as I visualized a stern authority figure who would investigate and accuse. Accuse whom?

I saw the rifle propped up against the wall.

"Is that thing loaded?"

"Not anymore," my husband had answered.

I saw Forrest's hands on Wilson's throat.

"I've a score to settle with you, Wilson, and you'd better hope we're not alone the next time we meet."

I saw the triumph in Wilson's eyes.

"I know some secrets even you don't know, shyster . . ."

No, I would not go for help, nor would I summon the constable. There must be no reason for the authorities to connect Wilson's murder with the Villa Montelano.

Before I could change my mind, I climbed back up

onto the coach. The buggy whip was still clutched in Wilson's dead hand. Swallowing my revulsion, I pried it loose and jumped to the ground. Then with a shout, I brought the whip down smartly on the horse's flanks.

He reared and headed for the road at breakneck speed, dragging the coach and Wilson's dead body along with him.

I threw the buggy whip in the deepest part of the stream and watched it sink out of sight. Then I trudged through the darkening woods toward the lights at the Villa Montelano.

Arriving home at last, I went immediately to my room, grateful for the fact that no one was about to see the bloodstains on my gown or bear witness to my distraught state.

Once safely inside the Blue Room, I shut the door. Still feeling nauseated, I headed for the bathroom, but as I passed the full-length mirror, I stopped suddenly and stared at my reflection.

The woman who stared back at me looked different, older, I decided, but a more subtle change was also present. Gone forever was the innocence of girlhood. I was a woman now and a desperate one. Coming face-to-face with the possibility that my husband might have committed murder, I had acted on that supposition by attempting to shield him.

God forgive me, but I shall go on shielding him, I thought, no matter what he has done. With that resolution voiced, my queasy feeling passed and an unexpected calm settled over me.

Later, when Fiona was dressing my hair, I caught a glimpse of my face in the mirror, and for the first time, I detected a resemblance to Gia in the artful expression I saw there.

The thought was so disturbing that I didn't answer Fiona until she repeated herself. "Beggin' your pardon, mum, I said, should I be getting the peach?"

I gave her a blank look. "The peach?"

"Your peach gown. This morning you told me to

press it so you could be wearing it tonight?"

"Oh, no," I said suddenly recalling Madam's reference to little brown wrens. "Not the peach. I don't think I'll ever wear peach again," I added. "In fact, you can have that gown, Fiona."

She gave me an incredulous look. "Oh, mum. Do you really mean it?"

"Yes, yes," I answered impatiently.

I was taking stock of my wardrobe and had mentally discarded gown after gown when suddenly inspiration struck me. The white lace by Worth had a detachable train. That should make it suitable for dinner.

"I'll wear the new white lace," I told Fiona. Then, feeling like a traitor to the unknown Roberto, I unclasped the locket I was wearing and handed it to her. "Put this away, please. I'll wear the diamond necklace tonight."

I went downstairs and met the others in the drawing room for cocktails. Marshall was the first to recover himself after I made my appearance.

"Charlotte, you look positively stunning," he said, coming forward and offering me his arm.

Carla took me in from head to toe and her eyes burned with envy as they assessed my gown and the diamonds at my throat. "We were beginning to worry about you," she murmured.

"Whatever for?"

"You're late, and Anna said Cal came back from the station without you."

They were keeping track of me and I felt threatened. "Really," I said. "I didn't know I was under surveillance."

Marshall looked at me in surprise. "We were concerned, Charlotte. It grows dark early on now, and the woods are dangerous. Have you forgotten about the poacher?"

Nicky came forward, walking stiff-legged and with his arms stretched out before him in a macabre attempt at humor. "And it's *All Hallows Eve,*" he said in a rasping voice. "The dead are supposed to walk tonight."

His sunken eyes and skull-like face turned my blood to ice water, but I managed to say, "So it is. I saw some children in the village playing spook."

"Poppycock," Victor said.

I was reminded that Wilson had used that same word before taking off in a huff after the Maestro's funeral. He and Nicky had been arguing, I recalled, and I suddenly wondered why.

"Oh, I don't know," Nicky said, eyeing Victor with amusement. "All Souls' Day," he mused. "It's tied in with theory of purgatory. The dead have to atone for their sins. How else can they do it, but to come back?"

Victor's lip curled in contempt as he glared at Nicky. "Since when did you turn priest, Faro?"

Dorcas suddenly appeared beside Nicky, and laying a hand on her son's arm, she said softly, "Don't antagonize him. He's drunk again."

What next? I thought, wondering how I should manage to get through this evening. What I would have given to be able to plead a headache and escape to my room, but I must be extremely careful, I warned myself. I must act perfectly natural and give them no cause to suspect that anything unusual has occurred today.

Dinner was announced and I was distressed to learn that we would be eating roast duck. My appetite immediately disappeared, for the duck only served to remind me that Forrest had been in possession of a rifle and the coachman had been shot.

My thoughts drifted back to that harrowing scene in the woods. Had it been wise to throw the buggy whip in the stream? What if it should be washed up on the bank and found by the police? Perhaps I should have tossed it back into the coach.

"The duck is excellent," Don Alberto said.

"The sauce is too tart," Dorcas commented.

"Not for my taste," Marshall said.

Victor's booming voice cut through their small talk like a scythe. "Why was McRae checking over the house?"

He was staring pointedly at me and I answered, "Owen McRae is an architect, Victor. Houses interest him."

I was relieved when Don Alberto channeled the subject into safer waters. "McRae is highly regarded. He designed a country place for Vidici in White Plains and of course Giusseppina's rather farcical château in Baltimore," he added with a chuckle.

I added that Mr. McRae had also worked on the Academy of Music. That led to a discussion of opera houses; and I was relieved to be shut out of the conversation.

Victor was silent for the remainder of the meal, and later, when we had all adjourned to the drawing room, he sat alone in a corner, drinking steadily.

I felt Carla's scorching eyes on my neck and my flesh literally burned. "Is your necklace new?" she finally asked.

"It's a family heirloom," I said.

Her eyes flashed. "That's not one of Gia's necklaces."

Meeting her gaze, I answered. "Of course not. This belonged to Forrest's family."

The unexpected reply antagonized her and she looked down on me with disdain. "And he gave it to *you?*"

"Of course," I heard myself say. "After all, I happen to be Forrest's wife."

She gave me an impudent smile. "For the present," she added, walking away from me.

I chatted with Don Alberto and Marshall, and when I heard the hall clock strike ten, I said my good-nights and made good my escape.

Victor followed me, and before I could reach the stairs, he grabbed hold of my arm. "I want to know what you intend doing about my proposition," he said, slurring his words. I felt myself in a grip of steel and knew there was no way I could escape his grasp, so I made no attempt to do so. "I'm not selling the house," I said in as steady a voice as I could muster, "and I'll thank you, sir, to unhand me."

It sounded like a line from some ridiculous melodrama and I almost expected him to laugh, but he only increased the pressure on my arm. "Gia saw this house and she wanted it. I was the one who got it for her and now it should belong to me. I won't be cheated out of it by you and that conniving lawyer you call your husband. *Capisci?*"

"Let me go," I said, and with a sudden burst of strength, I wrenched myself free of him and ran upstairs.

The moon was full, and I stood by the window in my nightgown drinking in the eerie stillness of the night.

Nicky's reference to All Hallows' Eve and the purgatory theory intrigued me. Could that be the answer? I wondered. Had the ghosts of the Villa Montelano been suspended in a netherland between heaven and hell, and had they been returned to earth to atone for past transgressions?

Surely Gia had much to atone for, I thought. And wasn't suicide looked upon as the ultimate sin? Those who died by their own hand were even denied Christian burial.

Somewhere in the distance an owl hooted. The spooky sound unnerved me and I glanced at the clock. Two more hours and All Souls' Day will come to an end, I reminded myself. All Hallows' Eve will turn into All Saints' Day and then I can rest easier.

I moved away from the window and let my eyes travel about the room. How could I while away two whole hours?

A thick book on opera lay on my bedside table. Written in textbook style, it was a little hard for me

216

to comprehend, but I had committed myself to studying it. Music held an almost obsessive fascination for me now, and I wanted to learn everything I could about it.

Nevertheless, tonight I needed something mundane and physical to do like the housekeeping tasks I used to perform when I was a shopgirl living alone in a tiny one-room flat.

Being a lady had its drawbacks, I decided, for in this spacious three-room suite Fiona had left me nothing to clean or even rearrange.

But, there is something to search for, I thought, settling about one last time to look for the Black Hand.

I double-checked the cedar chest and my bureau. I even took everything out of the closet and discovered yet another mystery. The richly plumed hat that matched my new velvet riding habit was missing. Had I taken it off and left it somewhere?

Forrest would not appreciate my carelessness. Rifling through the closet, I saw that the green riding habit was missing too, and then it suddenly dawned on me that Fiona had probably taken the whole outfit downstairs to clean it. At least one mystery is solved, I thought.

Not wanting to speculate any farther about the other one, I concentrated instead on the delicate little clasp of Roberto's locket. The piece of jewelry had become so much a part of me that I preferred keeping the diamond necklace in the drawer and the little locket around my neck.

The catch was a tricky one to close, and without thinking, I walked over to the mirror and peered at it.

I caught a glimpse of my own reflection and then the mirror suddenly turned into a swirling mist and I felt like I was peering into some kind of magical crystal ball.

Common sense told me not to look, but I couldn't tear myself away. Hypnotized, I stared entranced as the motion inside the glass accelerated, the clouds whirling faster and faster until they came together and formed a vortex.

Fascinated, I watched the spinning circles grow smaller and smaller, insidiously drawing my eyes to its center. I felt myself being sucked into the whirlpool, and then just as suddenly, all motion stopped. The glass cleared and I could see the locket resting on my bare bosom.

Confused, I raised my hand and felt the high-necked ruffle on my nightgown. My eyes immediately flew to the face reflected in the glass. Not my own, but an incredibly beautiful young Gia's stared back at me. She smiled, and with his back to the mirror, a man approached her from the other side of the room. He took her into his arms. They kissed and the scene wavered and began to fade.

I felt a vague sense of something lost or at least unfinished and I mentally willed the scene to return, but it grew fainter and fainter and finally disappeared altogether.

The nebulous clouds gathered again, and this time I was not so much frightened as intrigued by the frenzied activity inside the glass, for I felt certain another scene was about to materialize.

I saw the whirling circles, the vortex, all the same phenomena as before, and then the glass cleared and gradually an image appeared in the mirror. Again, it was the young Gia. She wore a shawl, a full, peasant-style skirt and her feet were bare. She must be in costume for *Carmen,* I thought.

The setting was that of a sumptuous bedroom, so rich and lavishly furnished as to be fit for a queen. Gia's dark, expressive eyes darted quickly around the room and then she walked over to a handsome desk and from it removed a curious-looking carved box. A satisfied smile lit up her face as she peered inside, and then wrapping her shawl around the box, she left the room.

The mirror dimmed and then picked Gia's image up again outside on a dusty, country road. A man was with her, but again, his back was to the mirror and I could only see Gia. She was gesturing wildly with her hands and her face was contorted in an angry scowl. They appeared to be arguing over the box, for they pulled it back and forth between them.

In the background I could see riders approaching, but Gia and the man didn't seem to be aware of their presence. They both kept pulling on the box, and then all of a sudden it left their hands and hit the ground.

Just as suddenly, the mirror cracked as though shattered by the force of the impact. I was immediately released from my hypnotic state, and as my mind snapped back into place, terror at the strange, supernatural phenomenon I had just witnessed overcame me and I fainted.

I wasn't sure if the incessant rapping I heard was inside or outside my head. It stopped for a moment and then resumed, and I finally realized that someone was knocking on the door.

"I'm coming," I said.

I was surprised to find myself on the floor. Had I been sleepwalking?

"Mrs. Singleton, wake up. It's me, Fiona." The Irish girl's voice was high-pitched and it was giving me a headache.

"I'm coming. I'm coming," I repeated, almost tripping over my nightgown to get to the door.

Fiona's small eyes were bulging, and with her flushed face and the unruly red hair that escaped her cap in feathery wisps, she reminded me of an excited chicken. "Oh, mum. You'll niver guess what's happened. Oh, it's that awful, it is."

"Come, sit down," I said, drawing her into the room.

She took a few steps and then stopped. "Oh, Lord. Oh, Blessed Mother of God!"

I followed her gaze and involuntarily gasped. Last night's strange happenings washed over me like a flood as I stared at the long crack that ran down the center of the mirror.

"That's seven years' bad luck," Fiona said, and turning terrified eyes in my direction, she added, "Oh, mum. I don't think I can rightly stay. There's too many bad things going on around here."

You should have been here last night, I felt like saying, but I surprised myself by remaining calm and giving the girl a motherly pat on the shoulder. "Don't upset yourself, Fiona. None of this has anything to do with you. I don't believe in the superstition about mirrors, but at any rate, it would be my bad luck, not yours. Now, what do you have to tell me?"

Of course I knew by now that Mr. Wilson's body would have been discovered, but I was anxious to hear what was being said about his murder.

Fiona took a deep breath and launched into an involved discourse. "You know we get milk and eggs from the Bosley farm. It's that one up there on the hill, you know."

I didn't know, but she was waiting and I said, "Yes, go on."

"Well, Mr. Bosley told cook that his son Willie has a sweetheart in town. Sunday's his courtin' day 'cause he has to help his pa during the week, you know."

Would she ever get to the point, I thought, but I nodded and said, "Yes, I know. Go on."

"Well, this girl's brother works at the livery stable and he said that long about dusk this coach comes tearin' into the livery stable, and what do you think?"

"I can't imagine."

"Mr. Wilson was slumped down in the coachman's box, dead as a doornail! Ain't that awful? Somebody had shot him. He had a hole right in between his eyes, Mr. Bosley said."

I tried to act completely shocked. "How horrible! Do they know how it happened?"

"The constable's gotta find that out. Now who do you suppose would do such a thing? Mr. Bosley says old man Wilson was a cranky old cuss and nobody really liked him, but folks don't get murdered just for being cranky."

"No, of course not, but it's no concern of ours, Fiona. I'm sure the constable will get to the bottom of it."

She seemed calmer after telling her story, and her eyes strayed to the mirror. "How did it get broken, mum?"

I wanted to deflect attention from the cracked mirror. "I knocked it over."

"Knocked it over? That big thing!"

"I was trying to move it close to the window. To get more light."

It was a plausible explanation and she nodded her head sympathetically. "Don't worry none. Tom Atkins can put a new glass in it."

"Oh, no," I protested vehemently, for I didn't want the mirror's spell to be broken.

She gave me a questioning look, so I said in a very calm voice, "Mr. Singleton may want to have it repaired in town. It's a valuable antique, Fiona, so we'll just push it into the dressing room and cover it over with a sheet for now."

I was frightened, but nevertheless intrigued by the mirror, for I felt the brief vignettes it had shown me were important glimpses into the past.

Could the mirror only speak to me on All Hallows' Eve? I wasn't sure, but subconsciously I knew that terrified or not, I meant to find out.

I dressed hurriedly and went downstairs to breakfast, for I was anxious to hear what was being said.

The news had evidently produced a similar reaction in everyone, for all the villa's residents were present when I entered the dining room.

A lively discussion was already in progress, and after ascertaining that I had been informed about the murder, the group to my relief excluded me from the conversation.

I lingered at the sideboard, taking an inordinate amount of time to make my selections. With my back to the others, I could listen and not have to worry that eyes far sharper than Fiona's might detect something in my facial expression to give me away.

"It's the hunting season," Victor was saying. "Could have been a stray shot."

I held my breath, but no one mentioned that Forrest and Owen McRae had gone duck hunting.

"Are you confessing, Victor?" Nicky followed the question with a sarcastic laugh. "The tiger and the waterboy. You told us about it yourself. Don't you remember?"

"Very funny," Victor said, "but I don't hunt no more."

"Well, somebody was sure hunting Wilson," Nicky said. "When a man's shot right between the eyes, that's no accident."

I brought my plate to the table then and had just sat down when Fiona entered the room. "Beggin' yere pardon, Mrs. Singleton, but there's a policeman outside. He said he'd like to ask you some questions about Mr. Wilson's murder."

Chapter 18

The sheriff, a heavy-set, middle-aged man, stood in the great hall. No doubt the Villa Montelano evoked in him the same curiosity and prejudice it elicited in the rest of the townfolk, for he looked uncomfortable and a little resentful.

"Good morning," I said, and though my heart was pounding in my chest, I managed to assume a cool, collected air. "I'm Mrs. Singleton, the mistress of the villa. Is there something I can help you with?"

The mistress of the villa. It was a title I had never associated with myself, and yet it had flowed quite naturally from my lips, taking me a little by surprise.

"Sheriff Atkins," he said in a deferential tone as he quickly removed his cap.

"You're related to Tom Atkins?" I asked.

"I s'pose. There's lots of Atkinses 'round these parts."

"Please, come into the library. We'll be more comfortable in there," I said. "Would you like some coffee?"

"Thanks, no. This won't take long."

A crazy thought entered my mind. *Does he want to know where he can reach my husband? Is he going to arrest Forrest?*

He followed me into the library, and steeling myself for what was to follow, I offered him a chair and a weak smile before closing the door. "Now, what can I do for you, Sheriff Atkins?"

"Like I said, Mrs. Singleton, this won't take long. I'm investigating the death of Eli Wilson. I understand from your maid that you people already know the coachman's been shot."

I nodded and he continued. "Well, ma'am, I understand that you was walking home from town 'long about the time the coach came back to the livery stable with Wilson's body. Been tryin' to pinpoint from what direction it come and I wondered if you might have seen it on the road."

I could hardly believe my ears. It had nothing to do with Forrest. It was just a routine question.

"I saw nothing at all," I heard myself say.

The lie left my lips with no trace of the stutter that had always plagued my speech when I was nervous.

Sheriff Atkins stood up. "That's all, then. Told you this wouldn't take long, but I thank you, ma'am, for your time."

As I opened the door, I caught a glimpse of someone making a hasty retreat down the corridor.

"Just a minute, Anna," I called, and she turned and faced me with resentful eyes. "You can show Sheriff Atkins out and then you may give your report to the Signora."

It gave me enormous satisfaction to see a ruddy glow creep up Anna's neck and brighten her sallow complexion.

I bade the sheriff good day and closed the door on his retreating back. Several minutes later, I went to the window and discreetly watched him mount a large gray and white horse and take off in the direction of the woods. Was he merely taking a shortcut into town? Or was he looking for something?

Feeling drained, I sat down and let the tears flow. Having anticipated the worst, I found it hard to accept the fact that my meeting with the sheriff had gone well.

Two days later, I had another visitor. Unlike the

sheriff, this was someone I was surprised but overjoyed to see, and yet that meeting was destined to set off a chain of events that would ultimately unleash my twin demons and give them the strength to overpower me.

Owen McRae arrived Wednesday morning with a briefcase full of blueprints and plans for the restoration of the villa.

"Of course we won't be able to start the actual work until spring," he said. "But since I was coming up this way on another matter, I thought I'd drop them off. You can look them over, and if you have any changes, we can work them out later."

"Has Forrest seen them?" I asked.

"Yes, but he wants you to have final approval, Charlotte. Oh, I almost forgot," he said, reaching into his pocket and withdrawing an envelope. "Forrest asked me to give you this note. One of his trial dates has been moved to Saturday, so he won't be able to get home this weekend. I've been asked to act as a consultant on a project in New Orleans and I'll be gone for several months," he added. "I wanted to get your reaction in person, so that's why I brought the drawings up here myself."

I took the note and stuffed it into the pocket of my skirt. I was bitterly disappointed, but I tried not to show it. This meant I wouldn't see Forrest for two whole weeks!

"I hope you'll stay and keep me company for a couple of days," I said.

Aware of the tense situation that existed at the villa, he gave me a sympathetic look. "I wish I could, Charlotte, but I'll be leaving for New Orleans next week and I have a lot of loose ends to tie up first. I'll have to catch the morning train back."

"Of course. It was good of you to bring the drawings up, Owen."

"Thank God," he said with a chuckle, and I gave him

a puzzled look. "I'm relieved that you're finally using my first name," he explained. "Now I feel like a friend and not a doddering old relic."

Strange, I thought. It seems perfectly natural to refer to him as Owen now, but only a few days ago I would have considered it an impertinence on my part.

I automatically reached for the bell cord, and when Anna appeared, I said, "Mr. McRae will be spending the night, Anna. Please see that his room is made ready."

"Sì, Signora."

Her expression remained sullen, but I think it was the first time that Anna had ever addressed me by that title.

After she left, Owen opened his briefcase and handed me an artist's conception of how the villa would look after its renovation.

The black-and-white drawing looked like it should be framed and I said so, but Owen laughed at my suggestion. "I'm no artist. That's just an architect's sketch."

Studying it, I could hardly believe my eyes. All traces of the ugly inkblot castle were gone and in its place I saw a gracious, stately mansion. "Oh, Owen. It's absolutely beautiful," I said.

"Your husband deserves the credit. He knew exactly what he wanted. I just followed directions."

Of course, I thought. This has been Forrest's dream.

And you have merely been a means to that end, my demon added.

I pushed the ugly thought aside and tried to concentrate on what Owen was saying.

"Do you want to look over the blueprints now?" he asked.

"Not really," I answered. "This drawing is all I need. I never could understand blueprints."

I felt sad, almost as if another period of my life was drawing to a close. Once Forrest had Lauraland back, would he need me at all?

Owen returned the blueprints to their long leather

carrying case. "I'll leave the sketch with you. Now, are you sure you don't have any questions?"

"No. Well, yes," I contradicted myself. "It's not about the renovation, but I was wondering, since you went over the house so thoroughly, if you found it contained any secret passages. I know it's silly," I added, feeling childish again. "But someone in town remarked about it and . . ."

"Oh, yes, indeed," he said casually. "The old wing has a secret passage."

Recalling Miz Bessie's explanation, I said, "People thought it was used to hide runaway slaves."

"That's possible, I guess, but it sounds like a romantic rumor to me. More likely the original owner did it for a lark. Lots of old mansions had them." He shook his head. "When people build a house, they want it to be unique in some way, even today. Take Josephine's whimsical château," he added with a smile.

"How did you know about the passageway?"

"I found the outside exit."

"You didn't go through it?"

"Only for a few feet."

Seemingly amused by my interest, he gave me an indulgent smile. "I'll show you the exit, but I'm not going through the thing, and I don't think you'd want to, either. Mice usually take up residence in these passageways," he added, "though I must say, what little I saw of it appeared to be fairly clean. Come to the garden and I'll show it to you."

The outside exit was concealed by tall bushes that grew close to the house, but even without them, the small door would hardly have been noticed.

Owen pushed against it and it swung open. "You can't see much without a lantern," he said, "but it goes down several feet. There's a small room and another stairway."

"Where does it lead?" I asked.

He stepped back and pointed to the window directly above us. "Isn't that the library?"

I nodded.

"Then it's my guess there's a secret panel behind one of the bookcases."

"Let's look," I exclaimed eagerly, and giving me another indulgent smile, he followed me back inside the house and into the library.

"They listen at the door," I said as I closed it. "So please, Owen, let's not talk. I don't want anybody to know what we're doing in here."

It sounded melodramatic even to my own ears, and he regarded me with a strange mixture of concern and pity. Did he find me irrational? Or had Forrest told him about my so-called *little fancies?*

Whatever the case, Owen nodded and quietly went to work. Removing a few books at a time, he proceeded to tap against the walls of the bookcase. After several minutes of this, he smiled and beckoned me to come closer.

Pointing to a small button that blended so effectively into the woodwork as to be almost unnoticeable, he pushed it and I gasped as the bookcase swung open.

I caught a brief glimpse of a landing and another set of stairs, and then a sharp knock on the library door threw me into a panic. "Close it up, quick," I whispered, and then hurrying to the door I called, "Just a minute, please." But the latch was already turning and suddenly Dorcas's huge frame appeared in the doorway.

Her beady little eyes looked down on me with contempt. "Am I disturbing something?" she asked in a sarcastic tone.

"Not at all," Owen answered behind me, and when I turned around, I saw that he was standing before a closed bookcase holding a heavy volume in his hands. Snapping it shut, he returned it to the shelf and giving me a knowing look, he said, "I'd suggest you look under *History of America, Volume II* by Hilary King if you want to check anything out, Charlotte." Then he turned to Dorcas and remarked, "Charlotte's inter-

228

ested in American history."

"Good. Let her concentrate on that and leave this house alone," she said, ignoring me and addressing herself exclusively to Owen. "Take my advice, Mr. McRae, and don't bother drawing up any plans for the Villa Montelano. Ownership will be changing soon and I wouldn't want you to waste your time."

Dorcas's unpleasant performance made me apprehensive. If she had no compunction about insulting me before a guest, what could I expect of the others? Suppose Victor and Nicky followed Dorcas's lead? Owen was a cultured gentleman of the old school. He'd feel duty-bound to defend me, and I shuddered at the thought of exposing him to Victor's coarse vulgarity and Nicky's sarcastic wit.

I wondered, too, what had occurred that would prompt Dorcas to act in such a reckless manner. What was it she had said?

Ownership will be changing hands soon.

She had sounded very sure of herself, and again my thoughts turned to the others. Was Dorcas acting solely on her own? Or, did they all know whatever it was that Dorcas knew?

My fears that the villa's dirty linen would be carted out and paraded before Owen McRae proved to be groundless. Except for Dorcas's earlier outburst, Gia's obnoxious heirs appeared rather innocuous and I wondered if Owen thought I could have exaggerated their faults.

Conversation over dinner was bland and no one alluded to the possibility that Owen had come to the villa on professional business, although I was certain they were all aware that Owen was an architect and that we had plans to renovate the villa.

I began to relax, and like a calm that precedes a storm, the evening passed without incident.

After a leisurely dinner, we gathered in the music

room and Owen prevailed upon Don Alberto to play the violin. Was there no end to these people's talents? I thought as our new maestro treated us to a virtuoso performance while Owen accompanied him on the piano.

The haunting strains of Tchaikovsky and Mendelssohn added a plaintive note to the evening and once again I experienced a vague and unexplained sadness, as though I had lost or was about to lose something very precious to me.

That night I dreamed about my father, and when I awoke his features were as clear as if I had seen him only yesterday. How could I have not known he was Italian? I thought—his deep olive complexion, his warmth, his expressive hands and soulful dark eyes.

What was it about his eyes? I suddenly wondered. Had my father been trying to reach me in the dream with those eyes? Trying to tell me something?

I dressed and went downstairs. Owen was already gone and I was a little disappointed that we hadn't gotten to talk again about the passage, but he had already provided me with the information I needed. *Behind Hilary King's* History of America, Volume II.

Like a mantra I repeated the words over and over all that day, but I never got an opportunity to explore the passageway.

My curiosity about it had turned into an obsession, and now, as I lay in bed listening to the clock strike two, a familiar voice spoke to my subconscious.

This would be the ideal time to satisfy your curiosity. Or are you afraid of what you might find?

Ignoring the insinuation, I thought that if the passage had been designed to conceal runaway slaves, it would most likely end in a small room like the priest holes in ancient castles. It would be interesting to see such a secret room.

I got up and began to dress. Thank God I didn't have to enter the passage from outside, for a quick glance through the window showed me a night shrouded in fog.

This won't take long, I told myself. I should be back and ready for a good night's sleep well before three. Then, stuffing a candle and several boxes of matches in the pocket of my old black skirt, I left the room and tiptoed downstairs.

The dimly lit great hall had always made me uneasy and I kept my eye on the tilting armor as I descended the staircase. I was aware that my fear was completely irrational, but nevertheless the weird-looking relic preyed on my imagination and I had a childish notion that there were eyes behind those black slits and that they were watching me.

I hurried past it and ran down the unlit corridor. Just enough light filtered through from the great hall to allow me to see my way, but the library was at the far end, and by the time I approached it, I had to feel along the wall to locate the door.

Once inside the room, I reached into my pocket for the matches. I was just about to open the box when I heard a light tapping sound coming from the window overlooking the garden. Paralyzed with fear I stood completely motionless for a moment, and then common sense prevailed and I told myself that it was only a branch knocking against the glass.

I lit the candle, but before proceeding to the bookcase, I parted the drapes and peered outside. The fog had thickened and it hung like a pall over the garden, giving even that lovely spot a sinister appearance.

Quickly I closed the curtain and turned away from the window. The last thing I needed tonight was to have the fog play tricks on my eyes.

Holding the candle high, I scanned the bookcase for *The History of America, Volume II*. The thick book was easy to spot and I hesitated, but only for a second, before removing it and pushing the button.

My heart pounded with excitement as the bookcase

slowly swung open. Replacing the book, I held the candle high and peered inside the passage. My first assessment had been correct. The stairs which began underground stopped at a landing and then continued up another flight.

Gingerly I stepped out onto the landing. Every nerve in my body protested and my teeth began to chatter uncontrollably.

I can always step back inside, I reminded myself, but at that very moment, the bookcase began to close. Too stunned to move, I watched in fascinated horror as it slowly swung shut.

The draft blew out the candle and I was plunged into total darkness. Waves of panic washed over me and I felt myself sinking into oblivion, but common sense had not deserted me yet.

You have lots of matches, I told myself. You can light it again, and inching myself down to a sitting position, I placed the candle on my lap and felt in my pocket for the matchbox.

Using my fingers for eyes, I took out a matchstick, scraped it against the flint, and relit the candle. Then, I stood up and examined the closed partition.

Running my fingers along the wall, I found the button. It was exactly like the one on the other side of the panel, but something made me hesitate to press it.

Had the bookcase swung shut of its own accord? Or, had somebody pushed it? If so, mightn't that person be waiting for me on the other side? To enter the library now could be a mistake, so I climbed the steps, knowing that if the passageway ended in a secret room, I would be forced to leave either through the library or the garden.

Neither alternative was to my liking, but as I stood at the top of the steps, I prayed that when I pushed the button this time, a fear that I had refused to articulate would finally be put to rest and I would find myself standing in an empty room.

I don't remember pushing the button or seeing the

panel swing open, but I felt a heart-wrenching stab of betrayal when I stepped inside and saw that I was standing in my own room.

The panel was located in an alcove off the dressing room, and the button that released it was very cleverly concealed under the molding. Forrest's grandfather had built this house. Forrest had been raised in it and only a fool would entertain the notion that he hadn't known about the passage.

My eyes filled with tears when I recalled how he had convinced me that I had been dreaming when I told him I had awakened to find him gone from the room.

No wonder he never told me the Villa Montelano and Lauraland were one and the same. This house is full of secrets, I thought, and Forrest does not want to share them with me.

My discovery had opened up Pandora's box and now a plethora of questions rained down on me like an avalanche.

Where did Forrest go that first night and why?

Was that the only time he had left me asleep and escaped through the passageway?

Or had there been times when I didn't know he was gone?

Once the questions began, there was no stopping them. One logically followed the other in rapid succession.

Did anyone else know about the passageway?

Suddenly, a chill ran down my spine as I recalled the Black Hand.

Of course someone else knew. That's how they had gotten in.

Chapter 19

"Signore Singleton, he's a not home yet?"

Coming from Anna, the question annoyed me, but I answered her matter-of-factly. "Mr. Singleton has business in town this weekend, Anna."

She looked perplexed. "That *poliziotto* . . ." She made a frustrated gesture with her hand. "That man . . . What you call him, a sher . . ."

"Sheriff?"

"*Sì*, that's it, sheriff."

She had my full attention now. "What about the sheriff? Was he here?"

"*Sì*. He coma this morning, but I say Signore Singleton won't be here until four, five o'clock."

"Why didn't you tell me?"

"I told the Signora," she said with a trace of her old arrogance.

My eyes ever wavered as they stared into hers. "As mistress of the Villa Montelano, I must insist that in the future all callers be referred to me. Is that clear, Anna?"

"But the Signora—"

"The Signora is not the mistress here, Anna. I am. *Capisci?*"

If she had seen a ghost, she couldn't have looked more startled, and to my utter amazement, Anna executed a quick curtsy and left the room.

Had my use of the Italian word astounded her? Or

could it be possible that for a split second I had reminded Anna of someone else? Gia, perhaps?

I hadn't time to speculate. Quickly turning my thoughts away from Anna, I faced the more immediate problem of the sheriff. What did he want now?

This time he had asked specifically for Forrest, and glancing at the clock on the wall, I saw that it was already after four. Sheriff Atkins would be here soon and I wondered if he would find it strange that Forrest would not be coming home as usual on this particular weekend.

The thought had barely entered my mind when a rather-subdued Anna returned. "Sheriff Atkins. He's a here now. Shall I send him in, Signora Singleton?"

"No. Show him to the morning room, and ask him to wait."

I took several deep breaths before joining Sheriff Atkins. "I must apologize for my maid," I said, after greeting him. "I could have told you this morning that Mr. Singleton would be staying in town. I'm afraid he won't be coming home for another week."

"Is that a fact?"

"Yes, he's tied up in court. I imagine you know how that is," I added.

"Yes, ma'am. I sure do."

"Perhaps I can help."

He hesitated a moment and then said, "Eli Wilson's landlady claims Mr. Singleton paid a call on the coachman Sunday morning. Would you be knowing anything about that?"

I felt the blood rush to my head, but I forced myself to smile. "No, but Mr. Wilson had been driving the coach in a very reckless manner. He almost overturned it in our driveway several days ago. My husband may have wanted to caution him about it."

I couldn't tell what he was thinking, but I told myself he was a long way from being a fool despite his countrified manner.

"You might ask your husband to stop by and see me

235

when he gets home, ma'am."

"Certainly, Sheriff Atkins. My husband should be back Friday." Then I casually asked, "Have you uncovered anything in your investigation?"

"We found a lot of money in Wilson's room," he answered, and then qualified the statement by saying, "A lot for a coachman, that is, which could mean he was blackmailing someone."

I was sorry I had asked. "That seems rather strange," I remarked.

"Yes, ma'am, and I'll tell you something else that's strange. Wilson had a pearl-handled buggy whip. Set quite a store by that whip, too. Used to carry it around town with him like a weapon. 'Course he never threatened nobody with it. I'd a run him in if he had."

"Maybe he sold it."

He looked puzzled and then broke into a broad grin. "Did I say it was missin'?"

I could have bitten my tongue off, but he kept right on smiling.

"No matter, the buggy whip *is* missin', ma'am, but it wouldn't bring no more'n ten or fifteen dollars. 'Sides, Wilson wouldn't have parted with it while he was alive."

I could feel my cheeks burning. Oh, why hadn't I thrown the thing back in the carriage? I thought.

Sheriff Atkins picked up his cap. "I'd best be runnin' along. Thanks for your help. You will have Mr. Singleton stop in the station soon as he gets back, won't you, now, ma'am?"

When he had gone, I paced the floor, trying to sort out what had been said. Why had Sheriff Atkins made it a point to bring up the buggy whip?

I pushed the disturbing thought out of my mind and left the room. In the hallway, I encountered the Signora.

"Anna tells me you wish to receive all the villa's callers yourself." Looking down on me with a patronizing smile, she shook her head. "That's not how

236

things are done. Mistresses of fine homes leave such matters to their housekeepers."

"That will no longer be the case at the Villa Montelano," I said. "So I would appreciate it if you would inform all of the servants about the new policy, Sophia."

I don't know what angered her more, the new policy or my inadvertent use of her first name, but I saw the silent rage that mottled her face with color and turned her eyes to black pupilless pools.

Anxious to avoid a confrontation, I heard myself say, "Thank you. That will be all."

Spoken in my clipped British accent, the words sounded supercilious and they hung in the air between us. She gave me one last murderous look and then turned her back and was gone.

I had too much on my mind to worry about the Signora, though, and feeling the need for a breath of fresh air, I changed into riding clothes and headed for the stable.

Cal was always in good humor and his warm greeting gave my spirits a much-needed lift. He was brushing Angelina, the horse he'd taught me to ride. Smiling, he said, "I tella this li'l filly you coma today. She been lonesome for her mistress, but I say you no stay in the house on a beautiful morning like this." Then winking his eye, he added in an aside to the horse, "See, Angelina, what I tella you?"

"I would have been here earlier," I said, "but Sheriff Atkins delayed me."

He turned suddenly serious. "*Sì*, I saw him ride up. He's wasting his time. He won't find what he's looking for 'round here."

His dark eyes locked with mine and I wondered what he meant. Did he know something or was he only making conversation?

Turning away then, he called out to the stablehand, "Hey, you boy! Bring Angelina's saddle. Mrs. Singleton gonna take her ride now."

Lost in my own thoughts, I gave Angelina her head, and before I realized where she was going, we had entered the woods.

"No, Angelina, not today," I said, grabbing the reins and steering the horse in the opposite direction. As I turned around, something caught my eye and I stopped to stare upward to the ridge where the hunting lodge loomed like a beacon on the horizon.

Someone was moving around up there, but I couldn't distinguish who it was. It could have been either a man or a woman, and in a flash the figure disappeared from my view.

Either the person had entered the lodge or just exited from it, I surmised, but having no desire left to explore the place, I hugged Angelina's flanks with my knees and urged her into a gallop away from the woods, away from the villa, and hopefully to forget all my problems in a punishing ride.

The steep hills and deep valleys that lay on the other side of the Villa Montelano were a challenge to a novice rider, but I did not even consider the danger, and despite my reckless behavior, Angelina and I returned home several hours later exhausted but safe.

"You boy," Cal called as he helped me dismount. "Rubba this horse down and cover her over with a blanket." Then he turned to me, his face full of concern. "You go back to the house now, Miss Charlotte. You get out of those damp clothes before you comma down with a heavy cold. You no worry, you hear me?"

The stableboy was already working on Angelina's sweaty body, and edging away from him, Cal's eyes captured mine in a mute appeal. Following his downward gaze, I watched as he unclenched a large hand and exposed the pearl handle that had once adorned a buggy whip.

Jagged, cut-off strips of leather protruded from it, and giving me a knowing look, he said, "Cal taka care of everything, Miss Charlotte. You no worry now."

Converstation that evening was strained, and after dinner I mingled briefly with my unwelcome guests and then retired early, not to sleep, but to mull over the events of this most disturbing day.

How had Cal gotten hold of the buggy whip? Had he accidently found it washed up on the bank? Or, had he been watching when I threw it away?

It mattered little, I supposed. What disturbed me was the fact that Cal knew the whip's significance, and I wondered if this also meant he was convinced of Forrest's guilt.

Of course he's convinced. Why else would he destroy evidence, my demon whispered.

I removed my jewelry—all but Gia's little necklace, which I had gotten into the habit of wearing even to bed. With shaking hands, I struggled to unhook my gown, and frustrated I wrenched it apart. I could have called on Fiona, but I wanted to be alone with my thoughts.

As I hung the gown in the closet, my hand accidently touched the mirror. It felt warm, and without thinking, I pulled off the sheet that covered it.

The crack was gone and the mirror was pulsing, like a beating heart. The closet was dark, but a ray of light had picked up the gold in my necklace and was reflecting it in a heat so blinding that I feared it would explode into flames.

Acting on an impulse, I pulled the heavy mirror out of the closet and into the center of the room. The light immediately went out, but the mirror continued to pulsate, and I watched fascinated as clouds began to emerge and swirl within it.

My eyes followed the circles as they were drawn into the vortex, and when all had been consumed, the glass cleared. Very gradually images began to take shape and form, and once again Gia's face appeared in the mirror. This time she was not dressed in peasant clothes;

rather she was resplendent in an exquisite gown that I immediately recognized as one of the costumes the Signora and I had packed away for the Metropolitan's museum.

Gia had worn it in *Traviata,* and the Signora had gone into ecstasies about her portrayal of Violetta and how Verdi himself had fallen in love with her because of it.

Gia stood alone on stage apparently taking curtain calls, for she bowed and threw kisses to an unseen audience. From the wings, an older, bearded man suddenly emerged. Walking purposefully he approached Gia, embraced her, and, smiling his approval to the audience, led her offstage.

The scene faded and another emerged. This time the setting appeared to be that of a dressing room filled with multitudinous arrangements of flowers. Gia sat before a dressing table and another woman stood beside her. The woman's face was contorted with anger and she threw what appeared to be money on the table. Then she marched out, and the flowers in the room shook as if from impact of a slammed door.

Alone in the room, Gia looked in her mirror and smiled.

The scene faded and I held my breath, waiting and hoping there would be more. I was not disappointed, for another scene immediately took shape.

The room was sparsely furnished. There was something vaguely familiar about it and I thought that it reminded me of the flat in my London boarding-house. It didn't seem a likely setting for Gia Gerardo, but she was there and, much to my disgust, writhing in the bed with a man.

She was older in this scene, but the man was older still and not the same one who had embraced Gia onstage. Feeling like a voyeur, I was embarrassed, but nevertheless, I continued to stare at the erotic scene depicted in the mirror.

Either a light was turned on or a door was opened,

240

for suddenly the couple sat up, exposing their nakedness to a shadowy figure who stood at the foot of the bed.

Gia's long, tangled hair masked her face, but the man's was completely exposed, and I don't think I have ever known shock to be more vividly portrayed in an expression.

This last vignette broke the mirror and the spell. I didn't want to see more, for the scene had both disgusted and affected me deeply. Who had been standing at the foot of that bed? The man's wife?

His face had emblazoned itself on my mind. There is no guilt like that which follows betrayal, and I wondered if Forrest would wear that same expression when I confronted him with the questions that could no longer be avoided.

It was much later that I awakened and sat bolt upright in bed. Had I been dreaming or had I really heard that mocking laughter again?

I turned on the light. This time I meant to find out if my grandmother's ghost was the only one who was mocking me.

Making no attempt to be quiet, I got out of bed, put on my robe and slippers, and walking with a heavier-than-usual tread, I entered the dressing room.

Low, spine-chilling laughter followed me.

"Fiona," I said loud enough for anyone standing in the passageway to hear me.

I heard it again, and edging my way quietly over to the concealed entrance, I pushed the button.

The door swung back with a *whoosh* and I found myself staring into absolute darkness. I heard a scuffling movement and I knew I had surprised someone in the passageway.

I had to know who it was. Throwing caution aside, I stepped into the black vacuum.

Recalling the sound I'd heard when the door had

swung open, I surmised that my enemy's light had been blown out, but staccato flashes on the stairs below told me that my tormentor had brought a flashlight and we were no longer equals in the dark.

Nevertheless, I was not turning back, and holding both hands on the rails, I felt my way down the treacherous stairway. Once I slipped and slid on my bottom several feet, but I was catching up to my prey, for the brief flashes of light were closer now.

My more cautious enemy grew bolder, leaving the flashlight on in a desperate attempt to escape as I narrowed the distance between us.

The tiny beam of light worked to my advantage too, for as I grew closer, I could see that the shadowy figure wore a cape and hood. It still did not give me a clue as to his or her identity, but this was a flesh-and-blood human and no ghost that could disappear in thin air.

The phantom figure reached the next landing, but kept on going, evidently deciding that the garden with its mazelike walkways and heavy shrubs offered more by way of concealment than the library.

I followed doggedly on reaching the bottom of the stairs just as my prey released the outside door.

I saw it swing open, and my demon whispered in my ear, *You've lost. Once outside, the night will swallow your enemy up and you'll never know who it was.*

"No," I shrieked, and my voice startled the figure, making it pause just outside the door.

In that split second, I was outside and I lunged for the retreating phantom, bringing it down with a thump on the dew-laden grass.

We grappled on the ground like animals, but it was dark and I still could not see the face of my tormentor. With one gigantic thrust, my enemy gave me a push and broke away. My head hit something hard, and reaching behind me, I found the flashlight.

Grabbing hold of it, I raced after the black-clad figure. When I caught up to it, I beamed the flashlight in her face. It was Carla!

242

Panting, we stood in our mud-stained clothes with our hair hanging down our backs and stared at each other.

Suddenly a light in the house went on and a window in the servant's quarters was raised. Fiona's voice broke the stillness of the night. "Something wrong out there?"

Carla answered. "It's nothing. We're talking. Go to bed."

The window closed and Carla's face contorted with fury. "You little bitch. I wish you'd broken your neck on that stairway."

"What a pity you couldn't have pushed me, like you did once before," I said.

"You're crazy. I never pushed you."

Then her face twisted into a smile and I shuddered. It was the same smile I had seen Gia wear after the woman in the mirror had thrown money on her dressing table.

"Perhaps it was your husband who pushed you. He'd like to get rid of you, you know." She pushed back the mane of black hair that fell across her face and regarded me with contempt. "Surely, you aren't naive enough to think he loves you!"

Laughter bubbled up in her throat and rang in my ears like a clanging bell.

"He does love me," I said. "You're just jealous. That's why you've been doing these things."

She laughed a little harder and I said, "Stop it. You're losing your mind."

She stopped and turned on me with fury. "No, *cara mia,* you're the one who's losing her mind. Can't you see? That was the plan. I'd help Forrest drive you crazy and then I would be the mistress of the villa."

"You're lying. I don't believe you," I said.

"How do you think I knew about the secret passageway? No one else knows, just Forrest and me. And now you, of course," she added, "and that meddling old Owen McRae.

243

"Forrest and I were lovers before he even met you," she said, smiling that contemptuous, Gia-like smile. "Do you remember the night he brought you to the villa? He used the secret passageway then. We met right here in the garden while you slept upstairs and we made our plans that very night." She threw up her hands. "Oh, why don't you just go back to England? You're going to lose the inheritance anyway and Forrest and I don't need the money. Vidici is going to make me a star of stars."

"I see you have more than one fantasy," I said.

"What do you mean by that?"

"You're a second-rate singer, Carla. You'll never be a star no matter how many beds you warm."

"You Cockney prude! What do you know about music or men and beds? No wonder Forrest is sick and tired of you." Her eyes, dark and piercing, bored into mine. "Take my advice, little shopgirl. Go home before it's too late!"

Chapter 20

"I'm sorry, Charlotte. I should have told you about Carla, but believe me, sweetheart. It was over long before I met you."

His admission fell like a heavy stone on my heart, but what had I expected? Where there is smoke, there is bound to be fire, or at least the dying embers of one.

Reaching over, he brushed a lock of hair out of my face. The gesture was a paternal one, and it annoyed me. I wasn't a child.

Surely you aren't naive enough to think he loves you. Carla's words rang in my ears and I looked away.

Forrest tilted my face up to his. "Charlotte, I'm thirty years old. Certainly there have been other women in my life, but none that I wanted to marry until I met you."

"Carla says you want to marry *her*. She says you're sick and tired of *me.*"

He pulled my unyielding body into his arms. "Oh, God, Charlotte. I'm so sorry. Carla's a mean-tempered bitch. She'll say anything when she's cornered."

"Maybe she was telling the truth."

Holding me out in front of him, he gave me an incredulous look. "Surely you don't believe such nonsense."

"I don't know what to believe," I said, jerking away from his grasp. "There's lots more you never told me, like the fact that this house and Lauraland are one and the same; like there's a secret passageway to our room and you used it for your rendezvous with Carla." My voice broke then, but I managed to add, "You made me think I was dreaming. You swore you'd never left our bed!"

He lowered his eyes and spoke almost in a whisper. "I was wrong not to tell you about the house, but I had my reasons. My memories of Lauraland are both painful and beautiful. I just wasn't ready to think about them then, but I did plan to tell you, Charlotte, and as for meeting Carla that night—yes, I met her, but it was no rendezvous. She came into the kitchen while I was fixing you something to drink. She threatened to make a scene if I didn't meet her in the garden, so I did. We talked. That was all. When I asked her to leave the villa, she refused and I told her if she made trouble for us I'd make trouble for her with Vidici. She agreed, and I thought everything was settled."

I wanted to believe him. Oh, God, how I wanted to believe him! "Forrest," I said. "Tell me you didn't marry me to get Lauraland back."

An expression of deep pain passed over his face. "I was afraid that's what you'd think and I guess that's another reason why I wanted to wait." His eyes grew misty as they locked with mine. "I married you because I fell in love with you. And if you can't believe that, Charlotte, our marriage has been a sham."

I couldn't stand to see him wounded like this and I threw myself into his arms. "Oh, Forrest, I'm sorry. I should never have listened to her. She's evil and sick. She's—"

"She's leaving," he said. "I'm throwing her out, will or no will, which is what I should have done in the first place." His arms tightened around me and his lips brushed my brow with quick little kisses. "When I think of the way she tormented you—that damned Black Hand and making you think there was a ghost."

"But, Forrest, there is a ghost, in fact there's two."

"Come now, Charlotte. Carla was your ghost and you caught her."

"No, there's been other things. I keep seeing Gia in the mirror and then there's the other ghost. I think it's your grandfather. I saw him hanging from a tree."

His face registered horror and then anger. "Who have you been talking to, Charlotte?"

"Mrs. Atkins, Tom Atkins's mother. She said your grandfather committed suicide. She said he—"

"Enough! I won't listen to this. You mean you've been discussing my family with gossips in the village?"

"No, I haven't. She just mentioned it. Are you telling me it's not true—that your grandfather didn't commit suicide?"

"Certainly not. I won't discuss this any further, Charlotte, and I'd appreciate it if you'd do the same."

His whole attitude had changed, and it bewildered and frightened me. "I'm sorry. If you say it didn't happen, it didn't happen."

He patted my shoulder awkwardly. "Forgive me, sweetheart. I didn't mean to scold you."

His choice of words sent me back to my place as child-bride. Children may be loved and petted, I thought, but they cannot be confided in. "Sheriff Atkins was here," I said in a dull voice. "He wants you to stop by his office. It's something about Mr. Wilson."

His expression never changed. "Fine. I'm going into town anyway. I let Owen McRae take my rifle back with him, so I think I'll stop at the gun shop and pick up another one."

Like a rabbit alerted to danger, I froze. "Why did you . . . What does Owen need your gun for?"

"I guess he plans to do some hunting in Louisiana."

"But doesn't he have his own gun?"

"It's a relic. He admired mine, so I let him have it."

"Oh, I see."

He came over and kissed me hard. "Don't give Carla another thought. She'll be gone by tomorrow."

After Forrest left, I paced the floor. Every nerve in

my body was taut and on edge. Recalling the swirling mists I'd seen in the mirror, I felt as if I too were caught up in a whirlpool. My head was going round and round and soon I'd be sucked down into the vortex.

I'd been so relieved to hear Forrest say he loved me, but then everything had changed when I'd mentioned the ghosts.

Why had Forrest had such a violent reaction to his grandfather's suicide? Mrs. Atkins and her mother-in-law weren't the kind of people who would make up wild stories, and yet Forrest had been so adamant.

Could it be possible that he hadn't been told? Recalling that he'd only been a lad of ten when his grandfather died, the theory suddenly made sense.

Of course he would be outraged that such a rumor had circulated. Forrest had dearly loved his grand-parents.

My sense of relief was quickly replaced by my worry over the gun. It bothered me that Forrest had neatly disposed of the weapon by sending it to New Orleans with Owen McRae. Couldn't bullets be traced through the guns they'd been fired from?

The disloyal thought filled me with guilt and feeling frustrated, I tried to console myself with the thought:

All seems infected that the infected spy,
As all looks yellow to the jaundiced eye.

I am reading suspicion into everything, I told myself. I need to get out of this room. I need to smell fresh country air. I need to feel the wind on my face. I need to ride.

Stepping out of my clothes, I raced to the closet. Where was my new green riding habit? I'd have to speak to Fiona. Nothing should take this long to be cleaned.

I pulled out my old brown one and slipped it on. It was true, I felt more comfortable in it, but Forrest was home now. He'd want me to wear the one he'd picked out for me.

I hurried to the stable and got the young lad who

helped Cal to saddle up Angelina.

"Cal's not here," he said, and then added proudly, "He left me in charge." Pulling out a big red handkerchief from his pants pocket, he wiped it across his forehead. "Whew, have I been busy! Cal said there wouldn't be much to do, but first off this morning I had to hitch up the buggy for Mr. Faro. Then Mr. Singleton wants his horse saddled, and soon's he leaves, Miss Pinetti come in. I been so busy, I ain't had time to clean out the stalls."

He gave me a leg up, and looking down at him, I asked. "Did Miss Pinetti go for a ride?"

"Yes, ma'am. She don't ride much and at first I thought she was you comin' in. She asked for a fast horse and I sure hope she knows what she's doing, 'cause I give her one and she went a-tearing outta here."

I was sorry he had told me. It was probably just a coincidence, but right now I didn't need anything else to worry about. Digging my heels in Angelina's flanks, I too tore out of the stable, leaving the boy to wonder who was the more reckless, Carla or me.

The weather was still unseasonably warm, and although Cal had said that the hillside would be covered with snow come winter, I found it rather hard to believe, as several hours later I once again returned a sweating horse to the stable.

I was anxious about Forrest's meeting with the sheriff, but it was over now, and the ride had calmed me down. Soon we'd be discussing it and Forrest would probably laugh and say it was nothing but a lot of nonsense.

"Has Mr. Singleton returned?" I asked the stable-boy.

"No, ma'am."

"Miss Pinetti?"

"No, ma'am."

His answers shattered my fragile composure, and I found myself longing to go back and lose myself again riding through that beautiful, peaceful countryside.

Please let everything be all right, I silently prayed. *All right about what? The meeting or Carla?*

Pushing the demonic thought aside, I entered the house and ran upstairs to my room. I'd take a warm, relaxing bath and then a nap. Things were turning out for the best. I'd be rid of Carla by tomorrow. Hadn't Forrest said so?

Filling the tub with hot water, I sprinkled a generous amount of bath salts over it. The warmth and the fragrance of the perfume lulled me into a false sense of security and my tightly drawn muscles began to relax.

Wrapping myself in a heavy bath towel, I slipped into bed. Perhaps I would awaken to find Forrest beside me and with that thought in mind, I drifted off to sleep.

All of the villa's residents with the glaring exception of Forrest and Carla were present for the customary cocktail hour that preceded dinner.

"Where's Forrest, Charlotte? Or shouldn't I be asking?" Nicky followed the impertinent question with an even more impertinent lift of his eyebrows.

"I suppose he's still tied up in town," I answered coldly.

Nicky laughed. "Tied up or locked up?"

I felt all the blood drain from my face.

"Just making a little joke, Charlotte," he added with a shrug. "I heard the sheriff was looking for Forrest. Do you know why?"

"A routine matter," I said.

"Well, that's a relief. They don't lock people up for routine matters. Maybe he's with Carla," he said, looking around the room. "She seems to be missing, too."

The conversation must have piqued Victor's interest, for as soon as Nicky and I had started to speak, I saw him open his eyes and uncurl himself from a couch at the far end of the room. The pallor on his face and the way he blinked and looked about him in confusion put me in mind of a corpse coming suddenly to life and popping up in a coffin.

I didn't feel up to coping with any drunken insults tonight, so I was relieved when he remained at the other end of the room, isolating himself from the rest of us.

Marshall tapped Nicky on the shoulder and asked, "Did I hear you say Carla isn't back yet?"

"Well, you don't see her here, do you?"

Marshall's customary composure evaporated. "Don't be so damn smart, Nicky. Of course she's not in this room, but has she come back from her ride?"

"I suppose not. Mother rapped on her door before coming down and got no answer." Nicky gave Marshall a sarcastic smile. "So, Carla and Forrest are both missing. What's the matter, Haines? Are you jealous?"

Marshall's urbane facade slipped and his eyes darkened in anger. "You're a filthy little cockroach, Faro. Take care. Somebody might step on you."

Marshall's challenge went unanswered, for at that moment the door opened and all eyes turned to Forrest as he entered the room.

Weak with relief, I supported my shaking limbs by leaning back against the arm of a chair. Thank God. Forrest was home. He hadn't been arrested.

"Sorry to be late," he said, giving me a quick kiss that landed on my forehead.

Marshall abruptly walked away and Forrest picked up a decanter of whiskey and poured himself a drink. Nicky waited until he had finished and then said, "Now that you're here, Singleton, there's something I think you should know."

Taking a large swallow, Forrest gave Nicky a look that was fraught with impatience and weariness. "What is it?" he said.

"I'm sure you're aware that Mother and I have engaged a lawyer."

I saw a muscle twitch in Forrest's temple and I knew

251

his nerves had been stretched to the breaking point. "This is neither the time nor the place to discuss wills."

"I have no intention of discussing wills outside of court, Singleton. I merely thought to inform you that our lawyer has turned up something else. Something that I feel I should warn you about."

Forrest's lip curled and he took another big swallow of whiskey. "Warn me about what?"

"About a thief, a convicted felon who resides here at the Villa Montelano. This man served twenty years in prison. He came into this country under false pretenses and should be deported."

Forrest's laugh was raucous and I couldn't help noticing that his glass was empty. "Who is it, Nicky? You?"

"Hilarious, but no, it's not I. It's Gia's wonderful groom, the one she endowed with a racehorse that should have been mine—Cal Marcus!"

Everyone heard and a hush settled over the room. Oh, no, I thought, not Cal. "I don't believe it," I said.

Nicky shrugged. "It's the truth. He served time in a penal colony for larceny." Nicky gave me a condescending look and shrugged. "I didn't have to tell you. I did it as a favor. I shouldn't imagine you'd want a thief and a convicted felon on the premises."

Forrest started to pour himself another drink and I prayed for dinner to be announced. Dismissing Nicky with a wave of his hand, he said. "The man served his time, right?"

Nicky looked self-satisfied. "But that's not good enough for immigration."

All he cares about is getting the racehorse, I thought. Maybe it's not even true, but a hollow feeling deep in my heart told me it was.

I looked up to see the Signora enter the room. Thank God, I thought. Dinner is being served—and not a minute too soon, because Forrest was just about to reach for the decanter again.

Something in her manner must have alerted Forrest,

and murmuring an apology, he left me and walked over to meet her.

She seemed excited, and when she pointed through the open door, I saw that the stableboy was standing in the hall.

No trace of the whiskey Forrest had consumed was evident in his voice as he addressed the assembled group. "The stableboy has just informed the Signora that the horse Carla was riding has returned to the stable without her. I've instructed Sophia to have the male servants form a search party. Any of you men who care to join us will be welcome."

Forrest left the room then and Marshall and Nicky followed after him. Victor started to rise, but it was obvious he could not stand, and his heavy frame hit the couch with a thud.

Dorcas, who considered food a priority, nodded toward him and said, "He's too drunk to eat, but we might as well have dinner ourselves."

Light from the torches and lanterns the men carried lit up the grounds and reflected in the dining-room windows. There was something alarming about the scene and I scarcely touched my plate, but Dorcas polished off first one course and then another with gusto.

Neither of us spoke, and in the silence my inner demons bombarded me with their insinuations.

Where is Carla? Has something happened to her? Why was Forrest so nervous and why was he gone so long? Were they together? Did he ask her to leave? Or could it be he's going to ask you to leave? You trusted Cal, and now it turns out he was a criminal.

I pushed my plate away and put a hand up to my head. "Please excuse me," I said to Dorcas. "I can't eat. I'm going to my room."

"It's all coming to a head, isn't it," she said. "Forrest knows it. Did you see how nervous he acted?"

The candles on the table flickered, casting a shadow across her face, and I thought how sinister and ugly she

253

looked. We were alone in the room, possibly alone in the whole east wing of the house except for the drunk in the parlor, and suddenly I was afraid. I had to get away from her.

"Good-night," I said, dashing from the room in the throes of a rising panic.

Once in the Blue Room, I locked the door and pushed a heavy chifforobe in front of the secret panel. Then I went to the window and looked outside.

I could see the search party's flickering lights as they fanned out over the grounds. More lights would be visible from the west wing, as the woods were on that side of the house and I was sure they would check the woods first.

"It's all coming to a head." Dorcas had said. Was it?

Although we were on opposite sides of this conundrum, I had to agree with her. I felt a strong premonition that events were spiraling us forward and that a climax was about to be reached. Set on a course from which there was no escape, I felt myself being propelled through the turbulent rapids of ignorance. Would the truth set me free or destroy me?

I jumped at the insistent knock on the door. Dorcas?

Crossing the room, I rechecked the lock. "Who is it?" I asked.

"It's me, mum—Fiona. I've come to say good-bye. I'm leavin' this house tonight. I'd rather take me chances on a dark road . . ."

My relief was tempered by panic. *Dear God. Don't let her leave. She's the only one left I can trust.* Giving the key a quick turn, I pulled her inside.

"Oh, mum, it's that awful, it is. I knew something bad was going to happen, but I didn't tell the others. Only you and me know."

My mind went blank. "Know what?"

"You know, mum. About the mirror."

Good God, I thought. Has she been fooling around with the mirror?"

"Don't you remember, mum? It cracked and I told

you that meant bad luck, but you said—"

"Never mind what I said. You don't have to worry about the mirror, Fiona. We were mistaken. It didn't break; come, let me show you."

I grabbed her hand and dragged her with me into the dressing room. Pulling back the sheet I exposed the mirror to her incredulous eyes.

"Saints above. It ain't cracked a'tall. How can that be, mum?"

God forgive me for the lie, but I was a drowning victim, reaching for an outstretched hand.

"It was probably a shadow. Don't you remember, it was dusk when we saw it.

She nodded her head and I covered the mirror quickly, for it was growing warm to my touch. "Now, come and brush my hair, and let's hear no more nonsense about leaving the villa."

For both of us, sleep was out of the question, and since I didn't relish being alone and Fiona preferred my company to the other servants', we spent the vigil together.

Fiona was optimistic now that the question of the mirror had been settled. "Lady Fitzwater, me mistress back in Ireland, was thrown from a horse once. Broke her leg, she did, but a woodcutter found her and took her to his cottage."

A simple enough explanation, but why was I so certain it didn't apply to Carla?

We busied ourselves with inconsequential things. I buffed my nails. Fiona took an inordinate amount of time spot-cleaning and brushing my gown, and as she was about to hang it up, I suddenly remembered something. "Fiona, where is my green velvet riding habit?"

Before she could answer, shouts from outside drew us both to the window. "They're carrying something. They've found her," Fiona cried.

Giving no thought to the fact that I was in my nightgown, I raced out of the room and down the corridor.

Standing on the upstairs balcony, I looked down on the great hall. My breath caught in my throat when the door burst open and two burly stablehands carried a makeshift stretcher inside. It was completely covered over with a blanket.

My hand flew to my mouth and I stifled the scream before it left my lips.

Other members of the search party came in and soon the hall was filled with men. Forrest's tall figure and stark white face stood out from the crowd. "Not here," he said. "Take her back to the study."

As they lifted the stretcher, the blanket slipped. I gripped the banister as Carla's dead body was exposed. She was wearing my green riding habit.

Chapter 21

Not wanting to draw attention to myself, I shrank back against the wall, but my presence went unnoticed. No one so much as looked up toward the balcony. They were all too engrossed in the macabre scene that was taking place below.

One of the men who had carried the stretcher crossed himself and then quickly covered Carla's face with the blanket again.

An uncontrollable trembling wracked my body.

"She'll be gone by tomorrow," Forrest had said.

But he didn't mean like this, I told myself.

The stretcher was carried away and the search party disbanded.

I returned to the Blue Room to find Fiona gone. No doubt she was in the servant's quarters wringing her hands and already preparing to pack her bags. I envied her the option, for this latest catastrophe had me baffled. What had happened to Carla?

"There's been an accident."

Hardly recognizing my husband as the disheveled man framed in the doorway, I stared mutely back at him.

"Carla's dead, Charlotte. We found her in the woods."

"She was shot?"

"Shot? Of course not. She fell from the ridge and broke her neck. What do you mean, shot?"

"The coachman was shot. I thought . . ."

A flicker of annoyance crossed his face. "For God's sake, Charlotte, that had nothing to do with Carla. She fell. Didn't you hear me? We found her at the bottom of the ridge."

"She was wearing my riding habit," I said, unconsciously putting my rambling thoughts into words. "She came in through the secret passageway and stole it from my room."

He gave me an incredulous look. "She was light-fingered, Charlotte. We all knew that. But she's dead, for God's sake. I know you didn't like her, but the riding habit and how she got it is not important right now."

I felt a wall go up between us. We spoke, but for all that we communicated, we might have been speaking in different languages.

Gathering up his night clothes, he said, "I'll sleep in one of the guest rooms."

I felt the wall grow higher and thicker. "Why can't you sleep here?"

"It's been a long day. I'm exhausted and I don't feel like talking right now."

"You're upset about Carla, aren't you?"

He stared back at me with cold blue eyes. "Is that so hard for you to understand? Look, what Carla and I had was over, I've already told you that, but her death was unexpected, untimely, and yes, dammit, I'm upset. And your attitude isn't helping. I think it's best if we just call it a night."

Without waiting for an answer, he turned and walked toward the door. Once I would have run after him, but there was that wall between us now. I heard the door close and still I sat, staring vacantly into space.

She didn't fall. She was pushed!

Remembering the hands at my own back, I shuddered, but the memory evoked an even more terrifying thought. If Carla hadn't pushed me, who had?

Forrest could have done it and he could have pushed Carla, too.

No, I protested. Forrest was surprised and shocked about Carla. I've never seen him so upset.

Perhaps he was upset because he mistook Carla for you.

Bile rose up in my throat, but I did not cast the thought aside. Once I would have found it preposterous, but Carla's words echoed in my head. *"Forrest and I were lovers before he ever met you."*

Had that been a lie? No, I told myself. Forrest had admitted as much.

"We had a plan. I would help him drive you crazy. Then I would be mistress of the villa."

If there had been a plan, it would have failed when I caught Carla in the passageway.

"Take my advice, little shopgirl. Go home before it's too late!"

"Oh, God," I cried in a heart-wrenching plea. "Why did she have to be wearing my riding habit?"

I saw Forrest only briefly the next morning. He informed me that he was going to the telegraph office to notify Carla's parents and Mario Vidici about the accident.

Mr. and Mrs. Pinetti arrived the following day, but Vidici, acting in the name of the Metroplitan Opera Company, merely sent condolences on the untimely death of a promising young singer.

The Pinettis were simple, peasantlike people, but they were outspoken in their disapproval of the villa and the life their daughter had embraced.

"We tell her not to come here, but she no listen," Mrs. Pinetti wailed. She was a short heavyset woman, and if she had ever possessed her daughter's beauty, hard work and hard times had obliterated it.

Angry-eyed, her husband stood beside her. "She wanta follow in the footsteps of that woman. That Gia

Gerardo!" He spat the name out like it was a curse. Then raising his fist he screamed, "You satisfied now, *figlia mia?* You follow that woman right into hell!"

Crossing herself, the mother sobbed. "Don't say such a thing, Angelo. We take Carla home. We talk to Father Donachelli. We bury Carla from church."

Forrest arranged to have Carla's body shipped home, and her tight-lipped parents were to accompany the plain wooden box to New York. It was obvious that the residents of the villa would not be welcome, and therefore none of us planned to attend the funeral.

Watching them leave from my bedroom window, I mused that like Gia, Carla had wanted it all. She had been Vidici's paramour as Gia had been Verdi's. She'd hoped someday to be a star and eventually the mistress of the Villa Montelano, but now Carla was going home to a little Italian settlement in New York where she'd be remembered only as the daughter of the butcher Angelo Pinetti and his wife, Maria.

Carla's death acted as a catalyst for change, for Marshall announced that evening that he would be leaving the villa.

He was going back to Missouri. Taking me aside, he confided, "I might stay in Clear Creek and give up the opera, Charlotte."

"But why? I thought you loved music."

"I do." He smiled rather wistfully and added, "But I suppose my father could use an assistant choir director."

I recalled then that he was a minister's son, and as if reading my thoughts, he looked around the ornate drawing room and added, "Here at the villa, I lost sight of the values I was raised on. The Pinettis brought that home to me and I guess I need to go back and find them."

Don Alberto, with no more pupils to train, would be leaving at the same time and that would reduce our unwelcome guests to only three, Victor and the two Faros. I wished it could have been the other way around, for those staying behind were the trouble-makers.

Nicky continued to agitate about Cal's immigration status, bringing the matter up again. "Leopards don't change their spots," he said. "Take Carla, for instance. She could be charming, but she'd steal the clothes right off your back if she got the chance."

Nothing had been said about the riding habit and I hadn't thought anybody but Forrest and I had noticed it. Yet I felt Nicky staring at me, and when I stared back, his skull-like face twisted into a macabre smile.

"That's enough, Nicky," Forrest said.

"Let the dead rest in peace," Marshall added, giving Nicky a look that could kill.

Marshall's interest in Carla had surfaced on the night she had been reported missing, and it was obvious to me now that at one time they, too, had been lovers.

Marshall walked away and Forrest turned back to Nicky. "As for this business about Cal," he said, "I told you before, I have no intention of doing anything about it."

Nicky shrugged, but he and Dorcas exchanged knowing glances and I knew that Cal, too, would soon be leaving. The thought distressed me, for Fiona had already left.

This time I hadn't tried to hold her. She thought the villa was cursed and I of all people could not deny it.

"Oh, mum. You leave, too. This house is evil," she had said. "Last night I heard the banshee and that was after they'd found Miss Pinetti, so you know what that means."

I knew what it meant, but I couldn't leave, for I still loved my husband, and to leave would be giving in to that ugly, nagging voice inside my head.

Forrest is the only one who would benefit from your death, it insisted in a calm logical tone.

"But who benefited from the Maestro's death, or the coachman's," I argued.

Both Forrest and Nicky were staring at me with puzzled expressions on their faces and, too late, I realized I'd spoken aloud.

Looking like holes in his skull-like face, Nicky's eyes grew larger and I had the insane feeling I was being sucked inside his head.

"I'm s-sorry," I said. "I'm afraid I lost track of the con—conversation."

"But what did you say?" Nicky insisted.

Struggling to overcome the stutter, I only made matters worse. "It was n-n-nothing. I was th-th-thinking ab—out s-s-something el—else."

I felt Forrest's hand on my elbow. "You're tired, Charlotte. I want you to go to bed." Giving Nicky a curt nod, he added, "Good night, Faro. Make our apologies to the others."

With his hand firmly on my arm, he led me out of the room. Once in the cavernous great hall, I felt cold, yet beads of perspiration dotted my brow and my legs felt too weak to support my body.

Forrest paused and, staring down at me, said, "You're as white as a sheet." In one swift motion, he had swept me off my feet and was carrying me up the long staircase to the blue room.

Depositing me on the bed, he very gently removed my clothes. "I've seen this coming on," he said, more to himself than to me. Naked, I shivered, and he quickly slipped my nightgown over my head and pulled back the covers. "I'm worried about you," he added almost gruffly, as he tucked me in.

"I'll b-b-be all r-r-right," I said.

He looked tall and powerful standing over me, and I involuntarily shuddered when he said, "I'm going downstairs to fix you a drink. Now don't you dare get out of that bed."

I don't think I could have even if the house was on fire. The events of the past few days had caught up with me and I was tired, tired of worrying and tired of wondering.

Forrest returned in an amazingly short space of time, and setting the tall glass on a table, he said. "I'll be leaving early tomorrow morning, Charlotte. I have a case going to trial, but I'll be back on Saturday and I'll be bringing Dr. Strauss with me."

His words snapped me to attention. "Who is he?"

"A friend of mine and a very wonderful doctor. You'll like him, sweetheart."

"But I don't need a doctor."

"Charlotte, I'm worried about your nerves. You've been under this terrible strain, and it's beginning to show. All this talk of ghosts, and if you could have seen yourself downstairs tonight . . ." Pausing, he shook his head. "You were confused and you looked like you were absolutely terrified."

"It was Nicky. His face, it looks like a skull, and I felt like his eyes were drawing me in. I . . ."

Oh, what was the use, I thought. It sounded crazy, even to me.

"Drink your drink and go to sleep, Charlotte," he said, leaning over and kissing my tear-stained face. "Everything is going to be all right, sweetheart. When I come back, we'll have a long talk, but not now. You need your rest."

He went into the bathroom and when I heard the door close, I sat up and grabbed the glass off the table. Before I could change my mind, I poured the contents out onto the plant that sat on the windowsill.

Remorse overtook me and I wept bitterly in silence when Forrest got into bed and very gently rubbed my back.

It was late when I woke up; Forrest was long gone. Sleep had not soothed my jagged nerves, nor erased my guilt, for the plant on the windowsill mocked me with its healthy green leaves.

Glancing up, I looked outside and saw that it was

snowing. The sudden change caught me off guard. Yesterday had been Indian summer, and like a thief in the night, winter had crept in. Forrest had warned me about the climate. In Maryland, all four seasons can appear in the space of a week, he'd said.

Reaching for the bell cord, I stopped, remembering that Fiona would not be answering it. Dressing quickly, for the house was cold, I went downstairs to breakfast.

Don Alberto and Marshall were alone in the dining room when I entered. They both stood up, and Don Alberto bowed and kissed my hand. "Dear Charlotte, Marshall and I were hoping you'd come down so we could say good-bye."

"But your train doesn't leave until two."

"We'll wait at the station," Marshall said, glancing out the window. "This is turning into a blizzard and we could get snowed in. The Faros have already appropriated the sleigh," he added wryly.

I was surprised. It was nine o'clock and Dorcas never got out of bed before noon. "Where did they go?" I asked.

Marshall shrugged. "They didn't say, but there's a telephone in Atkins' Feed Store and they've used it before to call their lawyer."

A shiver of apprehension ran down my spine and I laughed to cover my nervousness. "Everybody's leaving but me. That's a little frightening."

"The Signora will protect you," Don Alberto said. "I'll wager not even our mysterious poacher would tangle with old Sophia. And don't forget Victor," he added with a smile.

Marshall shook his head in disgust. "Much good he'd be. DeSantis'll sleep all day and then get drunk again tonight."

Don Alberto caught Marshall's eye and patted my hand. "Forgive us, Charlotte. We were only joking. You don't have to worry about the poacher anymore. The fellow's long gone."

I tried to smile back. The poacher was the least of my worries.

We had just finished breakfast when Anna appeared and announced that the carriage was waiting in the driveway. "Cal, he say you coma now. Roads, they getting bad," she added.

The two men followed her into the hall, and swathed in mufflers and great coats, they came back and bade me a last farewell. Marshall clasped my hands, and speaking low, so that only I could hear, he said, "Leave the Villa Montelano, Charlotte. It's an evil place."

I watched from the window and saw them swallowed up in the swirling white flakes. I couldn't even see the carriage, but I heard the wheels crunching in the snow and knew they had gone.

I felt alone and completely isolated from the rest of the world. It worried me that Nicky and Dorcas had gone to town, for I was sure that spelled trouble for Cal.

I still found it hard to believe that he could ever have been a thief. I remembered Cal's eyes. There was something about them, something intangible that I could never put my finger on, yet they had inspired me with trust and given me a warm, comfortable feeling.

Mesmerized, I remained at the window and watched the snowflakes fall. Back in England, I had loved the snow. Papa would stoke up the fire and I'd feel cozy and safe in our little cottage, but here the snow was an enemy because it made me an unwilling prisoner to this cold, hostile house.

I wandered idly through the downstairs rooms. The garish golds and bloody reds seemed tawdry and harsh against the pristine whiteness outside.

Not a servant did I see and it gave me a spooky feeling. Had they all defected like Fiona and left me at the mercy of Anna and the Signora?

Nonsense, I told myself. Fiona was an outsider like me. They were all glad to see her go, but the Italians were loyal to Sophia.

Somehow, I managed to get through the day, and without bothering to change my clothes, I ate a solitary supper in the small salon.

Nicky and Dorcas must have decided to stay in town because of the weather, and I was relieved that Victor did not choose to dine with me.

It was still snowing, but not as hard, and judging from English snowstorms, I rather expected it to clear before morning.

Having nothing else to do, I returned to the Blue Room, and picking up the opera book that Don Alberto had given me, I began to leaf through it. Would I ever understand and be able to appreciate all the nuances of this magnificent art form? I wondered; leafing idly through it. *Verdi!*

The name and the face popped out at me from the page. This was the man I had seen in the mirror, the bearded man who had presented Gia with flowers. What did the vignettes mean? I asked myself. Nicky had said something about purgatory.

The dead must atone for their sins.

Recalling the mirror's pulsing warmth when I had shown it to Fiona, I wondered. Did the mirror have more to tell?

Putting the book down, I walked back to the dressing room. If the mirror is cold, I won't even uncover it. But, if it is warm? I let the thought dangle, and as I entered the closet, I heard a low, soft hum.

Acting on impulse, I moved quickly to press the button and release the secret door. As soon as it swung open, I was on the landing ready to do battle with a second tormentor, but no one stood on the landing with me, and leaning out, I listened intently, but I heard no retreating footsteps.

Stepping back inside the closet, I pushed the button again and the door swung shut. Carla had laughed, but she hadn't hummed. Now I knew who did, and with trembling hands I reached out and touched the mirror.

It was warm and pulsing like a beating heart. Dragging it out of the closet, I pulled it into the bedroom. The clouds were already swirling when I removed the cover.

When the mirror cleared, I found myself looking at the very first scene all over again. Gia was young, she was in the richly furnished room, and she was dressed in peasant costume. I saw her take the box and go outside.

The scene shifted and again I saw her standing in a wheatfield arguing with the man. The riders approached on horseback and the box fell to the ground, scattering coins and jewels, but this time the scene did not fade.

I saw Gia kneel down, and scooping up the coins, she flicked them into her apron. Then, giving the man a quick kiss, she lost herself in the tall swaying stalks of wheat.

The man stood, his feet planted firmly in the ground waiting for the riders. They converged on the field, jumping off their horses and grabbing him roughly. In the split second before the scene faded, he turned and looked out at me from the mirror. I gasped. He was a very young handsome lad and there was something vaguely familiar about his face.

Engrossed in the scene, I hadn't heard the humming, but now it grew louder. Nothing could have persuaded me to leave, though, for following the mirror's familiar pattern, I knew another scene was about to unfold.

Gradually the forms inside the mirror took shape and I found myself staring at the dressing-room scene again. I watched Gia and the woman argue. The money was flung on the dressing table and the woman left as before. Gia scooped up the money and stuffed it inside her bodice. Then picking up a quill pen, she began to write. The mirror focused on the paper, and to my complete mystification, I found that although it was written in Italian, I could read it:

Signore Giuseppe Barranco
245 Chapelgate
London, England

I have sufficient money for lessons. I will be arriving in London within a fortnight. Please grant me an audition.

Gia Marconi

Giuseppe Barranco? And then it dawned on me. That was the old Maestro's name, but why did Gia sign herself Gia Marconi? Was Gerardo a stage name?

Don't stop now, I silently pleaded. If Gia went to England I should be able to find out if she is or is not my grandmother.

Eagerly awaiting the next scene, I was beside myself when I recognized Westminster Bridge and the Houses of Parliament. There could be no doubt now that Gia had gone to London.

Wearing a long black cape, she trudged along the crowded street carrying a market basket. The mirror followed her through twisting back alleys to a red brick building, which she entered. The institution's foyer was bleak and sparsely furnished, but there was a long bench and Gia set the basket down upon it. Her lips moved in a silent and anguished appeal to the woman who approached her.

The newcomer was plain, with a sharp ferretlike face and hair drawn tightly up into a skimpy knot that rested like a button on the top of her head. Looking down on Gia with contempt, the woman nodded.

She reached for the basket, but Gia held up her hand and then, peeling back the cover, stared for a long moment at the sleeping infant resting inside. Then Gia turned on her heel and walked purposefully out the door.

I stared into the mirror long after the scene had faded and tears filled my eyes. "Oh, Papa," I cried. "How could she?"

I didn't want to see anymore, but the mirror wasn't finished and my attention was reluctantly drawn back to it.

Once again, I was forced to witness a repeat of the erotic scene between Gia and her lover. The same sparsely furnished room dominated by the bed came into view. I recognized the man from the last time. He was probably in his fifties, but Gia was not young either, although her body was voluptuous and her face though hardened was still as beautiful as a rose in full bloom.

She was the seducer and I blushed at her display of raw sexuality. As before, a shadow crossed the bed and the writhing couple sat up. Again, Gia's long hair concealed her identity, but the man's face was as naked as his body.

The scene suddenly shifted and I peered inside the mirror with mounting excitement as the invisible camera moved slowly around to expose the shadow at the foot of the bed.

My hand flew to my mouth and I gasped. It was a child, a handsome, dark-haired little boy, and the expression on his small face was one I shall never forget.

"Oh, Forrest," I sobbed.

Chapter 22

The hurt, the anger, and the disillusionment I saw on that childish face told me all I needed to know. Overcome with guilt and devastated by the loss of his grandson's respect, Forrest's grandfather had committed suicide.

Oh, my poor darling, I thought, for now I also knew that Forrest blamed himself for his grandfather's death.

My heart ached for the little boy who had carried such a heavy burden alone, for knowing Forrest the way I did, I was also sure that he had never told his grandmother.

As I watched, the sad little face in the mirror began to fade, and clouds, darker and more turbulent than any I'd seen before, took its place.

Swirling violently, they generated a heat so intense that I backed away. The glass began to pulsate and then I heard what was unmistakably my grandmother's voice.

No tuneless hum, this was the great Gia Gerardo in full voice singing the most beautiful aria I have ever heard. Many years would pass before I was to discover that I had actually heard several arias that night, but since they were not sung in English, I did not understand their meaning at the time.

I cannot begin to describe her voice. Suffice it to say that nothing this side of heaven has ever equaled it. Voice of an angel, soul of a devil, I mused, but the plaintive notes held me spellbound and like a sleepwalker, I followed the sound out of the Blue Room and down the long dark corridor.

Hypnotized, I could think of nothing but the song and my grandmother's magnificent voice. I would have followed it anywhere, for never in my whole life had I heard anything so beautiful.

Always ahead of me, the sound would fade now and again, and frantic at the thought of losing it, I would follow blindly, giving neither thought nor care to where it might be leading me.

Crossing over into the west wing, I vaguely recall thinking that it was probably taking me to my grandmother's room, but the music's spell was so strong that I would not have hesitated to enter even that terrifying place.

The sound was not coming from my grandmother's room, however, and I passed it by, still following that beautiful disembodied voice. Softly, like the song of a Lorelei, it enticed me . . .

"Vissi d'arte, vissi d'amore."

I did not understand the words until years later when I was able to translate that poignantly beautiful aria into English:

I lived for art. I lived for love. I gave my singing to the stars—to the heavens.

Around the corner and down the steps, and when the beautiful voice grew faint and then stopped, I opened the door leading outside the house.

The absolute stillness of a winter's night confronted me and I felt an inexplicable sense of loss. Then suddenly across the snow-covered field, a high bell-like note exploded in the air.

I understood now that the baroness had meant when she said that Gia's high C was like a star. Mesmerized

271

by the sound, I stood at the open door oblivious to the cold and while I did not understand the words, the aria touched my heart with its poignant beauty.

Gradually the tempo of the music increased and as Gia's voice rose to a crescendo, the aria assumed an excited, frenzied tone. My heart began to pound and the blood rushed to my head. My grandmother's ghost was calling and bidding me to follow her across the rope bridge!

Without hesitation, I stepped outside. No longer falling, the snow covered the ground and it crunched under my feet as I followed the voice to the edge of the cliff.

Looking across to the other side, I saw a light in the window of the hunting lodge. The sound was closer now and I thought it was coming from inside the lodge.

The bridge was covered with snow, and I was terrified of crossing it, but a force more powerful than fear had me under its spell, and raising my skirt, I stepped gingerly out.

Gripping the ropes, I braced myself as the bridge began to sway. Every instinct I possessed told me to turn back, but that pleading, angelic voice would not be stilled. Like a magnet it drew me step by tortuous step across the narrow swinging span.

The wooden boards were slippery and once I fell, causing the bridge to sway violently back and forth. I landed facedown, and pulling myself up, I winced as the heavy ropes bit into my frozen hands.

A bright moon had broken through the clouds and looking down I saw it glisten on the icy stream that lay forty feet below me. "Oh, God," I prayed. "Don't let this bridge fall."

Clinging to the ropes, I inched my way the short distance that was left and stood on the other side, listening.

Absolute silence reigned, filling the night with the eerie stillness that seems to follow new-fallen snow.

The song? I wondered. Had I only imagined it?

Chilled to the bone, I lifted my heavy, snow-encrusted skirts and dragged myself up to the door of the hunting lodge.

Finding it open, I stumbled inside and was blinded by the bright light coming from the oil lamps. I saw nothing for a moment, but when my vision cleared, I noticed that there were papers strewn all over the floor and several chairs had been overturned. Puzzled, I stood in the middle of the floor and called, "Is anybody here?"

A grunting noise came from the direction of the bedroom, and without thinking, I followed the sound. The room was dark and I felt afraid. "Who's here?" I said.

Suddenly a figure rose up from the shadows and made a lunge for me. Heavy arms grasped me around the neck, forcing me to stagger backward into the sitting room. My own screams reverberated in my ears as the full weight of my assailant's body bore down on me in a crushing blow that forced me to the floor.

His face, distorted almost beyond recognition, was but inches from mine. "No, no, not you!" I screamed as the features of the man I had thought to be my friend swam before my eyes. "Not you, Cal," I whimpered as a black curtain was dropped over me and I lost consciousness.

When I came to a few seconds later, Cal's heavy body still had me pinned to the floor. His head rested on my chest, and with a strength born of desperation, I rolled away from him. It was then that I saw the blood.

He has stabbed me, I thought wildly as I stared with horrified eyes at the red stain on my breast. Terrified lest he stab me again, I inched myself away from him.

He made no move to restrain me, and looking closer I saw that it was Cal and not I who was bleeding.

"Cal, Cal," I cried, shaking him, but his body was limp and I sensed the angel of death hovering above him. "Please don't die, Cal. I'm sorry I was afraid. I should have known you could never hurt me."

"How touching."

The sudden intrusion of that ominous, sarcastic voice turned my blood to ice, and jerking my head around, I saw Victor DeSantis framed in the doorway.

"You did this to him," I cried, for Victor's presence alone was proof enough for me.

"You're right, Charlotte, and I'm so glad you came, *cara mia,* for now I can be rid of you both."

"But why?" I cried. "The house will go to Forrest at my death and surely you have nothing to gain by killing Cal."

Victor smiled, and shutting the door, he walked over and kicked the poor twisted body that lay on the floor. "He's already dead. That leaves only you."

By the light of the oil lamp, his black eyes glittered with malicious glee, and with mounting horror, I realized that he was insane.

"No hurry, *cara mia.* I explain it, nize and simple-like so even a little shopgirl like you can understand."

He's big and powerful, but he's old, I thought. If I can get out of this lodge, I can outrun him.

"Naw, *cara mia.* Don't even think about running away, 'cause I can stop you with this," he said, and still smiling he withdrew a small handgun from his pocket and pointed it at me. "Now get up off the floor and sit over there," he added, jerking his head toward the rocking chair.

Casting one last anguished glance at Cal's motionless body, I got up and sat in the rocker. "You killed him for a horse," I said.

He laughed. "The horse had nothing to do with his death, just as the villa has nothing to do with yours."

"Then why?"

"You sit there nize and quiet-like and I tell you."

The whole situation was bizarre—poor Cal lying on the floor—dead or alive I didn't know—and Victor holding a gun on me.

"A horse!" he said loudly, and I jumped. "I care nothing for a horse. Nicky wanted the horse. I wanted the villa, *sì*, but that's not why you're going to die, you stupid girl."

He was becoming excited and I thought to distract him. "Did you send me the Black Hand?"

He laughed again. "Naw, that was Carla. She wanted to frighten you away. I don't play such games. I sent Giuseppe the Black Hand because I knew it would scare the old fool to death and it did."

He seemed calmer and enormously pleased with himself. "Why did you want the Maestro dead?" I asked cautiously.

"To shut him up," he answered. "Nicky said he knew secrets about all the prima donnas and I didn't want him starting rumors about Gia."

"What kind of rumors," I probed.

"I thought he might say she had a child by Verdi and I preferred to believe that you were an imposter."

"But you don't believe that now?"

"Naw. Now I know different."

I waited, but he didn't go on and the expression on his face made my blood run cold. "Who killed the coachman?" I asked.

Again he laughed. "I did. Nobody toys with Victor DeSantis. Nicky hired Wilson to find the will. It was Wilson who broke into the Maestro's cottage looking for it. Then your husband's meddling uncle came in and Wilson hit him over the head, but the Maestro didn't have the will. It wasn't in Gia's room either," he added. "And incidentally, it was the coachman who pushed you down the steps so he could search the room."

So that's who had been hiding in the corridor, I thought. "But why did you kill him?" I asked.

275

"Bestia, he got greedy. He found the will and he thought I could pay more than Nicky, so he offered it to me. I met him in the woods, and when he told me he had read all the papers and what was in them, I killed him. I wasn't going to have him spreading Gia's indiscretions all over town. He was of no account," he added disdainfully.

Oh, God, I thought, and I had suspected Forrest. "And Carla?" I asked.

He shrugged. "An unfortunate mistake, especially for Carla. She and Marshall used to meet at the lodge," he explained. "Gia found out and there was a big row. Of course Carla got dropped like a hot potato. Pretty Boy Hains knew what side his bread was buttered on," he said with a smirk. "Anyway, she was certain he would be leaving the villa, and I guess Carla wanted to see him one last time. She was waiting for him outside the lodge and she was wearing your riding habit. I don't see so good when I drink," he added. "She was leaning over the cliff, looking down at the water. I thought it was you. The opportunity was there, so I pushed her." He laughed then. "Gia always told Carla her sticky fingers would get her into trouble someday."

I still didn't understand why he wanted to kill Cal, and if there was nothing to be gained from my death, why had he pushed Carla over the cliff thinking she was me?

He seemed to have an uncanny ability to read my mind. "You're wondering why I killed Cal and why I'm going to kill you," he said, and still brandishing the gun, he walked across the room and picked up a folder from the floor. *"All information pertaining to the race horse, Lady Baltimore,"* he read.

I recalled seeing that folder the first and only other time I'd come to the lodge.

"This is where Gia hid the will, but that's not important," he said. "Nicky would be disappointed to know there was only one small change in it anyway.

What is important, though, is what Gia attached to the will. Her 'Act of Contrition,' she called it," he added contemptuously. Then his face hardened and he started to pace the floor. "Over forty years we were together, and never once did she look at me as a man. I put up with her husbands, her lovers. I managed her career. I made her a star, and I always thought that someday when she was old, she'd turn to me."

Breathing heavily, he continued to pace the floor, and with his eyes glinting dangerously, he rambled on and on, waving the gun at me from time to time to emphasize a point. "I gave her everything and she kept me for a fool. She saw this place and she wanted it. It was called Lauraland then. *I'll turn it into a palace,* she said. *It'll make Patti's Craig-y-nos look like a pigeon coop.*" Suddenly remembering my presence, he looked directly at me and spoke.

"Your husband's grandfather didn't want to sell, but I wormed my way into his confidence. Got him to make some investments that would have forced him out, but Gia couldn't wait for that. Oh, no, she had to seduce him!"

Pointing outside the window, he said, "Singleton hanged himself right out there from the big tree. He couldn't have known about the investments then, so his suicide didn't make no sense, but it made things easy for us," he added. "His widow couldn't afford not to sell."

His callousness appalled me, but I was beginning to understand why I had been shown the mirror and why my grandmother's restless spirit had haunted the villa. "You still haven't told me Cal's part in all of this," I said.

Glancing contemptuously at the lifeless body that lay sprawled on the floor, Victor said, "He was her husband and the father of her *bambino.*"

I was astonished. "But, I thought Verdi . . ."

Victor's shoulders sagged and his voice trembled

with raw emotion. "I could have accepted Verdi, but not this . . ." His voice broke as he added, "This wretched drifter, this stablehand, and when I read in her confession that she had loved him . . ."

Scenes from the mirror went racing through my head. Gia barefoot and in peasant clothes. That hadn't been an opera scene. That had been real life!

I saw her take the money and then argue with a man. That young man had been Cal. Oh, God I thought. They said he'd been in prison.

"She let him take the blame," I said aloud, but Victor was too far gone to wonder how I could know that.

"So? She was an artiste. The world needed her voice. Roberto Marconi was nothing!"

Roberto Marconi. I repeated the name in my head, and recalling another vignette from the mirror, I saw the letter Gia had written to the Maestro. She had signed it, *Gia Marconi.*

Swallowing the lump in my throat, I touched the little locket around my neck and recalling the inscription, I whispered softly, *"Amore, Roberto."*

Victor had stood up, and with his face a mask of hate, he said, "She told me there was someone, but she wouldn't say who it was. She said, *I'll be a proper wife this time, if he'll have me."* He began to kick at Cal's lifeless body, *"Bestia,* pig," he shouted. "She wouldn't look at me, but she'd give herself to the likes of you!"

"Stop it," I screamed. "Leave him alone."

He turned on me with fury. "Get outside. I kill you now. You're nothing, just like him."

He was completely mad and it was useless to argue. Perhaps outside I would have a chance to escape.

Holding the gun at my back, he followed me out the door. The night was clear and cold and the frigid air heightened my senses. If I could keep him talking, I could stall for time.

"What did Gia change about the will?" I asked.

"Ah, the will," he said. His voice became oily and

sarcastic again. "*Sì*, I forgot to tell you, *cara mia*. Gia knew she was going to die and she wanted to make everything right. She left the villa to your husband instead of you. She said we'd stolen the villa from his grandfather."

He waved the gun in a gesture of impatience. "It doesn't matter now who lives in the house as long as it's not you or Roberto Marconi."

"What was wrong with Gia?" I asked.

He tapped his chest. "Heart. She never told nobody, not even me." He laughed then. "Gia wanted to buy her way out of hell, but I don't believe in hell, or heaven, either. The only hell I know is here, and I'll escape that after I take care of you," he added softly.

He was wearing a heavy overcoat and I wore only a shawl, but his blood was old and thin and the cold affected him more. Standing in the moonlight, I saw him shake, and the hand that held the gun looked like it was frozen to it.

Giving little thought to the consequences—for what did I have to lose?—I made a grab for the weapon. His fingers were too stiff to pull the trigger and, taken by surprise, he dropped the gun on the ground.

I found it before he did and with one kick I sent it flying, but the gun went off and a loud bang shattered the night's stillness.

"Bitch, I kill you without a gun," he muttered, grabbing me around the waist and dragging me up the embankment toward the rope bridge.

Young and quick I might be, but I was no match for Victor's superior strength and size. He's going to throw me over the cliff, I thought—just like Carla.

"No!" I screamed, digging my heels into the snow, but to no avail. When he had almost reached the edge, he slipped and I feared we might both be plunged forty feet down to the rocks below. Taking advantage of the first opportunity, I scrambled out of his reach only to be grabbed again and pulled even closer to the edge

279

of the cliff.

Somehow, he managed to stand up, and with one swoop of his powerful arms, he lifted me off my feet and raised my lightweight body above his head.

I closed my eyes, anticipating the terrifying sensation of hurtling through space, when I heard Gia's voice again. The clear magnificent notes seemed to come from another world.

Victor heard them too, and he staggered backward, dropping his arms. I fell, not through space, but into the soft bosom of a snowbank, and scrambling out of reach, I stared back at him.

"Gia, Gia," he called.

Walking forward, he tettered on the edge of the cliff. "Gia, wait," he shouted, and spreading his arms like a giant eagle, he soared over the side.

I ran to the edge and looked below. Arms still spread wide, he lay facedown at the bottom of the cliff.

The night was silent, but the moonlight picked up a figure standing in the shadows. She wore something white and gauzy and already she was beginning to fade and blend into the snow.

I saw the lanterns and torches then, but I was too cold and weak to cry out, and when the search party found me I was unconscious.

Drifting in and out of consciousness, I vaguely recall the tired and worried face of my husband, who must have kept a constant vigil by my bedside.

The nurse, a blur in white, seemed to float in and out of the room, and in my delirium, I mistook her for Gia.

I tried to sit up. "You saved my life. Why?" I asked her.

"Hush, Mrs. Singleton. Don't excite yourself."

Forrest's face, haggard and unshaven, suddenly appeared before me. "Don't give up, Charlotte. You're going to get well. Trust me, sweetheart."